Dear Carmine,
Thanks for your s[upport]
I hope you enjoy it.
Fred Abel

GOT AN EAGLE ON MY BUTTON

A NOVEL

F. W. ABEL

PublishAmerica
Baltimore

© 1995 by F. W. Abel.
All rights reserved. No part of this book may be reproduced, stored in a retrieval system or transmitted in any form or by any means without the prior written permission of the publishers, except by a reviewer who may quote brief passages in a review to be printed in a newspaper, magazine or journal.

First printing

ISBN: 1-4137-2819-7
PUBLISHED BY PUBLISHAMERICA, LLLP
www.publishamerica.com
Baltimore

Printed in the United States of America

*For Kathy,
who held the fort
against all odds.*

Acknowledgments

This is a work of fiction. From the introduction to the endnotes, it is written as it would have been by our fictional reporter/interviewer, "LeOtis Henry," in November 1917, as the United States was sending an army to Europe to fight World War I. Much of the action in which the characters are participants is based on historical events. I have tried to keep dramatic license to a minimum but admit to some alteration of the historical record, in most cases, by having fictional characters perform events that actually occurred. For example, I had the fictional Mercer Cavaliers performing almost all the cavalry actions at the battle of Belmont and the first day at Shiloh.

For historical information, I am indebted to the following: *The Civil War: A Narative* by Shelby Foote; *Who Was Who in the Civil War* by Stuart Sifakis; *Battle Tactics of the Civil War* by Paddy Griffith; *Billy Yank: The Union Soldier in the Civil War* by Bell I. Wiley; *Soldier Life in the Union and Confederate Armies* edited by Philip Van Doren Stern; *The Sable Arm: Black Troops in the Union Army, 1861-1865* by Dudley Taylor Cornish; *Forged in Battle: The Civil War Alliance of Black Soldiers and White Officers* by Joseph T. Glatthaar. Any errors in my text are my fault, not theirs.

I am also indebted to family and friends who read the manuscript and suggested improvements: my wife, Kathy, and Richard Boone, Herbert Lattimore, Gene Scarl and Donald Worch.

Finally, I have to acknowledge the inspiration of three authors: Bruce Catton for everything he ever wrote about the Civil War, which I read as an adolescent at the time of the Centennial; and George MacDonald Fraser and Bernard Cornwell, for creating two of the most memorable characters in military fiction.

"Once let the black man get upon his person the brass letters 'U.S.,' let him get an eagle on his button and a musket on his shoulder and bullets in his pocket, and there is no power on earth which can deny that he has earned the right to citizenship in the United States."

Frederick Douglass
August, 1863

INTRODUCTION

Jedediah Worth, 70, Distinguished Soldier & Lawman

One of Langston's most prominent citizens, Jedediah Worth, passed away yesterday peacefully in his sleep, just two months short of his 71st birthday.

Mr. Worth was well-known in Langston City, having served as our sheriff for more than a decade. Before settling here, Mr. Worth had a long and notable career in the United States Army, during which he rose to the highest non-commissioned officer grade, Regimental Sergeant-Major, in the celebrated 10th U.S. Cavalry.

He was the recipient of the highest award the nation bestows for bravery in battle, the Medal of Honor, not once, but twice, a feat almost unique in the annals of the American military. He was the first Negro to be awarded the Medal, for deeds of valor performed during the Rebellion, when he was only seventeen years of age.

A widower when he died, of Mr. Worth's children, two still survive: Jubal, a son, and Harriet, a daughter. His funeral will be held at 10:00 a.m. tomorrow at the Bethel Baptist Church.

This obituary, clipped from the *Langston Herald*, gave me deep sadness when it arrived from Oklahoma. For I had the privilege of knowing Jedediah Worth for more than twenty years.

I saw him for the first time in the spring of 1891, when I was a reporter for the Washington *Colored American*. Sergeant Worth was among the heroes from the Negro regiments sent to Washington as an honor guard in the nation's capital. It was a brief meeting. Because white soldiers objected so vigorously to their presence, the Negro soldiers were quickly sent back to the frontier.

I met him again in the fall of 1898, when he was the Regimental Sergeant-

Major of the 10th United States Colored Cavalry, the famed "Buffalo Soldiers." The 10th Cavalry had just returned from "the splendid little war" to free Cuba from the Spanish. Because the authorities feared the tropical diseases to which they had been exposed might become epidemic, soldiers returning from Cuba were quarantined. The men, white and Negro, were kept in a camp established at Montauk Point on Long Island, some 130 miles east of the city of New York.

The *Colored American* sent me out to Montauk to interview Negro soldiers about their experiences in the war. My editor was concerned that their contributions would not be acknowledged by the white-owned papers. Indeed, if you read only Hearst's New York *Journal*, you would have thought that the only regiment that did anything of note at all was the 1st United States Volunteer Cavalry, Theodore Roosevelt's headline-grabbing "Rough Riders." The *Colored American* was determined that the fortitude and pluck of the Negro soldiers be publicized.

I suppose things have not changed at that much since then, as the paper is sending me off to France with the 15th Regiment of the New York National Guard. We are determined that this latest group of Buffalo Soldiers not be ignored, either.

Upon my arrival at Montauk, the officer acting as the liaison with newspaper reporters and correspondents gave me leave to enter the camp of the 9th and 10th Cavalry Regiments, and the 24th and 25th Regiments of Infantry, all of which were composed entirely of Negro enlisted men. He advised me to make the acquaintance of each regiment's Sergeant Major, the highest-ranking enlisted soldier in the regiment. The Sergeant Major, even more than the regiment's Colonel, was the man who made sure the men were trained and disciplined, sheltered and fed, in short, the man responsible for having the men behave and carry themselves like soldiers. In this way, I was re-introduced to Sergeant Major Worth.

You might expect, given his responsibilities, to find a dour, humorless, authoritarian man, quick to admonish and slow to praise; harsh, even brutal, made narrow-minded by the need to enforce discipline and regulations.

As I interviewed his men, I discovered the affection and respect in which he was held, not only by the soldiers, but by the white officers also. I shy away from the term "legend," but there is no other way to describe the man, as can be intimated from just reading his obituary.

Of course I wanted to find out more about him, but when I approached him for an interview, he refused and insisted that my news reports be about his soldiers, of whom he was intensely proud. But I am a reporter, a "newshound" if you will, and over the course of several weeks was able to question Sergeant Major Worth about his life and military career, and learned even more in subsequent meetings through the years.

It took me a long time to get to know the man. Even now, I recall that when I first looked on his weather-worn and war-scarred visage, how I concluded that the crow's-feet around the eyes had to have come from squinting into the Southwestern sun and the lines about the mouth etched by the strain of having to immediately judge the correct course of action during battle. I know now that they were equally the result of laughter.

It is only now, years after I met him and two years after his death, that I am able to set his story down in chronological order. Apart from some endnotes I added in clarification or support of his reminiscences, the words are those of Jedediah Worth, a slave who became a soldier, a soldier who became a hero.

LeOtis Henry
New York City
November 1917

PROLOGUE

You're a newspaper man, so why would you want me to tell about things that happened more than thirty years ago? Those events are so old, they're no longer news. But I don't consider them history either. I've always been of the opinion that history is what happened in the distant past. It's hard to believe that events in my own lifetime could be considered historical.

Maybe when I have white hair and am sitting in a rocker on a porch, then it will be time to tell my life story. Of course, by then, who'd want to listen to the rambles of a senile old man? There's been a lot of dullness and monotony in my life, just as there is in any lifetime. Most life stories aren't nearly as dramatic as a play or novel.

You say that people will be interested, that our young people need to be reminded about the times of slavery. I think many of us who were slaves might prefer to allow the memory of slavery fade into oblivion, just like the institution itself has. Instead, as our people are discriminated against in so many ways, often with the connivance of the very government for which we fought, we need to devote our energies to ensuring our people are free in fact as well as name. I think the lesson to be learned is that emancipation of itself was no panacea, much to the chagrin of most abolitionists.

But, yes, the very idea of freedom for those of us who were slaves was a powerful impetus. Witness the great colored pugilist of the early century, Tom Mollineaux. The promise of freedom was enough to raise him almost literally from the dead.[1]

You remark about my choice of words. Do you think that journalists are the only people who know "nickel" words? I have to admit, I've gone out of my way to catch your ear. Many civilians, I've found, regard soldiering as being for those too ignorant or lazy to make a go of civilian life, so I wanted to dispel that notion right now at the start.

I was lucky to have learned to read fairly young and thus developed a taste for it as a leisure-time activity. Sitting in a dust-scoured fort in the desert allows ample time to read, in between the arduous living on the campaign trail and the excitement and terror of combat. Reading fills one's mind and time and goes a long way in keeping one from becoming a drunk or a deserter, the scourges of the frontier army.

Let me say, though, drunkenness or desertion happened less often in the colored regiments—a miracle given the undesirable locations in which we were usually posted—than in the white ones. The Seventh Cavalry was particularly prone to both, understandable in view of who their commander was.[2] But already I'm rambling.

Yes, I understand that there's a great deal of interest in the Rebellion, especially by the people too young to remember it. General Grant, with his memoir of the Rebellion, was probably read by more people, both American and foreign, than any American writer but Mark Twain.

I can tell you about the Rebellion, the fighting on the frontier and the war in Cuba as I experienced them, but don't expect a grand view of war like you got from General Grant's memoir. My range of vision is only as wide as a regiment, and that's when I was Sergeant Major. When I was a private, it didn't get much wider than my squad. Think of the descriptions of battle in *The Red Badge of Courage.*

Of course I read *Red Badge*. It's a most remarkable work, almost flawless, especially when you consider Crane's utter innocence of war. Just about any soldier, at any time, could read Crane's work and say to himself, "That's the way it really was."

The flaw? The protagonist, Henry Fleming, seems to believe he, himself, one soldier, could make a difference. By the end, he came to realize his insignificance. But there's none of the fatalism, almost despair, that afflicted many soldiers, especially the volunteers of 1861, during the autumn of '64 and the following winter. That's when the chilling thought that all the sacrifices might be in vain ran rampant, that the "Peace Democrats" could win the presidential election and end the war by giving the Confederacy its independence. But I've heard that *Red Badge* was set fairly early in the war, so maybe it's not such a flaw after all.[3]

That was why the enlistment of colored troops made such a difference to the outcome of the Rebellion. It wasn't just our numbers. It was said that the best men, on both sides, were those who enlisted in 1861. What they lacked in soldierly skill, they made up for in enthusiasm and determination. The men who followed, the conscripts and bounty men, just weren't up to their standard.

Except for us. The coloreds who enlisted in '63 and '64 possessed all the enthusiasm and determination of the volunteers of '61. We appeared at a propitious time, when many of the '61 men were war-weary and losing heart, or were dead. If the Confederacy had the wisdom to enlist slaves, promising freedom to those who enlisted, the war might have ended differently. I've often thought the Confederacy was akin to the protagonist in a Shakespeare tragedy, doomed by his own flaws. In the South's case, it was the fatal flaw of slavery. Most colored troops in federal service were from the South. Not only did the South not benefit from the fortitude of their own colored population, the valor of Southern coloreds was turned against the Confederacy. Except for an incident in which I was involved that occurred in the spring of 1865. The description of that will have to wait until its due time.

On the other hand, coloreds almost didn't get a chance to fight for the Union either. It may seem nonsensical, but powerful forces in the federal government were opposed to colored soldiers, at least at first. For coloreds, who had the most to gain or lose as a result of the war, the first battle was for the right to be Union soldiers at all. We had to fight for "Sambo's Right to be Kilt."[4]

You have to understand that, of all the things I've done, I'm most proud of having been in the first battle fought by colored troops during the Rebellion. It was small, so small we didn't even give it a name at the time. It's now called the battle of Island Mound, because it took place on a small island in the Osage River in Missouri. Given what a signal event it was, it's lamentable how few people today even know of it.

It occurred in the autumn of '62. That's right, before President Lincoln issued the Emancipation Proclamation. The real wonder of it all was the number of people who simply ignored the federal government and allowed us to soldier in the first place.

My road to Island Mound started with me in bondage in Kentucky. I went with my master's sons when they joined the Confederate army. I was with them at Belmont and Shiloh. Then I got the chance to run for freedom. While on the run in Tennessee is when I met my best friend, Samson, the African warrior who became Sergeant-Major Miner of the 9th Cavalry, and Effie, Belle and Josh, who became family.

Even now, as I relate it, I'm astonished at how simple my life seemed then. I suppose that one problem with living past one's youth is the amount of regret one tends to accumulate. I was young, not much more than a boy, really. But again, I digress.

I guess a good starting point for the story of how, to borrow from Frederick Douglass one of his noted phrases, I got "an eagle on my button," is a day in May of 1861. I recall that, as I awoke that morning, I had no notion it would be such an uncommon day.

I

"You're goin' to the army, Jed," old Gideon told me. "You and Obie both."

"The army? What army?" If I hadn't been so bewildered, I would never have talked back to Gideon, the slave in charge of all of us who worked with the master's horses.

"The master's sons are joinin' up. All the young masters in these parts are. Master Brady and Master Wade'll need servants." Normally, Gideon would never have bothered with an explanation, he would have just cuffed me one, but I guess he knew the news would be such a shock. He was the head groom on Wentworth Farm, one of the largest horse breeding farms in Kentucky. The farm produced some of the finest horses for racing and hunting in the state, famous for its horseflesh.

When I call it a "farm," you might get the idea that it was small, but Wentworth Farm covered more than six hundred acres and had more than sixty slaves, mostly to care for the horses. There were trainers, jockeys, grooms, stableboys, two blacksmiths and, the most expensive of all, a veterinarian. There were field hands to grow hay and vegetables and take care of cattle and pigs and mend fences, and house servants to take care of the four members of the Wentworth family.

To help with the horses was the reason I had been bought some three years prior, when I was twelve. I was somewhat tall for my age and working with my hands had made my shoulders broad and riding horses had given me well-muscled legs. Muscle is heavy, and my height and weight caused me some concern, because I wanted to be a jockey, and most jockeys were short and lightweight.

"You go on up to the main house now," Gideon ordered.

"Yes, sir," I said meekly, although I wanted to ask why. Gideon again took pity on me and explained.

"You're to be taught how to cook. The young masters're only takin' one servant each, so you and Obie'll have to know lots besides takin' care of their horses. Now get on up there."

"Yes, sir." I hurried to the house and knocked on the kitchen door. The door was opened by Libby, one of the serving girls.

"What d'you want?" she scolded. "You know you're not supposed t' be here. You eat in the shed with the field hands."

"I was told t' come in t' learn how t' cook. When the young massers go t' th' army, I'm goin' wit' 'em, t' take care o' 'em." At the time, I spoke with the soft drawl of the speech of central Kentucky. Most hard sounds at the end of words just dropped off. Words like "don't" and "sure" came out as "doan" and "sho" and everyone—not whites you understand—was addressed "you'all."

Libby scowled and made no move to let me in. I just stood, stupidly.

"What're you doin', girl?" snapped a voice, richer, deeper. "You let him in right now!"

Libby quickly stepped back and allowed me to enter the kitchen. Maddie, the cook, was the person who had spoken. She looked me up and down with a jaundiced eye.

"The first thin' you need t' learn about cookin' is you better be clean. You get on over t' the sink and scrub your hands right up t' your elbows."

I went to the sink, pumped some water and lathered up with a bar of brown soap. Maddie inspected my hands carefully before she nodded.

"Now get on over there with Obie," she said.

Obie was a groom like me, maybe a couple years older. We both tried to outdo each other in taking care of our horses. It was a competition that never went too far, and we were friendly toward each other. Today, I guess we each felt out of place in the kitchen, and we just nodded to each other.

"One o' the best ways t' learn t' cook is t' do it," Maddie told us, "and then eat what you cooked t' see how it tastes. I'm goin' to have you fix some ham and eggs and biscuits and coffee." Maddie showed us how to measure flour and milk and baking powder and mix it together to make biscuit batter.

"Ain't goin' t' be no stoves in the army," she told us. "So you'all need to bake in a Dutch oven over a fire."

While the biscuits were baking, Maddie showed us how to measure and boil coffee, how to slice and fry ham in a skillet and how to fry eggs in lard. I felt like I was "getting over," because eggs were a special treat for us slaves, only served on Christmas and Easter.

The biscuits that we made were a little hard, the eggs that I fried were brown on the bottom and runny on the top, and the coffee was weak, but I think it was a good first try. Maddie sampled our work and told us what we did wrong.

After breakfast, we cleaned the pans and plates and knives and forks we had used. Maddie inspected them all.

"The best way t' get th' trots is t' have dirty cookin' gear," she said. Obie and I both gave a laugh; "the trots" was another name for loose bowels. We abruptly stopped laughing when Maddie turned on us.

"Don't you'all be laughin' about th' trots, you hear? Th' trots likely t' kill you faster'n a Yankee bullet. Plenty are th' people died from th' trots. Now you get on outside and finish your mornin' work. When you come back at noon, you'all make sure th' first thin' you do is wash your hands," she called after us, as I raced Obie over to the tack shed to get bridles, saddles and saddle blankets.

Because the farm bred horses for racing and hunting, as well as for riding and pulling wagons and buggies, there were a lot of horses, and all needed to be exercised. Only the most trusted grooms got to ride the saddle horses, for the horses were too valuable and too easily hurt to let just anyone ride them. On many of the neighboring farms, a groom was only allowed to put a long halter on a horse and have it run in circles around the groom while he held the rope.

The other, equally important reason was that a slave might take a horse to try to run away. I remember the time a runaway from a neighboring farm was caught. It was soon after I had come to Wentworth Farm. The masters from the roundabout farms sent their own slaves, mostly the grooms and jockeys, to see what happened to runaways.

The man's hands were tied to a large wagon wheel and his shirt was ripped off his back. An overseer, one of the white men who made sure the slaves did what they were told, took a short, thick bullwhip to the runaway's back.

The man jumped as the first stroke hit him and raised a welt. After the third or fourth stroke, small trickles of blood bubbled up from his skin. By the tenth, blood flowed freely down his back, and by the twentieth, bits of skin began to come off and the man was screaming. By the fiftieth, the man's pinkish-white ribs and backbone were visible, but by then, thankfully for him, he had fainted.

"He's got another fifty comin'," said the overseer, "but we'll save 'em for another time. Be a waste of time if he can't feel nothin'." We were then marched back to our farms and plantations and told to tell other slaves what we had witnessed.

Maybe it was because I was so young, and so new to the farm, but the horror of that scene has stayed with me. Now, years later, the memory can still make me skittery.

On the other hand, I should probably mention that a whipping was an exceptional occurrence, at least in the farm country of Kentucky. The generation of coloreds born after Emancipation might think that slavery was how it was depicted in *Uncle Tom's Cabin*, but most masters would not dream of gratuitous cruelty to a slave, any more than to a horse.

This wasn't necessarily kindness; you have to recall that we slaves were valuable property. The punishment of the runaway had probably meant the loss of most of his value to his owner. A "prime buck" could cost more than two thousand dollars, and those were pre-war gold dollars, not greenbacks, so you see why we were treated the way we were.

In a way, that's the horror of slavery—the owners had so much money tied up in the institution that, to defend it, they invented all the notions of inequality that plague us to this day.

When the dinner bell rang for the noon meal, I ran to the kitchen door as fast as my boots would let me. I saw Obie coming, so I waited to knock until he got there. Libby opened the door and let us in, without sassing us this time. Heeding Maddie's words from that morning, Obie and I went over to the sink and scrubbed vigorously with brown soap.

Maddie showed us how to make cornbread in a skillet and fry Virginia ham. She had black-eyed peas soaking in water to soften, and showed us how to simmer the peas so they would be ready in time for supper. In between her lessons, Maddie made sure that Libby served the Wentworths properly in the dining room.

While Obie and I ate, we heard snatches of conversation every time Maddie or Libby pushed through the door between the kitchen and the dining room. Soon we could hear right through the walls as Mr. Wentworth began to shout.

"North Carolina secedes on the same day our damned legislature votes to remain neutral. Neutral! The very word leaves a bad taste in my mouth. It means Kentucky doesn't have the damned gumption to support one side or the other."

"Thomas, you can use any language you want outside or in the stables, but I will not have you swearing in this house," said his wife severely.

"But I was provoked beyond endurance, my dear. Kentucky is a Southern state and belongs with the Confederacy. Any fool, except maybe those in the legislature, understands that." Mr. Wentworth was not quite shouting, but he still talked loudly.

"Does this mean that Kentucky will not field any soldiers for either army, Father?" asked Brady, the older of the two Wentworth brothers. Wade, younger by three years, interrupted before his father could reply.

"Nothing's going to stop me. I'll go to Missouri to join up if I have to."

"Wade, do not interrupt your father," said Mrs. Wentworth. "And at seventeen, you're too young to be a soldier."

"But Father said..." Wade protested, but Mr. Wentworth hurriedly interrupted.

"Missouri has also not yet voted to secede from the Union. After all the damned trouble they caused in Kansas, they are not doing any more than Kentucky!"

"Thomas, I have already asked you not to swear in my house!" Mrs. Wentworth was close to shouting herself.

"Sorry, my dear. I was again provoked beyond all reason. Missouri men, by employing violence to try to force Kansans to permit slavery, greatly added to the ill-feeling between the two regions. The fools in Washington could maybe have patched together another compromise, had not the bigger fools in Missouri spilled blood."

"But, Pa! What about John Brown?" demanded Wade. "Not only did he kill Missouri men in cold blood, he tried to start a slave rebellion.[5] Nothing done by the Missourians could be worse than that!"

The greatest fear of all slave-owners was that their slaves would rise up in a bloody revolt. Small revolts did occur from time to time. Turner's rebellion in Virginia thirty years before saw the death of fifty-seven white men, women and children before it was savagely suppressed. John Brown's raid occurred only a year and a half prior, and the bitterness it had aroused on both sides was still fresh.

"I'm surprised that John Brown's trial, or rather his hanging, did not start a war sooner," Brady said quietly. "I thought the abolitionists would make him a saint and, under that banner, attack us then."

"Understand that most Yankees are not abolitionists," replied Mr. Wentworth. "Most of them could care less about coloreds. If the abolitionists got their way, coloreds would be free to slave in factories like Yankee workmen, and it's a well-known fact that we treat our livestock better than Yankee factory owners treat their workers. Our servants would be far worse off with the Yankees than they are with us." Like most Southerners, Mr. Wentworth rarely referred to the people he owned as slaves.

"However," he continued, "the election of Lincoln showed quite clearly that the North will not just allow us to leave the Union without trying to stop us. They believe that states do not have the right to make their own choices in this regard, even though the Constitution gives the states any rights not specifically given to the Federal Government. The states voluntarily entered the Union, therefore they should be able to voluntarily leave it."

"But what about Kentucky, Father?" Brady returned the conversation to his original question. "Does the vote of neutrality mean that the militia will not be called out?"

"I suppose that's exactly what it is intended to mean," replied Mr. Wentworth. "But as your hot-headed brother says, that will not prevent individuals from joining either side, even if they have to go to another state to do so."

"We sure…" Wade began but was again interrupted by Mr. Wentworth.

"Let us finish eating before the food gets cold."

At the time, I knew what a Yankee was, but I had never heard of an abolitionist. I thought Maddie might know, since she lived around the masters all the time, so I asked her.

"You hush!" Maddie whirled around and faced Obie and me. "Don't ever let white folks hear you say that word, or even that you know the word, or it's worth a whippin'." Maddie looked over her shoulder. "The abolitionists believe that colored people should be free to go do what they want, just like white folks. Now, don't let me hear you ask about that no more. Clean up th' pots and pans and go back to tendin' th' horses like you should."

That night, Obie and I were moved into the same loft to sleep. As we bedded down, Obie began to talk.

"Jed, remember what Maddie said today? What would you do if you were free?"

"I never gave it no thought before. It didn't ever seem possible."

"Why not? There's free coloreds, you know."

"I knew that."

"So what would you do if you were free, Jed? If you didn't have to tend the master's horses?"

"I like tendin' horses," I replied.

"You don't mean to say you like shovelin' manure," he said mockingly.

"No, not that part. I guess I'd rather be a jockey or a trainer, and just ride the horses and let someone else shovel the manure."

"That's all? You want nothin' more than that?"

"Well, there ain't no sense spendin' so much thinkin' about it," I said crossly. "You'all might as well go to sleep, cause there ain't anythin' you can could do about it, Obie. Freedom's about as real as whatever it is you'll dream tonight."

II

The next few weeks were more of the same: taking care of the horses while learning my new duties. Obie and I began to cook so well that Maddie would sometimes have something one of us cooked sent into the dining room. She wouldn't tell the family, so she could judge their reactions. Only rarely did they ever notice any difference.

We were learning other things as well. We already knew how to mend and polish leather from taking care of saddles and harnesses, but now we polished boots and mended clothing. Some of what we learned, like cooking, laundering clothes and making soap was rightly women's work, but we learned it and the dozen other things we would have to know when we accompanied the Wentworth brothers into the army.

We started to spend more time in the house, to train as personal servants to the brothers. Obie was assigned to Brady, while I waited on Wade. I was glad to get the easy-going Wade, with his sense of humor. Brady, who was serious and formal, almost stiff, made me feel uncomfortable.

As his personal servant, I cared for Wade almost like I cared for a horse. I heated and poured his bath water, emptied his chamber pot, laid out his clothes and polished his boots. The one thing that Obie did for Brady that I didn't have to do for Wade was shave him. Wade had not yet sprouted real whiskers.

The extra work did not take up too much time, because the Wentworth brothers were away from the farm most of every day. They constantly met with other wealthy young men like themselves to discuss the military unit they were forming to fight for the Confederacy. Because the young men were almost all horse breeders and racers, the unit would, of course, be cavalry.

One afternoon while Obie and I were in the kitchen cleaning up, Mr. Wentworth's familiar voice sounded from the parlor.

"Damn me!"

"Thomas, will you please stop swearing!" Mrs. Wentworth practically shouted. I left the kitchen and sneaked across the dining room so I could hear what was being discussed.

"Sorry, my dear. Events are again provoking me. Tennessee has seceded from the Union. *Tennessee!*" Mr. Wentworth said it as if bewildered. As he resumed speaking, his voice kept getting louder. "There is hardly a plantation there worthy of the name, and half the damned, sorry my dear, benighted state is full of Yankees, or people who are more like Yankees than any true Southerner should be, and yet even they have the fortitude to secede, and here Kentucky sits on the fence and does nothing!" Any comment that Mrs. Wentworth was preparing to make was interrupted by a shout from outside.

"Come look at us!" sounded Wade's voice, full of eagerness. While the Wentworths hurried out onto the front portico, Obie and I ran out the back and around the house.

Brady and Wade both sat very straight on their horses. Each had a drawn sword in his hand. At the same time, they brought the hilts up to their faces and then swept the blades down to the right in salute. The afternoon sun reflected off the gleaming brass and steel with painful brightness.

"First Lieutenant Wentworth, at your service, ma'am," Brady smiled at his mother. He sheathed his sword in the brass mounted steel scabbard that hung next to his left leg. The cock-tail plumes in his black slouch hat shook with a quiet rustling sound as he moved.

Brady wore a short gray jacket with strips of yellow frogging across his chest, with a yellow standing collar and yellow pointed cuffs. There were two horizontal bars of gold braid on each side of the collar and a strip of gold braid in an ornate pattern climbed up each sleeve past the elbow. I found out later that soldiers referred to the sleeve braid as "chicken guts."

A yellow tasseled sash encircled his waist under his sword belt. A narrow welt of gold braid bordered each side of the yellow stripe that ran down the outside seam of each trouser leg. His boots had large square tops that came up over the knee.

Wade was dressed the same way, except his uniform didn't have any chicken guts. Instead, his jacket had two downward-pointing, parallel stripes on each sleeve, on the upper arm.

"Corporal Wentworth, at your service, Ma," he said with a smile wider than Brady's.

"Oh, my! How magnificent. And how handsome you both look," Mrs. Wentworth gushed. Then she frowned. "I suppose this means you'll be going away soon," she said almost to herself.

"We wanted to surprise you, Father," said Brady. "We have an entire company already formed. 'The Mercer County Cavaliers.' I'm First Lieutenant and Jonathan Ballard was elected Captain. James Butler from up-county is the Second Lieutenant. You may recall he was introduced to you last Christmas season at the Ballards' holiday ball."

"I'm the youngest corporal," said Wade proudly. "We don't have our firearms yet, but they should be coming within a week or two."

"Wade ordered two pistols," Brady said with a hint of disapproval in his voice, "in addition to a carbine."

"I need them because I'm going to be actually fighting the war," Wade answered good-naturedly. "We can't all be officers like you, just waving swords and yelling orders, big brother. I mean, sir."

"What is a carbine?" asked their mother.

"A short rifle, especially for mounted troops," Wade answered. "As soon as everyone in the company gets their weapons, it'll be 'boots and saddles,' as we old soldiers like to say."

The Wentworths all laughed at Wade's mocking attempt to play the old soldier as they went into the house. Obie and I led the horses to the stables. That's when Obie started in.

"I sure hope the Yankees win this war." You may think it odd, even stupid, but I was shocked.

"You mean you'all want us to lose the war? How can you'all say somethin' like that?"

"What do you'all mean by 'us,' Jed?" asked Obie scornfully.

"Us. The South. This is our home, too. You'all want the Yankees to come destroy our land?"

"It's not our land any more than it's the horses' land," Obie said curtly. "What about abolition, Jed? Don't you want it to come true?"

"I don't think we should talk about it. You'all heard what Maddie said," I replied.

"Yeah, but what if we have a chance to be free? If it meant we'd be free, would you care if the masters lost the war?" persisted Obie.

"You'd better hush up like Maddie said. You'all are goin' to get in more trouble than you need if you'all not careful. You don't need that kind of trouble. Besides, ain't nobody done any fightin'."

"Yeah, but if there ain't goin' to be no fightin', why'd Brady and Wade join the rebel army? Why'd they have swords and guns?" Obie responded.

"Obie, the rebel army's the place where you and me's goin' to. You'all stop thinkin' about abolition, or you'all are goin' to say somethin' in front of the white folks that's goin' to get the hide whipped right off you." By the sound in my voice, I tried to make it clear that should be the final word on the matter.

"Yeah, but you'all still know the army we should be goin' to is the Yankee army. Even if you won't admit it out loud."

***

A week later, the pistols and carbine arrived. I carried the package to the parlor and watched as the Wentworths all gathered round as the weapons were unpacked. The brothers proudly showed their parents their new guns.

"It was made by Shawk and Maclanahan of St. Louis," said Brady, holding up a beautifully tapered, almost elegant-looking, pistol.

"It's thirty-six caliber, isn't it?" asked Mr. Wentworth.

"Yes, Father, it is."

"What does that mean?" asked Mrs. Wentworth.

"It means the diameter of the bullet is just over a third of an inch, Mother," Brady said. "It can fire six shots before it has to be reloaded. To reload, you put a cartridge into each chamber." Brady showed his mother the six chambers in the revolving cylinder and a bullet glued into a paper cartridge.

"Next, you use the rammer attached under the barrel to make sure the charges stay in each chamber securely. Then, you put a percussion cap on the nipple at the back of the cylinder, one over each chamber.

"This is the hammer. Before each shot, you pull it back, then pull the trigger. The hammer falls on the cap and it explodes, sending a thin flame through the nipple to ignite the powder charge in the chamber."

"How complicated it all sounds," Mrs. Wentworth commented.

"It's splendid!" exclaimed Mr. Wentworth. "When I was your age, we had to prime with powder…"

"Thomas, we are not interested in a history lesson," said Mrs. Wentworth, then she smiled. "Especially ancient history."

Wade unwrapped his pair of pistols. Compared to Brady's pistol, they looked squat, almost ugly. They didn't have any of the shiny brass; they were made of steel only.

"Mine are LeMats. They were invented by Doctor LeMat of New Orleans. The LeMat's a ten-shooter. Nine shots are pistol bullets, but you can pivot this little pin on top of the hammer to fire a charge of buckshot through this short barrel underneath the main one. This hook on the trigger guard is to help hold the gun steady when you fire the buckshot. The kick must be tremendous. I've also got a LeMat carbine."[6]

Wade displayed a gun which was like the pistols, but with a longer pair of barrels and a stock so it could be aimed from the shoulder like a rifle.

"I'm so distressed that you take this pride in such infernal machines," Mrs. Wentworth said, looking at Wade.

"I'm lucky to have received them," Wade replied, carefully not looking at his mother. "The shipper said that, because of the difficulty of obtaining raw materials, Doctor LeMat is going to move to France to manufacture his pistols."

"It's certainly lethal-looking, I'll give you that," Brady kidded, picking up one of the LeMat pistols.

"You both be careful with those things!" Their mother looked at them reprovingly, waving her hands at the pistol as if to ward off an evil. "You could hurt someone," she said sternly, as if they were children caught playing with matches.

***

A few days later, the brothers were ready to leave and join their company. Each of them took two horses, hunters. They were called hunters because they were specially bred for the speed, sure-footedness and endurance needed for fox-hunting.

Obie and I both rode saddle horses. A mule carried the brothers' spare clothing and personal effects, food, cooking gear and ammunition for each of the weapons, as well as Wade's LeMat carbine. The carbine came apart where the stock was joined to the rest of the gun, so it was a package somewhat longer than a pistol, but not much more bulky.

Obie and I had already said goodbye to Gideon, the jockeys and other grooms. Maddie made sure we got a special breakfast of ham and eggs. Even Libby wasn't as gruff as she usually was as she said goodbye.

We waited as Brady and Wade each kissed their teary-eyed mother and manfully shook hands with their father. The brothers then mounted their horses, waved goodbye one last time, then turned towards the gate. They rode side by side. Behind them, I led the spare hunters and Obie led the pack mule.

"Well, we're finally off on the great adventure," Wade said gaily.

"I just hope we don't live to rue the day," Brady replied somberly.

We followed the Wentworth brothers down the road toward Fair Oak

Farm. I hadn't been off Wentworth Farm since the whipping of the runaway, so, for me, being on the open road was a heady experience. Fair Oak was the home of Brady and Wade's friend, Jonathan Ballard, the captain of the Mercer County Cavaliers.

"Once we're all gathered at Fair Oak," Brady told Wade, "we'll ride southwest into Tennessee to join the Confederate army assembling around Union City."

"*Union* City?" asked Wade ironically. "Some choice of name. Why can't we stay here?"

"You know that Kentucky's neutral," replied Brady curtly. "Governor Magoffin favors the Confederacy, but he had to reject Jefferson Davis's call for troops, just as he had rejected Lincoln's call for troops to preserve the Union.[7] Tennessee just approved an ordinance of succession, so the state's officially part of the Confederacy."

"Tennessee's a long way to go," persisted Wade. "Why don't we head east, into Virginia?"

"Because a week ago, the Yankees pushed the Confederate army out of western Virginia, with their victory at Philippi."

Wade would probably liked to have argued further, but was cut off by the sound of hoofbeats. A horseman, dressed in the same uniform as the Wentworths, rode up from behind us.

"Henry Crump!" exclaimed Wade.

"Good morning to both of you," said Henry. "One of the field hands reported that you were riding by, so I came to join you."

"Where are your baggage and servants, Henry?" asked Brady. "Surely you're not going off just in the clothes you're standing in?"

"No, my servants are still packing. They'll join me at Fair Oak once they're done."

"Aren't you afraid they won't get there?" asked Wade. Henry looked befuddled.

"Why wouldn't they?" he asked, as if the answer to the question was self-evident. "We treat them well." There, in two sentences, was captured the attitude of many Southerners of the time toward slavery. They couldn't even imagine us wanting to be free. It's paradoxical, but many of them regarded their slaves almost as part of their families, at least in the way that pets are part of the family.

The three white men became so engrossed in conversation with each other that Obie and I were able to fall back a bit further so we could talk between ourselves.

"Do you know how old you are, Jed?" asked Obie.

"Around fifteen. I don't know what day my birthday is, but I remember my ma once sayin' I was born the day the war with Mexico started." I never knew if she meant the day that the fighting started, which would have been April 25th, 1846, or the day that war was officially declared on May 13th. I guess either date is close enough but I've since taken to celebrating my birth anniversary on April 25th.

"I'm seventeen," replied Obie. "I don't know my birthday either. I do know that I was born on a farm in Benton County, in Tennessee, but I don't know where that is. I remember it was close to a big river. The farm had a lot of milk cows and we used to milk them and take care of them. Some of the other slaves used to make cheese and take the cheese and pails of milk to town in a wagon with the master. I used to help take care of the horses that pulled the wagon. There were about ten or twelve of us slaves. One day when I was about ten or eleven, the master said he was selling the farm so a cotton planter could add it to his plantation. Some of us slaves got sold along with the land. My ma was one of them. I got sold to an agent and then went to the Wentworths." A faraway look crept crept across Obie's face. "I never saw my ma again." I could see the pain in Obie's eyes, but I didn't know what to say. To break the silence, which was uncomfortable, I started talking about myself.

"The first thing I remember was livin' in a town. Lexington. When I got big enough, I was put to work in a livery stable. I'd hold horses when the white gentlemen rode up. We'd unsaddle the horses and water and feed them if they were goin' to be there a while, or just leave the saddles on and water 'em if they weren't goin' to be there long.

"My ma was a maid in one of the big townhouses. Then she got sold to the Wentworths to serve in their townhouse. She begged the master to buy me. When he heard I had worked with horses, he bought me for the farm. He was goin' to send ma to the farm too, but she died before she could go." I paused, because I remembered something I hadn't thought of since my mother died. "Ma never called me 'Jed.' She always called me 'Jedediah.'"

You might have noticed that we didn't even mention fathers. You must understand that many slaves didn't know their fathers, although I found out later that one or two Southern states had enacted ordinances acknowledging the legal validity of slave marriages and forbidding breaking up slave families.

"I remember when you came to the farm," Obie replied. "I always wondered just how you knew so much about takin' care of horses, bein' new and all." We rode in silence for a little while before Obie spoke again.

"Jed, you ever think about runnin' away?"

"Were you there when they whipped that runaway two summers ago?" I asked. Obie nodded and I continued. "After lookin' at what they did to that man's back, I just never gave it no thought."

"That's when I started to want to run away, after I saw that. Master Wentworth never had us whipped like that, where a man almost died. I didn't know white folks would do somethin' like that. I never even thought about runnin' until I saw that," Obie said fiercely.

"I can't understand you wantin' to risk that same thing," I said, truly mystified that he hadn't reacted the same way I had.

"I can't understand you bein'…" He stopped, looking embarrassed, then changed the subject. "I always wondered why he ran in the first place. Was he runnin' away from somethin' worse than a whippin'? Or for some other reason?"

"Obie, why do you want to run?"

"I want to be free," Obie said with conviction.

"But what does that mean? How's it goin' to be different for you if you're free? You'all would still have to work. All you know is takin' care of horses. Do you think you're ever goin' to have enough money to have horses of your own to take care of? So what's the difference whether you're free and payin' for what you need to live on, or workin' for white folks and them givin' you your food and a place to live?"

"If I was free, and my ma was free, then nobody could ever keep us apart no more. You don't have a ma, so how would you know?" The remark stung me, but I kept my hurt from showing on my face. Obie was quiet for a while.

"I'm sorry. I didn't mean to say that."

"That's all right. I understand," I said, but Obie looked even more embarrassed than he had before. We again lapsed into silence.

Thinking about it, I guess I was not so much hurt by Obie's words as frightened by the realization that, except for being owned by the Wentworths, I was alone in the world. Now, I considered Obie my friend, but we were together because somebody else had decided we would be. I wondered what it would be like to live with people who accepted me, and not just because we were all owned by the same master. I wondered how I would feel if my mother was still alive and I had family.

"Jed! Obie!" Wade had dropped back to talk to us. "Things are getting a little tedious, so the three of us are going to ride cross-country to Fair Oak.

The ride'll probably turn into a steeplechase before we're done, so you won't be able to follow, leading the spare mounts and pack mule and all. Just keep on down this road and you'll come to a gate within about three miles. When you get there, go in back of the main house, to the servants' quarters. Somebody'll tell you where to stable the horses and bed down for the night." With a whoop, the three young men jumped their horses over the white plank fence alongside the road and raced away.

I could see from the look in his eyes that Obie was already thinking that this was a chance to run away. He looked quickly down the road behind us and then his eyes darted to the open field on the left side of the road. About two hundred yards beyond the field was a stand of trees that looked a few hundred yards wide. In the distance, there were more open fields.

I was suddenly afraid. I didn't know what I'd would do if Obie ran, whether I'd try to stop him, or go with him, or just do nothing.

I remember thinking of reasons against running, which were numerous. We didn't know where to go and the countryside would be full of soldiers. If we were stopped, we'd never be able to explain where we were going with four fine horses, a mule with a gun packed in its baggage, and no masters with us.

Then I heard the sound of galloping hooves coming up the road behind us. I turned to see seven Confederate soldiers overtaking us. I don't know whether I was alarmed at how close we might have come to running away and getting caught, or relieved that now we couldn't attempt it, or regretting the missed opportunity.

I glanced quickly at Obie and saw a wild light suddenly come into his eyes, like he had been caught doing something he shouldn't. Then, quickly, the gleam went out and Obie turned to face the soldiers, taking off his hat as he did so.

"Afternoon, sir," Obie said to the soldier in the lead. His uniform jacket had the same frogging across the chest as the jackets worn by the Wentworths. The soldier looked at Obie suspiciously.

"What are you doing on the road, boy?" he asked. Obie looked down slightly as he answered.

"Master Wentworth said to follow the road until we came to the gate for Fair Oak Farm, sir. The masters and Mister Crump just jumped the fence right here to race to see whose horse could get 'em to the big house first." The soldier looked at Obie through narrowed eyes for a few moments. I just sat in the saddle with my hat in my hands, trying to remain unnoticed.

"Well, do what your master said. But just wait a bit for our servants here. You can all ride together."

I looked back down the road and saw a group of riders leading other horses and pack mules trotting to catch up. They were all colored except for one white man in a Confederate uniform.

"Heywood, these two belong to Brady and Wade Wentworth," the man who questioned us told the soldier with the servants. "Make sure they get to Fair Oak."

"Sure thing, Porter." The soldier motioned for us to move into the column right behind him.

"Dandy, you stay with Heywood." Another soldier moved to ride behind us. The remaining five jumped the fence and galloped away.

"Let's move," said Heywood as he spurred his horse. We servants followed in silence. With the two soldiers there, none of us spoke, so I had plenty of time to ruminate on what had just happened. Would I have run with Obie, or would I have tried to talk him out of it? What would I have done if talking didn't work? Was the reason I so quickly thought of so many arguments against running because I was being sensible, or because I was afraid?

Would Obie try it again, or rather, what would I do when Obie tried it again, as he was sure to do?

The questions still chased each other around in my head with no clear answers for the rest of the ride, right up until the time I bedded down and tried to sleep.

***

By the second morning after we had arrived at Fair Oak, the other members of the company had arrived.

We had a quick breakfast, then the servants packed baggage on mules and took spare horses in tow. After an equal amount of confusion, the soldiers also were finally ready to begin the march to join the Confederate army gathering in western Tennessee. I say soldiers, but at that time, the only soldierly thing about them was their uniforms.

Just before we set out, Captain Ballard's mother presented the company with its guidon. A guidon is a small, swallow-tailed flag, used to mark the company's place on the battlefield. The guidon of the Mercer Cavaliers was modeled after the Confederate national flag, the "Stars and Bars."

Now, there are a lot of people who think the Stars and Bars were the red

Confederate flag with the two diagonal blue stripes crossing in the center. This was actually the "battle flag," used primarily in Lee's Army of Northern Virginia. The Stars and Bars resembled the United States flag, the "Stars and Stripes," except that, instead of thirteen red and white stripes, it had three broad bars. The top and bottom bars were red and on the middle bar was white. On the white bar of the guidon, Mrs. Ballard had embroidered "Mercer Cavaliers" in gold thread.

With much weeping by the women, cheering by the men and shouting by the children, the company set out for Tennessee.

We were able to travel by road almost the whole way, so the going was easy. The weather was mostly dry, so the three wagons that carried our food and the grain for the horses didn't get bogged down to slow our march. Captain Ballard's father had donated the wagons to the company, along with the teams and harness. He also donated three teamsters to drive them.

You remark that it must had been awful for those three men, to be considered as not much more than accessories of the wagons. I guess it was, but remember that there were over one hundred of us slaves. We had all been "donated," just as much as the teamsters had been.

We marched in the middle of the company, with the baggage and spare horses and pack mules, followed by the wagons and about twenty of the soldiers. Since there were no stables, at night the horses were tied in rows to long ropes by shorter ropes from their halters.

At the time, we felt like we were really living "in the rough," but compared to how we lived later, it was almost an extended picnic.

III

Almost three weeks after starting out, we rode into the camp of the Confederate army near Union City in western Tennessee.

Obie and I were split up then. Because Brady was an officer, he shared a large tent with James Butler, the company's second lieutenant. Wade shared a tent with three of the soldiers in his squad. Obie went with Brady, while I stayed with Wade.

We servants didn't get tents to sleep in. We were instructed to make lean-to shelters from oil-cloth, pine boughs and anything else we could find. The shelters were referred to as "shebangs." I found myself sharing a shebang with Daniel, who was a little older than me. The other two servants in our group, John and Isham, built their own shebang next to ours.

While Daniel and I were in the tent getting our masters settled in, Brady came to talk to Wade.

"You'll never guess who our commanding officer is, Wade! John Hunt Morgan, from Lexington," Brady continued before giving Wade a chance to answer.

"I never met the man, but of course I've heard of him," Wade replied. "I heard he raised the Lexington Rifles. They're infantry. So what's he doing in charge of us? We're cavalry!"

"The Lexington Rifles may be infantry, but Captain Morgan was a cavalryman in Mexico. I met him on a trip to Lexington with father. I'm glad he's our commander," Brady said with enthusiasm. "Tell Jed that if he's separated from us, he should ask for Company C of the Kentucky Cavalry Squadron. That's what we're called now."

Of course Brady was talking about General John Hunt Morgan, the famous raider. He was only a captain then, but I learned just about as much about cavalry tactics from eavesdropping when he talked as I learned on Grierson's Raid. Morgan had that much talent as a commander.

The squad soon settled into camp routine, with drill of some kind every day. Unlike many of the other men in camp, the men in the company didn't spend as much time at the "sinks," the latrine dug for bodily functions, as some others. Many men in the camp had the "trots" and a few had even died from it. The Mercer Cavaliers had servants to do the cooking and washing, and they all seemed to have heard a lecture similar to the one I had heard from Maddie about cleanliness.

The Cavaliers did lose a few men to other diseases. Like many Southerners, most of the men in camp came from rural areas, and they did not have the immunities to contagious disease that many city dwellers did. Wade was glad they stayed so healthy.

"How do you write to the folks back home to say that 'in defense of Southern liberty and states' rights, your son died heroically of the measles'?" he fumed.

One morning, after I cooked Wade's breakfast and saddled his horse, I asked if I could watch the squad at drill. I must have called him "master," because he told me not to anymore.

"Jed, from now on, just call me by my exalted rank, which is 'Corporal'," he said with a self-deprecating chuckle. "And sure you can watch, as long as you get your work done and have dinner ready on time. By the way, you're doin' a great job with the cookin'."

After I cleaned up from breakfast, I walked over to the field in which the company was drilling. Wade was with his seven men, practicing going from column into line.

The drill was important because cavalry marched in column. To be able to fight, they had to be able to go quickly and with no confusion from column into line. In line, each man faced the enemy and was able to use his weapons without fear of hitting someone from his own side.

After about twenty minutes, Wade's squad was fairly good at changing from column to line. I saw that with hindsight, having watched dozens of corporals and sergeants drill their men the same way. At that time, I had no idea of what was really going on.

When Wade told his men to take a break, I walked about a quarter-mile to where infantry regiments were drilling.

Some units were practicing getting into different formations. Others were doing rifle drill, learning how to shoulder arms and fix bayonets, thirteen-inch long blades, to the ends of their rifles.

I became so engrossed in what the infantrymen were doing, I started to follow their movements. The sergeant would commanded "On guard" and I would bring my hands out in front of myself, as if I held a bayonet-tipped rifle.

"Thrust" and I would stab forward. "Develop" and I'd twist the blade. "Recover" and I'd pull it out and return to "on guard."

"What ya'll think yer doin', boy? Think yer a sojer?" said a mocking voice right behind me. I was so startled, I probably jumped six inches off the ground.

I turned around to face a soldier maybe a couple years older than me. He had sandy-colored hair, freckles and a face that might have been handsome, if not for the sneer that seemed to be a permanent feature. I found out later his name was Martin Hawkins, and he was one of the few Southerners I met who I'd say absolutely hated colored people.

"No, sir. I'm no soldier. I just take care of Master Wade, I mean, Corp'ral Wentworth."

"A corp'ral with his own servant, huh? The corp'ral must be a cavalryman, ain't he, boy?"

"Yes, sir, Kentucky Cavalry Squadron. And I better get back there right now and start cookin' the noontime meal." I knew I didn't need any trouble from him, or any other soldier for that matter, so I hurried back to the company area.

I barely had the food cooked when Wade returned to the company area with his squad. They walked, leading their horses. I started to serve his food, but Wade stopped me.

"In the cavalry, the horses come first. Unsaddle him and take him down the creek for a drink. I'll serve myself."

Now, after some thirty years in the U.S. Cavalry, where all the enlisted men care for their own horses, I think back on the attitude of those Southern boys early in the war and it still makes me laugh sometimes. Especially when you remember that, for fighting efficiency, most Yankee cavalry couldn't touch them, at least at the time. But, by war's end, they were taking care of their own horses, that's for sure. And by then, the Yankee cavalry could touch them, and more.

Daniel, John, Isham and I unsaddled the horses then led them through the camp and over to the creek so they could drink.

"Give him some oats and tie him to the picket rope," Wade instructed me when we returned to the company area. "I'll use the mare for afternoon drill. Might as well get both horses used to bein' warhorses. Did you watch us, Jed? How'd we look?"

"You'all looked liked good soldiers, Master, I mean, Corp'ral. The Yankees see you ridin' down on them with swords wavin', they ain't goin' to wait around to ask who you are." Wade laughed.

"I hope we're as good as you think we are, Jed. All the boys are good horsemen, and most of us are good shots, but I think we have a lot to learn before we're good cavalrymen."

"Yes, Corp'ral," I said, but I was gratified that Wade had asked my opinion. I had hardly ever been asked what I thought before, and certainly no white man had ever sought my approval. Wade's question had made me feel mighty pleased.

That was the beginning of my affection for Wade. You might think it servile of me to have been grateful to be permitted to call him "Corporal," just like the soldiers did, and preen at his compliment, but I was grateful. It shows how little recognition most coloreds received, for something that small to have been such a big thing. But that's the way it was at the time. Most other masters wouldn't have thought to do it in ten years. To this day I admire Wade for trying to treat me like a person from the first.

The other servants and I were almost finished cleaning up after the meal, while Wade lounged around with the men from his squad, waiting for afternoon drill to begin, when we were all startled by a popping noise. The sound quickly changed to something like the sound of a brushfire in a pine woods, or maybe like heavy cloth tearing.

"Must be infantry learning how to fire in volley," Wade said as his puzzled look changed to a grin. "Let's go look." He said it to the squad, but I decided to take it as permission to go with them. When they walked off in the direction from which firing came, I tagged along close behind.

We came upon the infantry just as they cut loose with another volley. Although all the men were supposed to fire at once, the sound of firing lasted almost ten seconds. A cloud of dirty white smoke from the exploded gunpowder hung in the still air and almost hid the infantry from view. Even from a hundred yards away, I could smell the smoke. It had a faint tinge like rotten eggs. At the time, I supposed that was what old soldiers had meant by the smell of battle.

The infantry reloaded. It wasn't like now, with magazine rifles where you just snick the bolt and a new round slides into the chamber, ready to fire. In those days, we used muzzle-loaders. We didn't even have metallic cartridges, with the bullet and powder charge all one unit. Loading was a lot more laborious, and a lot slower process.

"Load at will—Load!" That there was just one command indicated that these soldiers were not completely untrained. If they were brand new men, the officers would have given them a separate command for each of the nine steps of the loading procedure. Or the sergeants would have been putting them through the motions, without their burning powder at all.

The infantrymen reached back into the cartridge pouches on their right hips and withdrew a cartridge. As they tore the cartridge paper open with their teeth, some of them rested their rifle butts on the ground and poured the powder from the cartridges down the barrel. Other infantrymen held their weapons in one hand, balancing them while pouring some of the powder in the lock before they put the butts on the ground and poured the remainder of the powder down the barrel.

"Some of them have flintlocks!" Wade exclaimed.[8]

Flintlocks were an older type of musket used back in the War for Independence, almost ninety years before. The newest type of rifle had a percussion lock. This used the same percussion cap as used on Wade's pistols to fire the main charge of black powder.

The infantrymen then wadded up the cartridge paper, put it on the muzzle, the open end of the barrel. They were firing blanks so there were no bullets to shove into the barrels on top of the paper. They then withdrew the long thin ramrods from their pipes under the barrels, and used them to send the wadded cartridge paper all the way down the barrels, right on top of the powder charges. If they had not been firing blanks, the ramrods would have pushed bullets down with the paper.

The men with percussion rifles fished around in the cap pouches on the front of their belts for a percussion cap. The lock was thumbed halfway back and the cap was pushed onto the nipple on the lock.

"Ready!" called out the officers. The men, whether they had percussion or flintlocks, thumbed their locks all the way back.

"Aim!" Rifles were brought up to shoulders.

"Fire!" commanded the officers, sweeping their swords down. The men all pulled their triggers, more or less at the same time. Even if they had pulled them at exactly the same time, percussion locks fired faster than the flintlocks.

When the flintlock's trigger was pulled, a flint was scraped down a piece of steel, throwing sparks into the powder that had been poured into the priming pan that was part of the lock. When this powder exploded, it sent a flame though a hole in the barrel that led to the main charge. There was a lag of almost half a second between the time that the powder in the pan exploded and the main charge fired. Sometimes it didn't fire at all. A flintlock was not only slower than percussion, it misfired almost ten times as often.

The smoke cloud from the last firing still hung in the air when the next volley rang out. The smoke almost completely hid the line of infantry. I could hear a sergeant yelling at a soldier who had left his ramrod in the barrel and shot it away.

"Why aren't they using bullets?" Charlie Rosser asked.

"They're still learnin' how to fire in formation and in unison," replied Wade. "Be a waste of lead to use bullets just yet."

"Boy, are they slow," Charlie's brother Rob snickered. Wade and the other men chuckled.

"They could blow you'all and your horses into food for the crows, fancy boy," said a voice behind us. We all turned around to face a group of soldiers, infantrymen by the light blue trim on the collar and cuffs of some of their uniforms. The one who had spoken was Hawkins, who recognized me.

"If it ain't the darkie who wants to be a sojer! Didn't I tell you'all to stay in your own camp, boy?"

"You tell your own boys anythin' you want," Wade replied, a hint of challenge in his voice, "but he's my property and he does what I tell him, nobody else. Got that, cornpone?"

"You damned horsemen think you're so high and mighty! I guess it's safer to gallop around on the back of a nag, so when a fight gets too hot, you can just skedaddle in that much more of a hurry." The infantrymen laughed.

"Any skedaddlin's more likely to be done by your flock of sheep," taunted Wade. "Don't tell me you walk because you like it. You probably tried out for the cavalry, but they don't let you in if the horses are smarter than you are."

"Now while you're down off your plug and can't skedaddle, maybe I should teach you some manners." I thought that Wade and Hawkins would begin throwing punches.

"Corporal Wentworth!" a voice boomed. "Why the hell aren't you and your men at drill?" We all looked around to see the large form of First Sergeant Moore bearing down on us.

First Sergeant Moore was the highest ranking non-commissioned officer in the company, ranking after the captain and the two lieutenants. He and Wade were friends, but Preston Moore was responsible for the men's training and drill, and he took his duties very seriously. Wade came to attention.

"I beg your pardon, First Sergeant. This here doughboy was castin' aspersions on the honor of the cavalry and I was just tryin' to get him to admit his error," Wade said mock-seriously.

"He was insultin' us," rejoined Hawkins. "I was just tellin' him that we could lick him and his fancy-pants boys and their nags in a real shootin' match."

"I don't know what military courtesy is like in the infantry," First Sergeant Moore responded, "but in the cavalry we address our superiors properly. What's your name, Private?" The sandy-haired soldier straightened up a little, but didn't quite come to attention.

"Private Martin Hawkins, First Sergeant."

"That's better. Fortunately or not, we're all on the same side, so we can't go shootin' each other. But it would be educational to see whether a line of infantry could stand up to charging cavalry. Corporal Wentworth, you get your men saddled up and back to drill. Private Hawkins, lead me to your First Sergeant."

I ran back and saddled Wade's second horse in record time. After Wade rode off to drill, I realized I was angry, but didn't know if I was more angry at Hawkins for mocking me as an inferior or embittered at Wade for referring to me as nothing more than a piece of property.

I had never questioned my lot as a slave before, even after the whipping of the runaway. Maybe Obie's idea of being free had affected me more than I thought, or maybe it was because I had started thinking of Wade as a friend. Quite a dangerous thing for a slave to do with his master, because friendship implies a lack of fear.

I knew better than to show anger in front of any white man, though. Coloreds who got angry, or "uppity" as the whites called it, were likely to find themselves sold, chained, or even whipped or hung.

By the next afternoon, the company was buzzing with the news that they would fight a mock battle with a company of infantry from Tennessee. Both first sergeants thought it would be a great way to motivate their men to do well in training. Each also intended it to give their men the confidence they needed to face a real enemy in battle.

It was to be a friendly contest, just between their men. They agreed that the highest-ranking participants would be sergeants; no officers would be involved. To add some "incentive, other than bragging rights," as Preston Moore said, the losing company would give the winners a full barrel of whiskey.

The Tennesseans staked "charcoal-mellowed, aged Lynchburg sour mash." To underscore just how smooth, the Tennessean First Sergeant had poured a generous tot from a jug he had close at hand, and offered it to Moore with his compliments. Against it, the Kentuckians wagered the finest bourbon in the company supply. That last part of the wager made many of the Cavaliers take notice; they hadn't known that the Supply Sergeant had bourbon. Many troopers started coughing and said they needed to get some of the whiskey for "medicinal purposes."

The two first sergeants decided that the contest would take place in a week or so. It would give both units some time to catch up on their training and also allow the infantry to accumulate the blank cartridges they needed. Because this was an unofficial exercise, with a wager to boot, both sides had to be careful so the high command wouldn't prohibit it. To keep officers from interfering, it would take place when the men of both companies were likely to be off-duty.

They set the date for what they assumed would be a holiday, right after the review and parade to welcome the new commanding general, Leonidas Polk. After the parade, the officers would attend a reception for the new general, so they would be out of the way.

Wade thought it would be a good idea to check from time to time on how well the Tennessee infantry were doing. He had me "wander over" to their training ground every few days and tell him about their progress.

"Jed, you make an excellent spy," Wade told me one day after I had finished reporting. "You have a good eye for detail and give real clear reports." Again, I warmed with pleasure at Wade's compliment, but Charlie Rosser broke the spell.

"Jed's a perfect spy," Charlie told Rob. "Nobody expects darkies to understand anythin' more complicated than a cotton gin."

I looked up sharply. It was plain from the look on his face that Charlie wasn't trying to be insulting; he really believed what he had said was fact.

Later, I wandered through camp, thinking about Charlie's remark. I recalled hearing stories about dogs saving people from fires and finding lost children and dragging injured people to safety. I was always amazed at how, in those stories, the dogs could understand the dangers the humans were in and know what to do. After all, they were just dogs.

The other assumption was that, even if a dog had put itself into danger to save the human, well, that was to be expected. Humans were the lords of creation and it was natural that an animal would have the need to please them. It made me wonder if the Rosser brothers and other white people regarded me, and all coloreds, as something like an intelligent and eager-to-please dog.

I was shaken out of my thoughts by a soldier brushing past from behind. I looked around and saw numerous soldiers gathering around an artillery battery that had just arrived in camp. I had never seen a cannon before and, from the look of it, neither had many of the soldiers. The cannoneers were pleased to be the center of so much attention. A sergeant with a red-trimmed uniform and a flair for the dramatic was explaining about the guns. I moved closer to hear what he was saying.

"Four of these guns are six-pounders and the two bigger ones are twelve-pounders."

"Even the small ones look heavier than that," some wag shouted. Only a few soldiers laughed before the artillery sergeant resumed.

"The number of pounds refer to the weight of the solid shot they fire. Smithfield, open the caisson and gimme a solid shot. Get out one of each of the other kinds, too." Smithfield opened the seat on the caisson, the two-wheeled cart that was hitched between the horse team and the cannon, and took out a solid iron ball. The sergeant took it and held it up with two hands.

"This is a twelve-pound solid shot, or roundshot as it's also called. It will carry about a mile. If it hit a file of men ten deep, dependin' on the range from the gun, it will tumble all ten, maybe only eight at extreme range. And the pieces of bone flyin' from the men it hits will wound the men next to 'em.

"Sometimes they don't even have to be hit. The wind of one of these passin' close can suck the air right out of a man's lungs and kill him without even makin' a mark. And if you see one of these rolling along the ground, just let it go by. I just know somebody is goin' to put out a foot to try to stop a rollin' roundshot. If you do that, you will have a nickname, I assure you. Something like 'Pegleg,' 'cause even if it's rollin' real slow, it will still take off your foot." The sergeant handed the roundshot back to Smithfield and was handed another iron ball.

"This is a case shot. It looks like a roundshot, but it's hollowed out and filled with powder and musket balls. This bronze plug is an Alger fuse. It's also been hollowed out and filled with powder. When it burns through, it ignites the main charge and explodes the ball into small pieces of iron and scatters the balls. What we like to do is cut the fuses so that the shells explode while still in the air, just overhead. That way, the ground doesn't soak up any of the force of the explosion. More death for the dollar, we like to say." The sergeant laughed and so did the cannoneers, but nobody else did. He grunted as he picked up a small bag netted with cord.

"Looks like a bunch o' grapes, don't it?" Since very few of the men had ever seen a bunch of grapes, nobody answered. "This is grapeshot. The 'grapes' are one inch iron balls, about twenty-five of them. When the enemy gets so close to the gun that we can't cut the case shot fuses short enough and we don't want to use roundshot 'cause they can only knock down one file at a time, we use grape. This will take care of more than one file at a time, I assure you." Again, the infantry just stared as the cannoneers chuckled.

Next, the sergeant held up what appeared to be a tin can and shook it, making a muted rattling.

"This is canister. What you hear rattlin' around are musket balls. About three hundred, I reckon, packed in sawdust. The charge just rips the can apart when it leaves the muzzle. Turns our cannon into one big shotgun. When the enemy is really close, we just shove one o' these down the barrel, touch it off, and before the smoke even clears, we can go back to playin' cards. Don't even have to bury the bodies. Not enough o' one left." Again, the cannoneers laughed, but everyone else seemed to be quiet and pale. The artillery sergeant finally appeared to notice the effect he was having.

"But, hey, boys, we're here to do all that to the Yankees!" The men cheered. Then an artillery officer rode up.

"Sergeant Ashley, I know you love an audience, but the horses need to be watered and fed, and so do the men."

"Yes, sir, Cap'n Rutledge, sir."[9] Sergeant Ashley did indeed look like he would miss his audience, but he got the artillerymen back to work. The crowd started to break up and I headed back to the Cavaliers' part of camp.

As I walked back, I was still in awe of the cannons. I couldn't believe all the ingenuity that had gone into creating the different types of shot, especially canister. How could a sane man have invented something like that? Did he just sit down one day and say, "Hmm, we still have the annoying problem of not being able to kill more than a single file of men at a time. What to do about it?" You have remember, this was before such luminaries as Gatling, Maxim and Browning had appeared to lend their respective genius to mass killing.[10]

I shuddered. For a fleeting instant was almost glad I was a slave and could never be a soldier.

IV

The morning of the review and parade finally arrived. Most men in the company awoke with eager anticipation, but not because of the parade. This was the day of the mock battle between the Mercer Cavaliers and the Tennessee infantry.

We servants had spent the previous day grooming the horses, cleaning uniforms, shining boots and polishing sabers for the grand review. Our newly-appointed general, Leonidas Polk, had recently arrived from Memphis. He had ordered the review to give himself a chance to inspect his troops.

I was ready with breakfast when Wade woke up. Wade was so excited about the review and the mock battle that he rushed through breakfast and almost choked. Everybody else seemed to be equally excited. They got washed and dressed with special care. Delaney Burns, known as "Dandy" for the elegance of his person and uniform, got a big laugh by mounting up barefoot. He then had John, his servant, put his socks and boots on his feet while he was in the saddle. He explained it was because he didn't want his beautifully shined boots to get dusty. Clinton Rockwell, almost as big a dandy as Delaney, sat in his camp chair and looked down at his already booted feet.

"Daniel, come pull my boots off," he ordered his servant.

"Your boots'll get smudged when I pull 'em off, sah. Won't have time to shine 'em up again," Daniel told Clint. Clint looked down at his boots with some distress. Then his face brightened.

"Wade, can I borrow Jed for a minute?" he asked.

"Sure you can," Wade replied. "But whatever you're thinkin' to do, do it quick. We've got to get into formation."

Clint had Daniel and me put our hands together and bend down, like we were getting ready to carry something heavy. Clint just stepped up into our hands and stood like a statue as we shuffled sideways over to Clint's horse. Everybody who saw it began to laugh. Even Daniel and I started to laugh, so hard we almost dropped him.

While Isham held the horse steady, Clint told us to heave him up into the saddle. I counted three and we threw Clint up into the air. At the top of his arc, Clint threw a leg over the cantle and managed to keep his seat in the saddle. He doffed his hat and with a flourish, he bowed to Dandy. Everyone was still laughing as Clint took his place in line.

"Settle down, girls, the ball is about to start," said Wade. The squad assumed their best "military bearing" and walked their horses out to the field where the Kentucky Cavalry Squadron was forming up, one company at a time. Daniel, Isham, John and I followed them and sat down at the edge of the field to watch the review.

When the whole squadron was in place, Captain John Hunt Morgan rode into the commanding officer's position centered in front of the troops. The infantry regiments were to the left of the cavalry and at the other end of the line was the artillery battery. The troops fidgeted for a little while, then the four-note trumpet call for "Attention" was sounded.

Captain Morgan gave the order to draw sabers. There was a long scraping sound as the blades came out of the scabbards. The troopers stayed at attention with the sabers held vertical in their right hands, the blades resting against their right shoulders.

In the center portion of the field, an officer saluted with his saber while reporting to an impressive-looking white-haired man on a horse. This was Major General Polk. Other high-ranking officers were ranged behind him.

You've probably heard of General Polk. After he graduated from the Military Academy at West Point, he became an artillery officer, but left the army soon after that to become a minister in the Episcopal Church. When the war started, he was the Bishop of Louisiana. Jefferson Davis had personally made him a major general and placed him in command of Department #2, the military designation for the western Tennessee area.

After a few minutes, General Polk rode to the right of the cavalry. He turned and rode in front of the line from right to left. Captain Morgan and the officers saluted with their sabers as he rode past.

General Polk continued down the line, inspecting the infantry and the artillery. When he was finished, he returned to his place in front of the men to make a short speech. Even with Polk's pulpit-trained voice, I couldn't hear all of what he said, but there were plenty of phrases like "great and noble cause" and "spirit of seventy-six" and "blessings of the Almighty."

When the speech was over, the company at the right of the squadron wheeled to the right and then wheeled left twice. This brought them on a course where they would pass in front of General Polk. They were followed by the other cavalry companies, then the infantry regiments and the artillery battery. As each company passed in front of the general, the officers saluted with their sabers and swords. When the artillery battery, which was last, passed the general, the review was over.

The officers left to go to the reception, leaving the men in the charge of the non-commissioned officers. This is what the Cavaliers were waiting for. They rode to a field on the other side of camp and waited for the infantry. The other servants and I, along with everyone else in camp who knew what was about to occur, ran through the camp to see the mock battle.

I got to the edge of the field and stood trying to catch my breath. The Cavaliers were already there and the infantry company was just marching onto the field.

First Sergeant Moore rode over to shake hands with the infantry first sergeant and then rode back to the company. It had been decided that, to be fair, a group of sergeants from the artillery battery would be the judges.

The Cavaliers were drawn up in two lines about four hundred yards from the infantry company, which was also in two lines. Each company had about the same number of men, so the cavalry lines were much wider than those of the infantry. This was because a man sitting on a horse occupied more space than a man standing on the ground. Although the usual practice for infantry when confronted by cavalry was to have their bayonets fixed, the infantry company didn't have theirs fixed, to keep the cavalrymen from getting hurt. Likewise, the Cavaliers didn't have their sabers drawn, but the men had cut willow wands to serve as mock sabers instead.

An artillery sergeant waved a red handkerchief to signal the beginning of the contest.

First Sergeant Moore turned to the trumpeter, who sounded the call "Charge." The company seemed to throw itself forward as one. The infantry fired a blank volley and immediately began to reload.

The cavalry lines started to get a little ragged as the faster horses started to get ahead of the slower ones. The men on the ends, who had no infantry directly in front of them at which to charge, began to angle in towards the center of the line.

The infantry were now pounding their ramrods down their barrels to seat the powder charges.

About fifteen seconds into the charge, the cavalry had covered almost half the distance to the infantry. The faster horses were already half a length ahead of the slower ones. Some horses were bumping others as the men on the ends continued to angle in.

The infantrymen were putting their percussion caps onto the nipples. There were no flintlocks today; the Tennesseans had borrowed from other companies to make sure every man had a percussion rifle. Two seconds later, the infantry fired their second volley. I, and almost everyone else watching, gave a start as two horses went down with their riders.

"Did some of those fools use real cartridges?" cried a bystander.

"More likely one of 'em forgot to take out his ramrod before he fired," someone else answered. Actually, the center of the charging line was so densely packed, the two horses had probably just collided.

The infantry snatched new cartridges out of their pouches and bit them open. They rammed the paper on top of the powder as the cavalry charge started to lose cohesion.

The faster horses in the second line began to catch up to the slower horses in the first line. As the men on the ends continued to angle in, some of the troopers rode knee to knee. The cavalry had covered almost all the remaining distance to the waiting infantry when the infantry fired again.

This time, only the front rank fired while the rear rank held their fire. The men in front rank got into position to "guard against cavalry," holding their rifles rigidly in front, muzzles angled chest high to a horse.

If bayonets had been fixed, the horses would have been in danger of being impaled.

I caught the sound of galloping horses behind and turned to see numerous officers ride up. They must have had heard the trumpet call and the firing, and, like good soldiers, had ridden as fast as they could to the sound of the guns.

"Are the Yankees attacking?" shouted one.

"No, looks like we got a little inter-service scrimmage going on here," another answered after a pause.

"They're ragged," a voice behind me noted sagely. "The purpose of a cavalry charge is to shock the enemy by all the horses hitting the opposing line at about the same time. They began the charge from too far away." I turned and saw that the speaker was Captain Morgan, talking to two cavalry lieutenants from another company.

I guess some infantrymen must have lost their nerve as the horses closed in on them, because they ran out of the line to the rear. A few cavalrymen angled out of the charging line to intercept them.

The rear rank of infantry now fired. Many of the front horses stopped, startled by the noise and the stinging of the wads of burning paper that erupted from the muzzles of the rifles. One rider sailed over his horse's neck to land with a thump just in front of the kneeling infantrymen. Other horses were jostled and one was knocked down when the horses coming from behind collided with them. Most of the horses refused to ride any closer to the lines of infantry and the troopers in the center started to try to push their way out to the sides.

"Even horses trained as hunters will not ride into an obstacle they can't jump over or see a way around," Morgan told the two lieutenants. "The men on the ends should have remained there to ride around the edges of the infantry line to take it from the rear, instead of angling in."

By then, the line of infantry was bending back into a circle so the cavalry could not get behind them. The infantrymen who had fled the line had all either been knocked down by the horses or corralled together and captured, except for one man who smacked a horse in the nose with the muzzle of his rifle. He ran off the field as the horse reared and threw its rider.

"When charged by cavalry, the correct formation for infantry to adopt is a square, but they waited too long to get into it. That circle they're in looks ragged, but it still may be as effective in preventing an attack from the rear."

We didn't get the chance to see whether the circle would work, for the artillery sergeants ran onto the field to declare the battle over. Slowly, the two sides disentangled from each other. Some of the men on both sides looked really angry, especially the infantrymen who had been knocked down by horses and the cavalrymen who had been thrown. Two cavalrymen looked severely injured, as did an infantryman who had been kicked by a horse. One thing I noticed was that none of the infantrymen who had held his position in the encircled line had been injured.

Tempers on both sides were flaring, so the two first sergeants quickly got together to shake hands so the angry men could see that it was all over before any fist-fights could start. The first sergeant of the artillery battery loudly called for silence.

"The cavalry couldn't break the infantry's formation. On the other hand, the infantry were surrounded by the cavalry and tactically neutralized. I declare this contest a draw."

Some men on each side cheered. Some looked like they still wanted to fight. A few went off to tend to their injured friends.

The sergeants in each company got their men into formation and marched from the field. The two first sergeants decided that right after the evening meal, the two sides would get together back in the field and fraternize by sharing each other's whiskey.

The crowd of soldiers started to go back to camp, but I stayed behind to listen to Captain Morgan lecture the lieutenants.

"During the war, the last war that is, when I was in Mexico, I heard how a Mexican cavalry charge was completely broken by one infantry volley. It happened near Buena Vista, a big ranch. The men of a volunteer regiment saw they were about to be charged by Mexican cavalry. Some say there were a thousand cavalry, others say it was almost two thousand. The volunteers should have formed square, but they either didn't know they should or didn't know how." Morgan chuckled. "But they *should* have known how. The regiment was the Mississippi Rifles, commanded by our illustrious president, Jefferson Davis. He was then Colonel Davis, and he had been a soldier for a long time.

"Anyway, the Rifles formed a line. As you just saw, if the line of cavalry is longer than a line of opposing infantry, the cavalry can envelop the flank of the infantry and cut them down from the sides and rear. The Mexicans cantered up to get close, so they could charge effectively. As I just said, cavalry charges are more effective over short distances, because the horses don't get as tired and the lines do not get as ragged.

"Before the Mexicans charged, another volunteer regiment, one from Indiana, ran up to the right of the Rifles. The Indiana boys couldn't even fall in on a straight line with the Rifles, so the two regiments together formed a big vee, with the arms of the vee toward the Mexicans. The Mexicans were already within the arms, so they charged to break through at the point, where the two regiments abutted.

"Our troops fired once. The Mexicans were between the two regiments, so they were caught in a cross-fire. Half of them were shot out of the saddle by that one volley.

"Some of the survivors looked as though they still had some fight left and were getting set to charge before the volunteers could reload. The Mississippi boys threw down their guns, drew their Bowie knives and, on foot, charged the Mexican cavalry. They actually caught some and dragged them from their saddles and stabbed them. The rest of the Mexican cavalry withdrew from the field.

"The lesson to be learned is that a saber charge cannot succeed against steady infantry, men who do not run. Even the cavalry of the great Napoleon himself could not break the infantry at Waterloo. What I'm trying to tell you gentlemen is that, against good infantry, especially when supported by cannon, a cavalry charge is just a heroic way to die." Captain Morgan walked away with the two lieutenants.

I hurried back to camp to get Wade's supper ready. As I walked, I wondered if it would have made any difference in the success of the charge if the cavalry had not bothered with sabers, but used their pistols instead. Although pistols could not fire as far as rifles, they were repeaters, able to fire five or six times before reloading. I figured that the cavalry could just use their pistols to blast a gap in a line of infantry, then pour through the gap to destroy their formation from the sides and rear. I was still mulling this over when I got back to the company area.

Wade and the other members of the squad were larking about, telling each other that they had really won and that the contest was declared a draw just to keep the infantry from feeling humiliated.

"We had those doughboys surrounded and they were ready to surrender," Wade crowed. "They would have, too, if that stupid cannoneer hadn't stopped it!" All the soldiers and servants were nodding and smiling. Wade looked over at me and said, "Ain't that right, Jed?" Without thinking, I blurted out my rendition of Captain Morgan's great lesson.

"Saber charges against infantry that won't run away is nothin' more'n dyin' like a hero, Master Wade." Wade looked stunned. "I mean, Corp'ral," I added softly. There was a long moment of silence. Everyone, soldiers and servants alike, was staring at me.

"Now what gave you call to say somethin' like that, Jed?" Wade demanded.

"Don't mean nothin' by it, Corp'ral. Heard Captain Morgan say it, that's all," I replied. Wade stared at me for what seemed like an eternity.

"Oh. Well then. Captain Morgan was just an infantryman himself, so of course he'd say that. He don't know nothin' about cavalry," Wade said to the squad and servants. He looked back at me.

"You sounded like an infantryman yourself there, Jed," Wade laughed. "Don't you forget, you're with the Mercer Cavaliers, boy."

"Yes, sir, Corp'ral. I'm with the Cavaliers. And besides, if them doughboys didn't give up, you'all could've shot 'em down with your pistols, right, Corp'ral?" I smiled, trying to get back in his good graces. Wade looked startled again. Then he smiled and slapped me on the back.

"Sure, Jed. We could've just shot them down. Captain Morgan say that, too?"

I instantly realized my mistake. I didn't want Wade to realize that I had drawn that conclusion by myself. White people were innately distrustful of coloreds who could think for themselves and reason things out. So I lied.

"Yes, Corp'ral. That's who said it."

***

One evening about three weeks after the mock battle, I sat with Obie, tending a small fire. Obie had just put coffee on to boil. The squad was sitting around the fire in a circle, waiting for the coffee to be ready. The men were complaining to each other about how the squadron, and the whole army, was being run. They had heard about Captain Morgan's comment about the futility of saber charges. Every one of them thought Captain Morgan was wrong. Wade summed up their feelings.

"Maybe steady infantry wouldn't cut and run, but Yankees will. One look at us wavin' steel and all we'll see of them is the seats of their pants. One of us is worth ten of them." Nobody in the squad disagreed.

"You know what bothers me?" Dandy Burns piped up. "We know how to ride and shoot. Why do we have to spend so much time on useless things like learning how to salute or stand at attention? The war will be over soon and we don't need to know any of that. We should go east to Virginia before we miss the big battle."

At the time, many men on both sides were sure that one big battle would decide the war. It seems naive now, and it was a memory that would excite rueful amusement a year later, but they were concerned that the war would be over before they got a chance to fight. Many were sure that the one big battle of the war would take place in northern Virginia, somewhere between the Confederate capital, Richmond, and Washington, the United States capital. Of course, they all wanted to be in it.

The Cavaliers had already gotten two scares that they had missed the big one when news had arrived that there had been two fights in Virginia, one at Rich Mountain and another at Corrick's Ford two days later. They consoled themselves with the thought that each was a relatively small fray. They read in the newspapers that the main Yankee army had not yet left Washington. The big battle wouldn't happen until it marched.

One evening, as the men were discussing this for what seemed the hundredth time, a shout came out of the darkness beyond the campfire's light.

"The Yankees are marching on Richmond!" William Knowles, a soldier from another squad, stepped into the circle around the fire. "I just heard

Ballard, Butler and Wade's brother talking. The Yankee army marched on Richmond three days ago. There was a fight at a place called Blackburn's Ford the day before yesterday."

"It wasn't the big one, was it?" Rob Rosser asked, almost fearfully.

"It doesn't appear to be, but the big one can't be far behind," Knowles replied.

"I hope we didn't put up with all this tomfoolery just to miss the war," shouted Clint Rockwell. The whole squad jumped up and hurried toward Captain Ballard's tent to get more news. After they were gone, I turned to Obie.

"They're sure itchin' to get into the fight. I wonder why none of 'em are scared." I imagined going into something like the mock battle, only with real bullets, grapeshot and canister, and knew that I wouldn't be able to help being scared. Obie gave a dry laugh.

"What d'you mean, they ain't scared? I don't know for sure, but I'll bet every one of 'em is scared some."

"They don't sound scared to me. They sound full of vinegar, like they can't wait to get at the Yankees," I retorted. Obie looked thoughtful.

"Like I said, I don't know for sure but I think they're all talkin' like that to make sure nobody *thinks* they're scared. Maybe they're tryin' to tell themselves they ain't scared. Everybody is scared of somethin' and a war seems like a good thing to be scared of." Obie changed the subject. "You want some of this coffee, Jed? It smells ready and there'll still be enough for all them when they get back."

I sipped coffee and wondered if Obie said what he said about everybody being afraid of something just to make me feel better. I was certain that I'd be too scared to do anything in a battle. I'd never be able to even remember how to load and fire a rifle, let alone do it. I'd probably shake so much I'd spill all the cartridge powder on the ground, instead of down the barrel. I consoled myself with the thought that it didn't matter, and would never matter, because slaves couldn't fight.

***

Three days later, news came that the Cavaliers had indeed missed the big battle. The two armies had met less than forty miles from Washington, near a town in northern Virginia named Manassas Junction. The Confederate army whipped the Yankees so badly that they hadn't stop running until they reached Washington.

The morning after we heard the news, Wade was kind of quiet. I helped Wade put on his uniform and held his sword belt to buckle it around him. Wade looked at the saber.

"I don't need that today," he said morosely. "The war is over, I guess."

"You'all don't seem too happy about that, Corp'ral. We won, didn't we?" I asked. As you can see, at the time I still struggled with where my loyalties lay.

"Jed, I really don't know if I'm happy we won, or I'm more let down that the Cavaliers didn't have a part. I wish we had been in one battle, even a small one, just so I'd know how we'd have done." Wade gave a short laugh. "Somebody said it's like goin' to the circus to see the elephant and goin' home without seein' it. If that's why you went, you're bound to be disappointed. Oh, well. Let's see whether there's goin' to be a parade or celebration or somethin' in honor of the victory."

A day or so later, there was still no word that the Yankees had surrendered or that they would sign a treaty agreeing to Southern independence. A few of the soldiers started to believe that there would be more than one battle to this war.

The other bit of news that greatly interested the cavalrymen was the account of how, after the infantry and artillery had shot at each other all day, it was the cavalry that finally sent the Yankees running.

"Listen to this!" Wade read from a week-old newspaper. "Here's what the paper says. 'Instrumental, perhaps decisive, in putting the federal army to flight was the charge of the First Virginia Cavalry, commanded by Lieutenant Colonel Stuart. Colonel Stuart, while a captain in the United States Army, played a leading role in the capture of the notorious John Brown at Harpers Ferry, Virginia. With drawn sabers'... You'all hear that!... 'with drawn sabers, the gallant Virginians, heedless of the danger to themselves, rode headlong into the line of federal infantry and put them to flight after their brief and futile attempt to resist.' Who says sabers can't win a battle, huh?"

The squad, which had gotten lax in their training after the news of the Southern victory, now couldn't get enough of saber training. Wade borrowed a well-thumbed copy of *Patten's Cavalry Drill & Sabre Exercise* and copied the chapters detailing saber drill.

The officer who owned the manual told Wade a story, which he gleefully recounted to the squad. During the war with Mexico, a patrol of twenty men of the 2nd Dragoons were confronted by a force of over one hundred Mexican cavalry. They had reached for their carbines, but their leader, Sergeant Jack

Miller, told them that if they couldn't rout a hundred Mexicans with their sabers, he'd give up riding and join the doughboys, as infantry were nicknamed then. The dragoons charged and killed, wounded or captured eighty-nine enemy troopers.

"That's what we're goin' to be like, only better," Wade told the squad. "Figure that those twenty dragoons probably had Germans and Irish among them." Like many Americans of the time, Wade looked down on immigrants. "If *they* could scatter a hundred Mexicans, imagine what we'd have done. Now, I'm not sayin' Yankees ain't braver than Mexicans, because they are. They're still Americans. But facin' us, they'll scatter like Mexicans!" Everyone in the squad shouted in agreement and threw themselves into saber drill like men possessed.

The servants and I watched them practice the different movements: backward slash, downward slash, thrust en tierce, guard, parry, and all the others. They first practiced while on foot, imitating Wade while he demonstrated each movement.

When he thought the squad was ready, Wade had Isham and me remove the rails from between some fence posts. Wade had begged some spoiled vegetables from the Commissary Sergeant and we set a squash or melon on the top of each of the posts. Each man in the squad was supposed to ride zig-zag through the line of posts, cutting with his saber at the vegetables, imagining them to be enemy heads.

Henry Crump went first. He missed the first three posts he tried to slash, then split a melon. On the next post, he cut through a squash, but his saber also cut into the top of the post. It got stuck and was pulled out of his hand. Isham and I, standing by to replace the cut melons, tried not to laugh.

Heywood Stewart saw what had happened to Henry and remembered to tighten the saber's wrist strap. He missed the melon on the first post and cut into the front of the second post so hard, his saber also got stuck in the wood. When his horse kept running, he was pulled out of the saddle by his wrist strap. He fell with a crash, but only his dignity seemed to be hurt. Everyone laughed, including me and Isham.

Porter Lawliss was next. He completely missed with a downward slash to the right at the first post. At the next post, while trying a downward slash to the left, he cut the top of his horse's ear off. The horse was so startled by the sudden pain, it bucked Porter off. We all were convulsed by laughter, even Porter, after he had picked himself up off the ground.

"Reckon your horse is a Yankee, Porter?" asked Rob sarcastically.

"You invent that move yourself, Porter?" added Charlie. "Never did see nothin' like what you just did anywhere in the manual."

The men were thinking that maybe they had enough saber drill for one day, when we noticed Captain Morgan sitting on his horse, watching. I could see from their faces that the men in the squad were feeling pretty foolish, especially knowing his view on the saber. They just stared at him, waiting for the ridicule that was sure to come.

Captain Morgan walked his horse slowly forward. Wade called the squad to attention and saluted. Captain Morgan returned the salute.

"Afternoon, Corporal. Doing some extra training with your squad, I see," Morgan said pleasantly after he dismounted.

"Yes, sir. If them Virginia boys can whip Yankees with sabers, so can we," Wade said defiantly.

"Corporal, those Yankees were whipped before the Virginians ever got close. Not one of those Yankees had probably ever even seen a cavalry charge before.

"Now, I got to admit, sabers in the hands of some devils screaming blue murder has got to be a frightening sight. Know why? Most men know what a blade can do to them. You live on farms and have seen hogs butchered. Most of you have probably cut yourselves accidently with knives or razors on occasion. You know what it feels like.

"It gets magnified in your mind because a saber is so much bigger than a razor. That's why it's so fearsome." Morgan asked to see Wade's hand-copied manual and quickly thumbed through it.

"Spend much time learning these moves?"

"Not much, Captain. But the boys'll get better at it."

"Corporal, as your commanding officer, I could just order you not to spend any more time on it," Morgan said mildly. "But I've always found that most people learn best when they learn something by themselves. Instead, I'm going to give you two easy rules for when to use sabers.

"First, only use them against troops who are running away, or look like they're about to run away. Second, don't wave the things around, trying to cut with them. If you're going to use a saber, stab the enemy with the point.

"But even better than that, shoot them. Firepower will always beat cold steel, no matter how brave the men behind it." Morgan remounted his horse. As Morgan started to ride away, Wade called after him.

"That doesn't take very much valor, now does it, Captain?" Morgan checked his horse and gave a short, mirthless laugh.

"You think war is about a chance to win glory, don't you? Of course you do; you're a Southerner. We Southerners all have a yearning for glory, to win a name for ourselves that will be remembered by generations of schoolboys to come.

"You call yourself 'The Cavaliers,' but war isn't about chivalry. It's about winning. Use any advantage that you have: greater numbers, better weapons, surprise. Nobody is going to care how gallant you are if you lose. I do not intend to lose." Morgan's gaze challenged us for a long hard moment, then he rode away.

V

It may seem puzzling, but when they heard news of another Confederate victory—a sharp little engagement at Wilson's Creek in southwestern Missouri—the men griped bitterly. This was so close, it seemed local, and many of the young men couldn't abide having been left out of the action once again.

We were still camped around Union City, Tennessee. Polk's army had grown since the Cavaliers had joined it in early summer. There were now almost 11,000 men but many of them had only shotguns or hunting rifles for weapons and many more did not have firearms of any type at all.

Not fifty miles away, waiting just north of the Kentucky state line at Cairo, Illinois, was a Yankee force under Brigadier General Ulysses S. Grant. Neither side wanted to enter Kentucky first and violate that state's neutrality, for each knew such a move would likely drive the Kentuckians to join the other side.

One afternoon in late August, while I was grooming one of Wade's horses, Obie walked over, trying very hard to look casual. I knew him well enough to know that he must have some great secret inside him and, if I left him alone, he'd tell me soon enough. Sure enough, after some small talk, Obie got down to it.

"We've been here so long, almost feels like home, don't it? But next week, we'll be goin' home." For a moment, I thought that Obie was talking about running again. Then I realized what he meant by "we" was the whole army.

"Kentucky? We're finally goin' to cross the river? Where'd you'all hear that?"

"I hang around with officers. Cap'n Ballard was tellin' the lieutenants. We goin' to move soon, next week the latest." Obie paused. "I wonder how close we are now to Benton County?"

"Obie, how you'all goin' to get there if you don't even know where Benton County is? What're you goin' to do if you do get there and your ma ain't even there no more?"

I was alarmed that Obie was again planning to run, but as I spoke, I realized that I was concerned about the practical problems connected with running away, not the fear of running. I didn't want anything to happen to Obie, but at the same time I appreciated his need to find his mother.

"All I'm sayin, is, don't go off half cocked. If you're goin', make sure you know where you're goin' and how to get there. Wait until the army moves, then try to slip away. With this number of people movin' all at once, it may take a day or two till anyone even knows you're gone. Even when they do find out, they might have other things on their minds, like the Yankee army." I was sharply aware that if anyone found out I was encouraging another slave to run, I could be whipped. I was also aware that the thought didn't frighten me so much any more.

Obie just looked back at me without saying anything. At that moment, Charlie Rosser came trotting into the campsite. Obie walked casually back towards the officers' tents, while I tried not to look as guilty as I felt.

"Hey, Jed! Hold my horse a minute. I just need to get my carbine." As Charlie dismounted, he looked into my face. "Feelin' a little sick, Jed? You're all sweaty and look a little jittery."

"I hope I'm not gettin' sick, sir," I replied more calmly than I felt. "There's way too much to do around here." Charlie just pushed past me, poked around in the tent, and leaped back into the saddle with his carbine.

"I'll tell Wade, uh, the Corp'ral, not to work you so hard." Charlie laughed and rode away, while I tried to force my heart to stop hammering.

It turned out that Obie was correct about the army getting ready to move. We were going north into Kentucky.

The people of the town of Columbus sent word that the Yankees were going to occupy their town, to gain control of the rail line that went south into Tennessee and Mississippi. Because of the scarcity of good roads on which to move the armies and their supplies, control of the rivers was very important, as were the railroad junctions and terminals. It was easier, and faster, to move troops by train or boat than to have them march.

The morning we were to move out, all the servants were kept busy getting everything packed and ready. I went down to the creek with a small bucket to get some water for Wade's horse. Wade had been detailed as Captain Ballard's messenger. All morning, he had galloped back and forth from the head to the tail of the column, and his horse was thirsty.

I waded out a few steps into the creek, but not far enough for the water to come over my boot tops, to get clear-flowing water. Closer to the banks, the water was brackish, covered with green scum and even had a few fish floating belly-up. I filled the bucket and turned back toward the bank. Standing on the bank was Hawkins, festooned with canteens.

"I got sent down here to fill canteens, but since you're here, you do it for me, darkie. No sense both of us getting our feet wet," he sneered. He held the canteens out.

I knew from seeing him around camp that Hawkins was a "shirker," a soldier who avoided work. He got out of work by feigning illness, at least most of the time. Those few times I did see him work, he was usually "dogging," that is, he appeared to be doing what was expected, but, if you looked closely, you could see that he wasn't. For example, if he was digging a rifle pit, he didn't move his shovel too often, and when he did, he didn't come up with a full shovelful of earth. More often, while his company was digging rifle pits, he would carry his musket and cartridge box and pretend to be on guard. These past thirty years I spent as a non-comm in the United States Cavalry, no soldier has been able to get away with shirking or dogging with me, just from what I learned about it watching Hawkins.

I don't know why, since it was so trivial, but a feeling of anger took hold of me. Maybe I was angry because I knew he hated coloreds. Of course, I had been a slave too long to let it show. I held out my hand and took the canteens.

While Hawkins went to sit with his back against a tree on the bank, I waded back out into the creek and filled the canteens. When I looked back at Hawkins, his head was thrown back and his eyes were closed.

I quickly put a dead fish into one of the canteens, then corked it. I draped all the canteens over my shoulder, except for the one with the dead fish.

As I splashed back to the bank, Hawkins sat up. I held out the canteen with the dead fish and, as I expected, Hawkins took it and draped it over his shoulder. Then he took the other canteens for the rest of the men. He didn't say thank you, just kicked over the bucket and walked away.

I just stood, imagining the scene when Hawkins, thirsty during the march, tipped the canteen up to his lips. I knew that there would be a reckoning with Hawkins someday. I also knew that Hawkins wouldn't make himself look foolish by telling anyone about how he had been tricked by a colored, so when the reckoning came, it would be between just the two of us. I didn't exactly look forward to it, but I didn't shrink from it either.

With a grim smile, I refilled the bucket and walked back to water Wade's horse.

***

The march to Columbus took only a few days. From the look of things, it was hard to tell we were back in Kentucky. The scenery didn't look any different from that part of Tennessee.

Every morning during the army's march to Columbus, I made sure to go past the company's headquarters to see if Obie had run away during the night. Each morning, I felt relieved when I saw that he was still around.

The Cavaliers didn't stay in Kentucky very long. A small Yankee army, under Grant, had countered the Confederate move by occupying Paducah, where the Tennessee River met the Ohio River. Polk realized that from Paducah, Grant could attack down the Mississippi River and hit Columbus head-on or he could outflank the Confederate positions by marching down the western bank of the Mississippi, in Missouri.

To make sure he received word if the Yankees tried to outflank him, Polk sent a regiment of infantry, a battery of artillery and two companies of cavalry across the river to Belmont, Missouri, to set up an observation post. The Cavaliers was one of the two cavalry companies.

During the crossing of the river, I made sure I got on the same boat as Obie. I hadn't had a chance to talk to him since the day I had cautioned him about running away. Rather than bring that up, I told him about putting the dead fish into Hawkins' canteen. Obie laughed at the story, then quickly turned serious.

"Why'd you'all do that? You don't need no trouble like that."

"Hawkins'd make trouble anyway. He looks at all coloreds like we were scum. I know I'm a slave, but that don't mean I ain't a man."

"You'all ain't a man, you're still a boy, not even sixteen years old," Obie teased gently, then grew serious again. "Better watch your back, Jed. Nothin' says Hawkins won't get some of his friends to help him get even. I'll watch out for you as best I can." The boat bumped on the far bank.

"And you can count on me if you need help on the other thing," I replied. Obie knew I meant about running away and just nodded his thanks.

When all of the small force had been ferried over from Columbus, the infantry regiment, with the artillery battery, began taking up defensive positions around the village of Belmont, which didn't seem to be much more than a cluster of three or four shacks next to a steamboat landing. Looking back across the river, I could clearly see the fortifications around Columbus, with their heavy cannons. All the same, we felt isolated. If the Yankees did come this way, we would be totally on our own until help could be sent from across the river.

The infantry sent out pickets to cover the main positions. A picket was a small group of soldiers, usually four to eight men under a corporal or a sergeant, that guarded against surprise attacks. The soldiers on picket usually had one- or two-man posts a few hundred yards in front of the main defensive position, preferably with something like an open field or stream in front of them, where the enemy would have trouble getting close without being seen first.

If the enemy attempted to surprise the main force, they would first run into the picket line. The pickets would shoot at the approaching enemy to try to slow them down and, more importantly, to warn the main force of danger by the sound of their gunfire. The pickets would then withdraw back to the main position.

The cavalry companies were assigned to provide patrols and vedettes. Vedettes were like mounted pickets. Because they could move faster, vedettes were usually placed further out than pickets, or in places, like the far side of an open field or a stream, where a man on foot would be at a disadvantage in trying to get back.

Patrols were small groups of cavalrymen that scouted the areas between picket and vedette positions and scouted in front of the picket lines, seeking information about the enemy while they were still far away.

The squad soon settled down into a routine: on vedette every second or third night and on patrol every third or fourth day. They usually took only one servant when they were assigned to these duties. The servant didn't have to do any cooking or cleaning, just lead a spare horse. The spare horse was there in case any of the soldiers' horses got hurt, lamed or threw a shoe and couldn't be ridden. The spare also carried a small amount of oats and some extra food for the men, in case they had to stay out on patrol longer than planned. When they weren't on patrol, the squad was allowed to stay in camp with little to do but get ready for the next patrol.

Brady still sent newspapers to Wade when the officers had finished reading them. The papers could be anywhere from a few days to several weeks old. Wade would read items out loud to the squad, then pass the papers on to another squad.

I usually listened when Wade read, mostly news of the war in other areas of the country. My ears pricked up one day while Wade read a story from a

Memphis paper. The article spoke of a marching column "of several hundred stout Negro men in military order, under the command of Confederate officers."

For a second, my heart beat more quickly at the thought that the Confederacy had allowed colored men to become soldiers, but then Wade read how the coloreds carried only shovels, picks and axes.

Another time, when Obie came with newspapers for Wade, he stayed to listen while Wade read out loud. In the middle of reading a story, Wade suddenly stopped, apparently too angry to go on.

"Damn it all," he shouted. "This changes everything. The damn Yankees are allowing coloreds to serve on navy ships!"

"So what, Wade?" said Henry Crump. "The Yankees need cooks and servants just like we do. I'm glad they're allowing coloreds on board their ships to do all that. Shows 'em for the hypocrites they are."

"You don't understand," said Wade. "They're allowing coloreds to enlist."

"Freedmen or runaways?" asked Dandy.

"What does that matter?" said Clint.

"They don't ask what their status is," answered Wade.

"That's somebody's property!" shouted Porter Lawliss. "Damned thieves! Stealin' somebody's property and puttin' them on ships where they got no chance of gettin' them back."

"Quiet down! That's not the worst part," continued Wade. "The slaves are allowed to serve in gun crews. The Yankees are letting slaves fight us!"

The men were so shocked they were struck speechless. Finally, Wade broke the silence.

"I know it was the abolitionists wanted the war to free the slaves, where most Yankees just want to reunite the country," he said quietly. "But I never thought they'd do something so low as to arm slaves to murder their masters."

I carefully kept my head down, not looking at anyone. I knew better than to draw attention to myself at a moment like this. But then I had the feeling of being watched and raised my eyes. Obie gave me a long, significant look.

I could see in his face a greater determination than ever. If I knew him, now that there was a means of fighting to be free, Obie would run and somehow make his way to the sea and join the Yankee navy.

I also knew that for the first time since he started talking about running, I wouldn't try to stop him.

***

The squad's routine of patrol persisted monotonously as September passed into October, which flowed into November. The men again became discontented from the lack of action.

One morning in early November, I brought up the rear as the squad patrolled a wooded area to the north of Belmont.

"Know what we're doin' today, Charlie?" Rob Rosser, one of the last two riders in the column, groused to his brother. "We are wearin' out the seats of our pants, and nothin' more." Charlie was a little less melancholy, but more sarcastic, than his brother.

"Of course we are. You know why? There's no such thing as a Yankee. You know that, don't you, Rob? I mean, if Yankees were real, how come we've never even seen one?" Wade, at the front of the column, turned in his saddle.

"Quiet! You all hear that?" I heard a distant rumbling, then looked up at the sky. The sky was mostly blue, so the noise wasn't a thunderstorm. The rumbling sound was immediately followed by a whole host of crashes crowded on each other.

"Cannon fire, that's what it is!" Wade hollered to the squad. "It has to be. The Yankees must be attackin' Columbus!"

"I guess the phony war is over," Henry Crump said.

"Just our luck," Clint Rockwell said disgustedly. He turned to Wade, who was next to him at the front of the column. "Finally, the chance of some action after all these months, and we're on the wrong side of the river."

Suddenly, there was a ragged popping sound. Puffs of smoke appeared from the treeline on the far side of the field.

"Tarnation!" shouted Clint, as his horse collapsed under him. Clint threw his right foot out of the stirrup as the horse went down, but he didn't get his left foot clear. I heard a sickening crack as Clint's left leg broke. We all just sat our horses, dumfounded.

I guess I recovered from the shock first. I put spurs to my horse, leading the spare mount to where Clint lay pinned under his dying horse. I leaped from the saddle, yelling to Wade.

"Shoot! Shoot back!"

When I grabbed Clint under the arms and pulled, he screamed in pain. The scream must have startled Wade back to reality, for he finally made sense of what I had said.

"Get into line!" he yelled at the squad. "Form in front of Clint and start shootin'." The men pulled their pistols from their holsters, thumbed back the hammers, and sent a hail of bullets toward the men in blue running at them from the treeline.

The Yankees stopped to fire back. Some of them went down on one knee to take steadier aim, but nobody in the squad was hit.

"Hurry, Jed! Get him up!" Wade shouted without looking back.

Clint pushed against the horse with his right foot, trying to help me free his left foot. I had my right foot against the horse's side also, pushing it away while continuing to pull Clint. His foot finally came free, and I almost fell backwards. I dropped him and he screamed in pain again. He screamed some more as I dragged him over to my horse. I tried to lift him into the saddle, but he was too heavy.

The men in the squad had emptied their pistols. Some raised their carbines. Wade's carbine was on the spare horse, so he drew his other pistol and resumed firing.

"Jed, hurry! Here they come!" Now that the Confederate fire had slackened, the Yankees were again up and advancing.

Desperation seemed to give me tremendous strength. With a grunt, I heaved Clint up into the saddle so hard that he almost fell off the other side.

"Got 'im!" I yelled to Wade, leaping onto the unsaddled spare horse. I grabbed the reins of the mount on which Clint kept a precarious seat and, not bothering to get permission, I galloped both horses back away from the advancing line of Yankee soldiers.

I didn't slow down until I got Clint in among the trees. The rest of the squad caught up. Wade looked back to the open field. The Yankees were still following and occasionally shooting at us.

"It looks like about sixty men," Wade estimated. "That's a company skirmish line which means there's the rest of a whole regiment followin'." It was still fairly early in the war, so a federal infantry regiment might contain eight or nine hundred men, a real danger to the small Confederate force in Belmont.

"We've got to get back and warn the rest of the army," Wade told the squad. "We also got to get Clint to a doctor. Let's go!" He galloped away, followed by the rest of us. We galloped all the way back to the first line of infantry pickets. Wade found their sergeant.

"The Yankees are comin' this way. They'll be comin' from the north. You'd better get ready for them." Without waiting for a reply, Wade led us on back to Belmont.

Wade went to find Captain Ballard, to report what had happened and the Yankee force we had seen. The rest of us rode over to the shack where the infantry's regimental surgeon had set up his office.

Dandy Burns helped me get Clint off the horse and carry him through the door. The surgeon told us to put Clint on the table and called for medical orderlies to come help him. He then ordered us out.

"It will be too crowded to work if you're all hanging about." Dandy and I left the surgeon's office and remounted our horses. I again took the reins of the spare horse.

Now, for the first time since we had been shot at, I had time to think. While the fighting had been going on, I hadn't really thought at all, just reacted. I had taken the correct actions purely through instinct, but I felt pleased with myself.

Just then, the realization of the danger overwhelmed me. I felt my stomach contract into a hard knot and my face break out into a sweat. I looked up at the squad to see if anyone noticed.

Henry was just staring at the ground, apparently not seeing anything. Rob was talking loudly and quickly. He didn't seem to care if anyone was listening or not. Heywood had a look in his eyes like a hunted animal that just had escaped being cornered. All the rest of the squad seemed to be affected in some way, except for Charlie, who was yawning. I didn't know it at the time, but each of the reactions, including the yawning, were the reactions of men whose bodies and minds were coping with fear.

I suddenly felt pleased again, because they all seemed to have been affected at least as much as I had. In fact, I seemed to be the best off of any of them, so I kind of took charge.

"We'd better find the Corp'ral," I told them. "There's goin' to be a fight." I led them to where the company officers camped. Wade was already there. When we rode up, Captain Ballard was telling Wade that, while they were out on patrol, the Confederate force at Belmont had been reinforced by four regiments of infantry.

"We're to screen General Pillow's brigade as they move to contact with the enemy. The general doesn't want to wait behind the breastworks. Get your men ready to move. Your squad will lead, since you know where the enemy are. We'll start in a few minutes, as soon as the outlying patrols come in." Wade saluted as Captain Ballard rode away, then he turned to us.

"How's Clint?"

"We left him at the surgeon's," Dandy replied. "The surgeon told us to leave, so he could work on him. Guess he'll be all right."

"Fine. Well, you all heard the orders, so get yourselves ready." Wade pulled me aside. "You did a real good job back there, Jed. If not for you, Clint, I mean Private Rockwell... ah, I mean Clint. He might've been captured, or worse. I'm glad you were with us, Jed."

"Thanks for sayin' that, Corp'ral." I didn't need to feel grateful for his compliment. I knew I had performed well. Looking back, I think that was the exact moment I decided I should no longer be a slave.

Wade moved back to the front of the squad to wait for the infantry. He must have felt the mood.

"Well, we've seen the elephant. Don't look like nothin' we can't handle, now does it?" No one in the squad spoke, but they all snapped out of their individual preoccupations. Without orders, they formed up in a column of twos to wait for the infantry to get ready.

Since the number of men in the squad was now uneven, Heywood Stewart, at the back of the column, had no one next to him. I moved my horse into the empty space in the formation. Heywood glanced over at me with raised eyebrows, but then he gave me a tight little smile and faced front, waiting for the order to march.

A few minutes later, we got the command to move forward.

VI

The squad led the company north, out of Belmont to screen and fix the location of the Yankee force. Once we found them, the company was to form a firing line to try to slow the Yankees down. Infantry regiments would come up from behind the cavalry to make the main attack.

We rode less than a mile before we saw soldiers in blue in the woods. The leading company was still in skirmish order, but they had halted. I saw an officer at the front, facing his men. He looked to me as though he was making a speech.[11]

Wade immediately halted the squad.

"Go find the Captain and get him over here," he told Charlie Rosser. "You others, dismount and grab your carbines. Jed, get me my carbine and hold the horses."

I leaped off my horse, pulled Wade's LeMat carbine off the spare mount and handed it to him. I then grabbed the reins from each member of the squad and struggled to keep the horses quiet.

Captain Ballard rode up with Brady and Charlie. Charlie dismounted and also tossed me his reins, then, carbine in hand, took his place in the firing line next to Rob.

"Let him keep talking," Captain Ballard told Wade, meaning the Yankee officer. "It will give us a little more time. We'll form up on each side of you. Lieutenant Wentworth, have the even-numbered squads form up to the right of Wade's men. Odd-numbered to the left." Brady rode off.

"Corp'ral," I said urgently to Wade, "it looks to me the Yankee's finished his speech."

"Aim at those Yankees in front of us. Range, three hundred yards. Fire!" Seven shots rattled sharply, and I saw three blue-coated soldiers fall.

The other squads came up from behind and began fanning out to each side. The troopers dismounted and tied their horses to trees. They ran forward, extending our line until almost eighty troopers were blazing away with their carbines. Most of them were single shot weapons, unlike Wade's LeMat, and it took them almost twenty seconds to reload after each shot. Their firing slackened a little after the first few shots as they began to tire, so the Yankees resumed their advance.

The Yankee soldiers were infantry with rifles. Rifles shot farther, but they also took about twenty seconds to reload. The Yankees seemed to work in pairs. After one man fired and began to reload, his partner ran up ahead of him and stood behind a tree or got down on one knee, ready to fire. When the first man was finished reloading, the second man found a target and fired, then himself began reloading, while the first man ran forward and took position behind another tree.

Behind the skirmishers, other companies came forward in closely-ordered lines. The Yankee skirmishers fired their last shots, then they also formed a line and took position at the left flank of their regiment.

The Yankee line halted about a hundred yards away and they brought their weapons to their shoulders. As the officers' swords swept down, they fired. Here and there along the line, Mercer Cavaliers fell backwards, or forward onto their faces, and didn't move again. Others screamed, wounded. They started streaming to the rear, in two cases accompanied by unwounded men. First Sergeant Moore was close enough to grab one unwounded man and roughly shove him back into the line.

One of the men in Wade's squad was shot down, but I couldn't tell who it was. He had fallen on his face. I was too busy trying to hold the frightened horses. One of the horses kept rearing back, whinnying shrilly. I finally realized it had been struck by a stray bullet, but I couldn't do anything to help it. I couldn't even let the horse loose, because all the reins were tangled up in my hands.

I also realized that I had been wrong when I thought that the smell of battle was the rotten-egg smell of gunpowder. The true smell of battle overlaid the gunpowder smell with the stink of a privy, as men lost control of their bowels through fear or they were torn open by bullets.

By this time, the Yankee line had advanced out of the smoke of their last volley. They came forward another twenty yards to fire again. Again some Confederates fell. The Yankee line continued slowly forward, the men flitting from tree to tree as they reloaded.

Some Cavaliers, both wounded and unwounded, left the firing line, making for their horses. Dandy Burns, wild-eyed, suddenly turned toward me, looking for his horse.

I felt, rather than heard, a volley split the air and saw about a dozen Yankees fall. The first of the Confederate infantry regiments had arrived.

The Yankees halted their advance and began trading shots with the Confederate infantry, while soldiers on both sides came up and took position on the firing line.

I heard some horsemen galloping up from behind and moved to get out of the way. A bewhiskered man with buff trim on his uniform shouted at me.

"Where's the cavalry commander, boy?" I realized the man was a general and pointed out Captain Ballard, crouched behind Wade's squad. Instead of riding there himself, the general dismounted behind a large tree and sent a major to get Captain Ballard.[12]

Other Confederate infantry continued to come up, while Captain Ballard returned from his short conference with the general. He shouted new orders to the company.

"Most of our infantry is still to our rear. They're forming to attack. We'll fire a volley then let them pass through our line."

The general, still behind the tree, talked to another Confederate officer, an infantry colonel by his uniform. The general looked around the tree only long enough to point to two flags, one the Stars and Stripes and the other dark blue with an eagle on it, just behind the Yankee line. The colonel nodded, then mounted and rode back to where I stood with the horses.

"Hold my horse, boy," he said, throwing me the reins. The officers from the leading company of the newly-arriving infantry regiment ran up to the colonel.

"We'll attack in column of companies," he shouted to be heard above the noise. "Guide on the Yankee colors. The cavalrymen to our front will let us pass through. They'll fire a volley to cover us, then we'll just charge towards those colors. Captain Ashton, your company will lead. I'll be right with you." Captain Ashton saluted and ran to his company.

"Fix bayonets!" he shouted to his men. The infantrymen quickly pulled their bayonets out of their scabbards and fixed bayonets. They brought their rifles out in front of them to the "Charge bayonets" position. Captain Ballard watched them, then turned to the Cavaliers.

"Fire!" he yelled. The line belched smoke and flame as the cavalry fired.

"Follow me!" shouted the colonel. With a high-pitched keening yell, the Confederate infantry went forward at the double-quick.

The Yankees fired another volley, then seemed to disappear in the smoke. The front of the Confederate column seemed to run into an invisible barrier that knocked men to the ground. Continuing their high yipping yell, the men in the succeeding ranks jumped over their downed comrades and ran straight into the Yankee line.

The line just seemed to crack where the gray column hit it and swung back to the left and right, almost like barn doors. The Confederates poured into the gap and disappeared into the smoke.

The sound of a tremendous amount of firing and an enormous amount of smoke erupted from the gap. After a minute or two, the Confederate infantrymen reappeared, walking backwards, firing as they withdrew. Yankee soldiers followed them, firing as they advanced.

When the Yankees reached the spot where their line had cracked, they stopped. The gap was gone and the Yankee line was solid once more. The Confederate infantry rallied on us and began trading shots with the Yankees.

I heard Wade calling, so I tied the horses to tree branches, then ran over to him.

"Jed, we're running low on ammunition. Find the First Sergeant and tell him we need more, fast!" I nodded and ran off in the direction that I had seen First Sergeant Moore shove the man back into line. I ran just to the rear of the firing line and heard a sound I had never heard before, but heard too many times after that. It was a very distinctive sound, kind of a *thwack!*. It was made by a minie ball hitting the flesh and bone of a body close by.

I stumbled and fell as a cavalryman crashed into me. I looked down at the man, who had a small hole in his chest just starting to ooze blood, then got back to my feet and continued running. I found First Sergeant Moore just behind the line, yelling at the men not to fire too high. He turned as I skidded to a halt in front of him.

"What is it, boy?" he asked curtly.

"Corp'ral Wentworth's squad is almost out of ammunition, sir. He sent me to get some more."

"You tell him some should be coming forward soon, but right now the only extra ammunition we have is in dead men's pouches." I heard the *thwack!* sound again. As if to emphasize what the First Sergeant had just said, a man spun around and fell on his face right next to me.

Looking down at the dead man, I took my clasp knife from my pocket. I knelt down and cut the loops that held his cartridge pouch to his waist belt.

"Thank you, First Sergeant," was all I said as I got back to my feet. You might think it was just bravado, and at least some of was, but I was really driven not to let the men in Wade's squad down. I ran back to the squad, stopping only to cut cartridge pouches from dead men. This time, I also remembered to cut away pouches of percussion caps.

When I got back, I handed Wade a cartridge box and cap pouch. Wade winced at the blood on the pouch and almost let it slip from his hand. I moved away to hand out the other pouches. As I did, I looked down at a crumpled form. The man who had been killed was Heywood Stewart. I knelt and took his pouches, too.

I had just finished handing out the ammunition and moved back to the horses, when an invisible force threw me down on my back. A shell had just exploded about thirty yards away, killing three men from another squad and wounding two more. The Yankees had thrown artillery into the fray. Before I could stop them, two of the horses, terrified by the noise and concussion, broke their halters and bolted away.

Because the Confederates were in line and the artillery rounds were coming in from a great height, little damage was done unless a shell landed close. Hardly any damage at all was done by the solid shot, most of which landed in front of the Confederate line, then bounced harmlessly overhead.

"Where's *our* artillery?" Henry yelled plaintively to Wade.

As if in answer, a Confederate battery rode up slowly, threading its way through the trees. The gunners unlimbered their guns, moved the caissons about fifty yards behind the guns and got ready to fire.

Just like with rifles, in those days, loading and firing a cannon was much more laborious than today. At each gun, one man ran clumsily with a shell in his hands from the caisson to the gun. He handed the shell to the loader, then reached into the heavy leather pouch draped over his shoulder and pulled out a cloth bag of powder for the cannon. He put it in the cannon's muzzle and then ran back to the caisson for more ammunition.

The rammer pushed the powder bag down the barrel with the ramming staff, then stepped back and waited as the loader put the shell into the muzzle. The rammer used the staff to push the shell down the barrel on top of the powder charge.

In the meantime, behind the gun, the assistant gunner shoved a sharp spike into the vent at the top of the barrel to pierce the powder bag. The gunner screwed a friction primer into the vent and attached the lanyard cord. He turned toward the sergeant in charge of the gun and waited for the order to fire. The captain commanding the battery waited until all the guns were ready.

"Fire!" The six guns went off almost simultaneously and jumped back on their wheels. A blinding cloud of smoke immediately enveloped them.

The crews manhandled each gun back into its firing position. They didn't need to move the trail left or right at all. The Yankee line was so wide that they would hit someone as long as they had the correct elevation.

One of the gunners held his thumb covered with a thick leather thumbstall over the vent as the rammer swabbed out the gun with a wet sheepskin sponge attached to the staff. This was to prevent any sparks in the barrel from igniting as the next powder charge was rammed down.[13] The sponge made a curious hollow sound, like when you blow into a half-empty jug, as the rammer pulled it from the barrel. After sponging, the loading sequence began again. Rather than wait for the slowest crew, the battery commander had each fire at their own speed.

The battle continued with little change in form. Each firing line continued to shoot at each other, supported by their artillery. Each man's rate of fire slackened as exhaustion set in and the battle's overall volume of fire also slackened as men were killed, wounded or skedaddled.

After a while, the artillerymen got too tired to push their guns back after each shot and the recoil slowly drove the cannons back until they were almost to the caissons. Then the battery ceased firing altogether and the men limbered up the guns. They moved back through the trees the way they had come.

The lack of artillery support made the men in the Confederate firing line uneasy. Slowly, almost imperceptibly, they began to look back. Then they began to move back.

I caught sight of a bearded man on a horse, just behind the Yankee line. I guessed he was an officer, because he wasn't dressed neatly enough to be a typical cavalryman, although he handled his horse like one. As I watched, his horse went down, throwing him clear. A neatly dressed officer dismounted and offered the bearded man his horse. Not only was the bearded man an officer, then, he had to be a high-ranking officer, maybe even a general. He mounted, then rode back, away from the firing line.

A few minutes later, the Yankee infantry suddenly leveled their rifles in the "Charge bayonets" position and began moving forward. They didn't move fast, but they advanced steadily.

As I watched the glittering points come closer, it seemed as if each bayonet were reaching for me. I tried to control my fear but an empty feeling washed over me as I concluded that it didn't look like anything could stop them.

All along the line, cavalrymen started running for their horses, mounting and riding back toward Belmont and the river. The Yankee infantrymen, seeing them go, gave a deep-throated cheer and charged for the gap the skedaddling cavalry had left. The Confederate infantry, seeing the cavalry retreat and a gap open in the Confederate line, also broke and ran to the rear.

"Jed, bring the horses, quick!" yelled Wade. With undue haste, the Cavaliers mounted, not caring whether the were on their own mounts or somebody else's. I leaped aboard my horse and rode right behind Wade, with the squad all around us. We got to Belmont and kept right on going until we came to the riverbank. We leaped off our horses and slid down the bank until we were practically lying in the river. The men avoided looking each other in the eye as they huddled away from the shooting. After a bit, the shooting petered out. A short while later, I thought I heard music.

"Well, I'll be!" exclaimed Charlie Rosser. "The Yankees brought a band." We all looked over the top of the riverbank and, sure enough, I saw some Yankees with shiny brass horns playing music while the rest of them looted our camp.

"Go back! Don't land!" Dandy Burns jumped up and yelled. "You'll only be captured. We've been whipped." He was shouting to the boatloads of Confederate infantry coming over from Columbus.

Wade angrily told Dandy to shut up, but other men had taken up the cry. The boats altered course, but not to go back to Columbus. They went north, so they could land and form a line without getting tangled up with the beaten men. Landing to the north would also cut the Yankees off from their own boats.

"Look!" shouted Porter. "Our camp's burnin'." Sure enough, the camp was on fire and the Yankees had started to flee the flames.

The cannons in Columbus fired across the river, and the Yankees, now in near panic, broke ranks and began to run toward their boats.

The first boatloads of Confederate troops landed just north of the camp, almost three full regiments along with a boat full of officers and horses. The man in front had grayish white hair.

"It's General Polk himself!" somebody shouted, then Wade and every man in the squad took up the cry. The company ran back up the bank. The infantry who had retreated with us also came back up the bank. They went to link up with the three newly-arrived regiments that were getting into battle formation.

On the riverbank, all was confusion for a few minutes as cavalrymen tried to find their horses and get them calm enough to allow them to mount up. Finally, Captain Ballard led us all in pursuit of the Yankees, swinging to the left so the company would not get stuck behind the Confederate infantry. After a hard ride on half-blown horses, we got to the river just as the last of the Yankee riverboats pulled away.

One man seemed to have been left behind. It was the bearded horseman that I had seen earlier in the battle.

"Let's capture him, boys!" Wade whooped, but before the squad could form up and move, a plank was run out from the riverboat. The Yankee urged his horse over the bank. The horse slid down on its hindquarters and stepped, almost daintily, onto the plank.

"He's one heck of a horseman, even if he is a Yankee," Wade said admiringly. Just then, an officer from General Polk's staff rode up.

"Shoot him! The general says to shoot him." Everyone was so startled that no one moved. The Yankee on the horse safely reached the deck of the riverboat. The staff officer shook his head.

"Perdition! He got away." He turned to the squad. "Don't you know who that was?" he asked no one in particular. "That was General Grant."

***

I could still smell the burnt powder hanging in the air as Isham and I threw the last shovelsful of earth on a grave and packed it down.

The Cavaliers had nine men killed during the fight at Belmont, including Heywood Stewart. They were buried in a small clearing in the woods where they had fallen. Clint Rockwell, although his left leg was in splints, insisted on coming to the burial service. He held himself against a tree and saluted while a party of soldiers drawn from each squad in the company fired a volley over the fallen. When the service was finished, the soldiers moved off and left us servants to fill in the graves.

When I finished, I helped Daniel get Clint onto one of the boats which had come to ferry the wounded back to Columbus. The boatmen, Daniel and I were the only unwounded men aboard. Some of the wounded were Yankees who had been left behind when their comrades retreated.

Apart from the color of their uniforms, there was little discernable difference between Yankees and Confederates. It still amazes me how people so much alike could kill each other so wantonly.

Most of the soldiers in the company were young men, and with the resilience of youth, they soon seemed to forget the terror of combat. The way most of them bragged and carried on, an observer would have thought the last one who spoke had been single-handedly responsible for winning the battle, itself no more than a glorious game.

I knew why the soldiers were carrying on so, because I felt the same way. They were reacting to fear. During the battle itself, they had to control their terror, for they couldn't lose their honor in front of their friends. They couldn't let their friends down by not doing their part. They had all grown up together and, after the war, they would all go home together, at least the ones still alive. They knew they couldn't live with the shame of cowardice among the men who would have witnessed it first-hand.

When they ran, they had all run together, except for a few who had slipped back out of the firing line first. They didn't run until their artillery support retired, and then they ran almost as if they had come to a common consent. As they sheltered behind the riverbank at Belmont, most of them realized, without ever articulating it, that each of them had some breaking point, some point at which they would lose control and react to their terror. For some it came sooner than others.

Later on, I would find that the nature of the peril seemed to make a difference in many cases. Some men would stand as long as they weren't bombarded by artillery, with death seeming to come from nowhere. Others would stand and trade fire with enemy infantry, as long as the enemy didn't get too close or more enemy soldiers seemed to be falling than friends. Others wouldn't be able to face a charge by cavalry, terrified of big horses bearing down on them.

Curiously, I had little sensation that I myself had really been in a battle. During the skirmish when I had pulled Clint from under his horse, I was doing something I had experience with. When training hunters for the jumps, jockeys and grooms were sometimes thrown or had horses fall down on them. We all knew the flailing iron-shod hooves could easily crush a man's skull like an eggshell, so our first reaction was to pull the rider away from his downed mount. When Clint's horse fell, I had reacted the way I would have had I been back on the farm.

I felt I had been almost a spectator during the battle itself. I had had a lot of work to do, trying to control the horses and running around for more ammunition. That left me little time to think. Then too, I had not fought, and there had always been a line of Confederate riflemen between me and the Yankees. You might think that trivial, but whole companies and regiments decide to stand and fight or to skedaddle based on such trivialities.

All the same, I knew that I had behaved well during the fight.

VII

The Cavaliers expected to spend the winter in Columbus, riding patrol and manning vedettes, just like they had at Belmont. They figured that with the Southern victory at Belmont and winter coming on, the Yankees would just sit tight where they were until spring.

Columbus was still the strongest of the Confederate fortresses built to resist Yankee control of the rivers that flowed through the middle South. The Confederate command knew that if the Yankees were able to dominate the major rivers, they could not only carry the war into the Deep South, the rivers would act as barriers to prevent one region of the South from aiding another. The rivers would be like slices of a blade, cutting Confederate territory into pieces which could then be conquered in turn.

I was cleaning the mud off Wade's boots one morning after the squad had ridden in from patrol. Wade lay on a cot in his stocking feet, reading an old newspaper. Porter Lawliss was collecting his equipment. He hadn't ridden patrol that morning. He had just been promoted to corporal and was leaving to take over another squad whose corporal had been killed at Belmont. Every squad was a few men understrength, but the company was reorganizing, trying to keep roughly the same number of men in each squad.

The Cavaliers were lucky that they had extra mounts, so no men were lost that way. In the Confederate army, the men owned the horses, not the government. The government would only reimburse the owner if his horse was killed in action. If a cavalryman's horse was otherwise killed or disabled, he had to take leave and go find a new one. If he couldn't replace his horse, he had to transfer to the infantry.

"My, my, those chevrons are so new and unfaded!" From the cot, Wade spoke teasingly. "Remember, Porter, if you forget any commands, just come on back here and talk to the expert."

"Anytime you want to see how an efficient squad looks, just come on over and I'll show you," Porter quickly rejoined.

"Maybe I'll take you up on that. It's not like you're goin' so far away." Wade stood up. "Good luck," he told Porter. Both men shook hands. Dandy helped Porter with his equipment and the two men pushed their way through the tent flap.

"Mornin', Captain," they both said outside.

"Is that you, Captain?" Wade jumped back up from the cot where he had just sat down..

"It is a captain, but not the one you're probably thinking of." A head poked through the tent flap. It was Captain Morgan. "Mind if I come in, Corporal?"

"Yes, sir. I mean please come in, sir. Jed, go get the Captain some coffee, some good coffee, not the stuff made from blackened peanuts." Morgan held up his hand.

"I appreciate your hospitality, but there's no time. I'm here on urgent business, Corporal. Are you familiar with the area around Bowling Green?" Bowling Green, Kentucky was where the main Confederate army in the west was concentrated. A Yankee army was rumored to be getting ready to move against it.

"I've been to Bowling Green, sir. I'm pretty familiar with the town and the area around it," Wade told Captain Morgan.

"I need someone who knows the terrain, especially to the north of town, intimately. Where roads are that don't appear on maps, from Bowling Green north to Louisville. Are you the man I'm looking for?"

"No, sir, but whatever you're goin' to do, I'd like to come along," Wade said earnestly. Then he joked, "Me and the boys would even leave our sabers behind." Morgan just grinned.

"I appreciate your offer. I'll keep it in mind. Thank you for your honesty, Corporal." Morgan swept out of the tent.

"I wish we were goin' with him," Wade said wistfully. "He's goin' to do somethin' spectacular, I just know it. I should've told him I knew the area."

"If you said you knew somethin' you don't, and men got killed for it, you wouldn't be able to live with yourself, Corp'ral," I told him. You might think me bold, but by that time, I knew I could tell Wade something like that. He looked back at me, but made no reply.

The next day, we heard that Captain Morgan was riding toward the Yankee army in Kentucky, accompanied by only thirteen men.

"Maybe it's a good thing we didn't go, after all," Wade told me, and I silently agreed.

We again settled down to a routine dominated by patrols. A day was distinguished from another only by whether the squad was on morning or evening patrol. Occasionally, they were given a day off, more to rest the horses than the men.

One day when the squad was off duty, I sat in Wade's tent, cleaning his LeMats. The men of the squad were engaged in a heated discussion about the news Wade had just read in a month-old newspaper.

"I guess allowin' them into the navy wasn't enough," Wade said. "Now they're proposin' usin' them in the army, too."

"It could hurt them more than it helps," Henry said. "Darkies can't be good soldiers. I mean they can take orders and all, but they don't have what it takes to fight a real battle." Rob disagreed.

"You ever hear of an insurrection where they didn't murder a bunch of folks?"

"That ain't soldierin', it's murder," Henry retorted. "I'm not sayin' that they can't do a fair job of killin', especially in an attack, when their bloodlust is up. But how about in a stand-up fight, like we had at Belmont? Nobody's goin' to tell me that darkies'll be able to just stand there, men fallin all around them, and trade shots."

"Well, it just says that Cameron 'advocates' using colored troops," said Wade. "Like Henry says, it could be more trouble for them than it's worth, havin' to feed and clothe the darkies like soldiers, without bein' able to use them as soldiers. They'll probably just have them dig and do hard labor, like we do."

"Who is this Cameron, anyhow?" asked Clint.

"The paper said he's their Secretary of War," answered Wade.

"He sounds more like the Secretary of Stupidity," declared Dandy. "This should tell those folks back home who say the war is to preserve the Union that they are dead wrong. The Yankees are tryin' to provoke a slave insurrection."

"If they do that, there can be no goin' back," Charlie said vehemently. "All we can do is beat 'em and go our own way." They all agreed. I just kept my head down and continued to clean weapons, not daring to let the hope show on my face.

A few days later, Obie came over with the news that Captain Morgan had ridden all the way around the Yankee army north of Bowling Green.

"There was fourteen of them, countin' the Cap'n. They brought in thirty-three Yankee prisoners," he told me. "Some were Kentucky men."

"I heard that there's a lot of Kentucky men fightin' in the Yankee army," I replied. "Some families have brothers fightin' on different sides. I wonder what would happen if two brothers on different sides saw each other in a fight. I can't imagine a man tryin' to kill his own brother."

"Whatever it is they're fightin' for," said Obie softly, "they'll kill their own kin for it. I don't know what it is, though. Seems to me, they're fightin' awful hard, but they don't have as much to fight for as we do." I stayed quiet for a long time, knowing what he was thinking. Finally, I spoke.

"When the time comes to run, I ain't goin' to help you get away, I'll be goin', too. We'll join the Yankee navy, or the army. But we've got to plan it.

"We'll wait until the army moves. We'd be missed too soon if we ran while we're camped here. We'll have to know where to go and how to get there. We'll need food and horses. We'll plan it right, and we'll go when the time is right."

"You really mean it, Jed? You're really comin'?"

"Way back, when you said the army we should be with is the Yankee army, you were right." I looked around at the squad campsite. "These are people we know, people we've known almost all our lives. We work for them and they take care of us, at least the good ones do. But they're not *our* people. The Yankees may not be our people either, but at least they don't keep slaves. When it's time to go, you can bet I'll be goin'."

***

The first Christmas of the war came, followed by New Year's Day, 1862. A few weeks later, the men were all depressed by the news of a Confederate defeat at Logan's Cross Roads in eastern Kentucky. Not only did the Confederates have to retreat back across the Cumberland River, the general leading the Confederate force had been killed.[14]

To change the subject, Wade took great satisfaction in reading to the squad how Simon Cameron, who had endorsed the use of colored soldiers, had been removed from his position as Secretary of War.

"It says here he's to be the ambassador to Russia," Wade said.

"Maybe even Lincoln has some sense then, if he got rid of that fool," said Dandy. "Now maybe we can get back to fightin' a civilized war between brothers."

"It isn't between brothers," Rob said. "Look at all that Irish and German trash the Yankees enlist. They probably drag 'em off as soon as the ships land. If they'll do that, I'll bet we still ain't heard the last of colored soldiers."

One morning when the squad wasn't assigned duty, we awoke to find the earth covered with a blanket of snow. It wasn't that deep, maybe three or four inches. Daniel and I trudged through the snow to feed and water the horses, while John and Isham took care of fixing breakfast.

After breakfast, we servants cleaned up. John and Isham went into the tent to put the mess gear away. While they were in the tent, I quickly made a snowball. As John came out of the tent, I threw the snowball as hard as I could and hit him right in the chest. I whooped in triumph.

John bent down to scoop up some snow to throw back. Daniel started packing snow into balls, waiting for Isham to show himself. John yelled to Isham to warn him. Isham charged out of the tent so quickly that Daniel didn't even get a chance to throw. Isham slid to the ground next to John.

Daniel and I threw snowballs at John and Isham as quickly as we could make them. Isham and John threw back, but were quickly forced to retreat. They took cover behind the tent.

Daniel and I continued to throw snowballs. I had just launched one when Wade came out of the tent to see what the commotion was about. The snowball hit Wade on the side of the head. Wade put his hand up to his ear and yelled in pain.

No matter what the relationship I thought Wade and I had, I felt a pang of fear. Slaves didn't hit their masters, not even with a snowball, not even by accident. The others stood with "slave" faces, the blank expression we all used to hide our emotions, by looking off at nothing. But I couldn't look away from Wade.

Wade no doubt saw the looks and knew what they meant. I didn't know what to do or say to salvage the situation but, to his credit, Wade did.

He quickly scooped up some snow and, packing as he ran, got behind the tent. Then Wade turned and threw the snowball back at me. It hit me right smack on the forehead and the next thing I knew, I was on my backside in the snow.

"Take that!" Wade shouted. "C'mon! Make more," he said to John and Isham. "We got 'em outnumbered."

Wade, John and Isham stayed behind the tent and pelted Daniel and me with what seemed like a blizzard of snowballs. We two couldn't pack near enough snowballs to return the volume of snow smacking us. Then I got an idea.

"Daniel, you'all stay here and keep on throwin'. When I call, run back." I ran back a few dozen yards and get behind a large tree. I packed snowballs, but I didn't throw them. When I had made about four dozen, I covered them lightly with some snow. Then I made another dozen, and called Daniel back.

"We got some buried. Take these and go around the left. I'll go around the right. Throw what you have, then run back here. We'll let them chase us back to here, and when they get close, we'll let 'em have it."

By now, the whole squad had come out of their tents to watch the fight. Daniel and I each took a half-dozen snowballs. Daniel headed toward the left of the tent just as Wade, John and Isham came from behind it. He threw a snowball, hitting Isham. The three turned toward Daniel to pelt him. When they did, I threw all but one of my snowballs in quick succession, hitting Isham in the back of the head with one and John in the chest with another.

Wade, Isham and John just stood in surprise for a few seconds, getting battered by snow. I threw my last snowball, then ran. Daniel threw his, then he ran, too.

"After 'em!" shouted Wade. The three ran around the tent, each with three or four snowballs, figuring they could just pummel us at will. They threw on the run, but scored no hits.

Meanwhile, Daniel and I reached the cache of prepared snowballs. We just stooped and threw, stooped and threw. Isham was knocked off his feet. Wade turned his back to avoid being hit in the front. The snowballs came so fast, he couldn't turn towards us to throw back. John was hunched down and couldn't stand up without getting thoroughly pelted.

"Daniel, stop and wait," I told him when he was about to throw another one. Sure enough, Wade turned around. "Now!" I shouted.

Wade turned just in time to have a snowball smack him right in the nose. Tears came into his eyes as he fell on his back.

"Grab them all, Daniel!" I shouted. Daniel and I grabbed all the remaining snowballs. "Let's get 'em!"

We ran at the three, throwing as hard as we could, and reached them without a single snowball thrown our way. We stood over the three men, and threw a few more snowballs at the huddled forms.

"Give up?" I cried, waving a snowball menacingly. I still had three and Daniel had two.

"You win," said Wade, blood trickling from his nose. As Daniel and I dropped our snowballs, Wade took one he had concealed and hurled it at me. I heard it whiz past my head.

Daniel and I pounded Wade with snow, then with my last snowball held threateningly, I yelled in what I hoped sounded like a commanding voice for

Wade to give up. It was only then that I noticed the shocked silence that permeated the men in the squad. Even in the heat of winning what was essentially a game, it did not do for a slave to cross the invisible, but nonetheless very real line of behavior which could be construed as defiance. It appeared I had crossed it and the excitement of winning was replaced by another spasm of fear.

Then Wade put up his hand.

"All right, Jed. You win. For real this time," Wade joked. I never loved that man more than I did right then. Wade, John and Isham stood up and brushed off the snow, then started laughing. Behind us, the squad good-naturedly jeered.

"The worst whuppin' I seen since we licked the Yankees at Belmont," mocked Henry.

"Better let me take care of your nose, Corp'ral," I said, but Wade just shrugged. I put my hand on Wade's shoulder and he let me gently push him toward the tent.

***

A month later, the weather turned unseasonably warm. News came that Yankee gunboats had taken advantage of the mild weather and attacked Fort Henry on the Tennessee River, less than sixty miles away.

"Guess we'll get the word soon to go reinforce the fort," said Henry.

"I doubt it," said Rob. "What good are cavalry inside a fort? Now, I don't doubt the infantry will go, ain't that right, Wade?"

"I doubt if any of us go, cavalry or infantry. I heard that the warm weather melted the snow and raised the level of the river. The water's so high, the fort is almost under water. Besides, even if the Yankees do take Fort Henry, Fort Donelson is only twelve miles away from it. They'll have to take that, and Columbus too, before they can go anywhere. We're in the strongest fort on any of the rivers. I don't think that the 'Right Reverend' will do anything to weaken Columbus." General Polk's title as an Episcopal bishop was "Right Reverend" and some of the men irreverently used that title to refer to him.

A few days later, word went around Columbus that Fort Henry had surrendered. The only good news was most of the garrison had withdrawn to Fort Donelson before the surrender. Only fifty-four men had remained in the fort to try to hold off the federal fleet. They had severely damaged an ironclad gunboat but could do no more before they had to surrender.

Two days later, First Sergeant Moore told the squad leaders to get their men ready to move. General P.G.T. Beauregard, hero of the first Confederate victory at Manassas, was coming to take command. Wade relayed the orders in high spirits.

"He wouldn't come all this way just to have us just sit in earthworks. 'Ole Borey' is coming to lead an attack. While the Yankees are tied up tryin' to take Donelson, we'll attack them from the rear. You mark my words."

Orders had come down to the company from Captain Morgan that most of the servants were to be sent back home. As I said before, just about every Cavalier had his own servant. There was a great deal of concern about the extra supplies, especially food, that we consumed. Morgan permitted the company officers to keep one servant among the three of them. The men would no longer have personal servants. Only the teamsters for the three wagons, a few grooms for the spare mounts and skinners for the pack horses and mules would be allowed to remain.

Daniel, John and Isham were among those to be sent back home. I was ordered to take charge of one of the twelve packhorses and mules that the company kept to haul extra equipment. I hadn't heard which of the three officers' servants was to stay. I didn't know if I hoped it would be Obie.

On one hand, he might have a better chance to run on the way back to Mercer County. If nothing else, he would be out of the danger of the battle sure to be coming. On the other hand, we were good friends, almost like brothers, and I would sorely miss him.

"Jed, take the stock off my carbine and pack it," Wade told me. "Two pistols should be enough until we get where we're going."

"You'll definitely need it when we get to Donelson," said Charlie. "It'll probably be another stand-up fight like Belmont."

Charlie, like the others, was getting rid of items he really didn't need. Since the new orders, the squad only had one packhorse for all their extra gear. The squad had already discarded most of their cooking equipment. Some of the men had even tossed away their shaving gear and started raising beards. They had all agreed, even Wade, that the sabers were useless.

"Maybe keep one saber," said Wade.

"What for?" Rob demanded.

"Always come in handy for a roasting spit," Wade said, grinning. They put the sabers with the items to be sent back home with the servants.

"I want my saber to hang on the wall in the study," Henry said, "so after the war, I just have to look over at it to remember what a hero I once was." Everyone chuckled.

Dandy had just put on the brand-new boots he had brought from home. His old ones weren't in that bad a shape, but he couldn't see carrying the new ones around while waiting for the old ones to wear out.

"You want 'em, Jed? Your feet look about the same size as mine."

"Thank you, Private Burns." I pulled off my old boots and put on Dandy's. They were slightly big, but almost a perfect fit. I threw my old boots onto the pile for the garbage pit. They were old when I got them. Back on the farm, all the servants who worked with horses had boots, but only the jockeys and trainers ever got new ones. When they got worn, the farm's cobbler mended them and then the boots were passed down to a groom or stableboy.

Word soon circulated around Columbus that Fort Donelson had been taken. Beauregard had not come to lead the Confederate army north, he had been sent to make sure that General Polk followed orders and withdrew south from Columbus.

General Albert Sidney Johnston, who commanded all Confederate forces in Kentucky, Tennessee, Missouri and on out to Indian Territory, had decided to abandon Kentucky and most of Tennessee for the moment. Confederate forces in the West would fall back to northern Mississippi. When they were all gathered together, they would again turn north and go on the offensive.

For better than a week, the entire Columbus garrison, working at night, helped move and load heavy artillery onto riverboats. One night, they were attacked by a federal gunboat but they got the artillery away without the Yankees suspecting that Columbus was being evacuated. The artillery pieces and 7,000 men were floated down the Mississippi to New Madrid, Missouri. The rest of the army, some 10,000 men, marched south along the river. The Cavaliers, along with the rest of the cavalry, led their horses instead of riding them.

"Well, at least the weather's nice. Spring must be comin' early this year," said Rob cheerfully. They had all given me their overcoats to load on the packhorse.

"Don't count on it," muttered Charlie to his brother. "Even if we are headin' south, it's still only March. You know what they say about weather in March. 'In like a lamb, out like a lion.'"

One evening, as I was unloading the pack horse in the squad area, someone came up behind me.

"Glad to see you'all." I spun around. It was Obie.

"Glad to see you, too. Happy you didn't get sent back."

"Me, too," Obie smiled back, then turned serious. "When should we go?"

"Real soon. Right now, the army is headin' south, which is the way to the ocean and the Yankee navy. We should stay with the army as long as they keep marchin' along the river.

"While we're on the march, put by a little food each day. Come on down and visit me every night. That way, they get used to seein' us together. It's natural anyway, since we're from the same farm.

"Each night, we'll go a little farther away from camp and stay away a little longer. Soon, they'll get used to us bein' away but comin' back. One night, we just won't come back."

During the next day's march, the roadside was littered with discarded equipment. Not many Confederates had overcoats, but even so, there were more than a few by the roadside.

I picked up two overcoats as well as a canteen and a haversack for food. I hoped that, in the dark, the overcoats would help deceive any observers into thinking we were Confederate soldiers.

When we halted, I quickly unloaded the pack horse so no one would see the overcoats, haversack or canteen. I hid them under bundles that didn't need to be opened. The company was part of the rear guard, so the squad might not get in until after dark.

When Obie came over, we picked up canvas buckets and walked down to a large creek to fill them.

"This would be a good time, with the company on rear guard," I told Obie. "And with the creek as shallow as it is, it might be a good way out of camp. We could walk in the water for a ways so we wouldn't leave footprints."

We walked back to camp. Obie put some blackened-peanut coffee on to boil. We still had plenty of sugar, so it wouldn't taste too bad.

At dusk, the company still hadn't come in. A drizzling rain began falling and so did the temperature. It was easy to see that it would soon be a miserable night. I looked at Obie.

"The pickets ain't goin' to be none too watchful tonight. If we could get clear of camp before morning, the rain might wash away our footprints." I threw an overcoat over to Obie. "Put it on and just walk out of camp with a bucket and the canteen. Wait for me by the creek." Obie walked slowly through the camp with the bucket and canteen.

I quickly crammed all the food I could into the haversack then passed the strap over my shoulder. I put the overcoat on to hide the haversack and then picked up a bucket. I walked out of camp, following the path that Obie had taken.

The distance to the creek wasn't that great, but by the time I got there, the rain had started pelting down so hard it was difficult to see. I strained, willing my eyes to pierce the liquid dark and see Obie. I didn't see him and, for a moment, I thought I wasn't in the right place. I looked around again. As I became certain it was the right place, fear clutched my heart.

"Hold it right there, boy!" I was so startled, I almost screamed. Then I realized the voice came from about fifty yards away to my right. Squinting through the rain, I made out a figure holding a rifle. It had to be one of the pickets. He kept his rifle pointed down towards the bank of the creek.

"Come up outta there, boy!" the picket said again, more menacingly this time.

I looked around for a stout stick or a rock, but couldn't find any. I began to move quickly toward the picket, trusting to the falling rain to cover the sound of my movements. As I moved, I unbuttoned the overcoat and let it fall to the ground. I pulled the food-filled haversack off my shoulder and wrapped the strap around my hand so I could swing it like a club if I had to.

Meanwhile, another figure had appeared from the bottom of the slippery bank. It had to be Obie. The picket kept the rifle pointed at him.

"Just take it nice and easy, no sudden moves, hear me, boy?" the picket said loudly. Obie nodded and put his hands up.

By now, I was only about fifteen feet from the picket. I debated whether I should try to get closer or just charge him from where I was. Then I figured he would march Obie back away from the creek, so I slipped behind a tree that bordered their likely path.

Heart pounding, I carefully peered around the tree. Sure enough, the picket was motioning Obie back toward where I was hiding. I wrapped the strap around my hand a bit more tightly and brought the haversack up, ready to strike with it.

I knew that if the rifle went off, the rest of the pickets would be on us in a minute. I had to knock the picket unconscious, or at least knock the rifle from his hands before he could pull the trigger.

Just then, Obie walked past the tree. He was startled when he saw me hiding there. The picket must have noticed Obie's reaction, because he shouted.

"Who's there?"

Swinging the haversack, I charged around the far side of the tree, appearing almost directly at the right side of the picket. I guess he supposed that I would come from the other side of the tree, where Obie had seen me, and seemed surprised by my appearance from the unexpected quarter.

I hit him in the face with the haversack. He staggered, but didn't go down, so I swung the haversack back from the left, aiming at the back of his head. He turned to his right, trying to block the impact with the barrel of his rifle. He got it up just in time, but the force of the blow knocked the muzzle back into his mouth. Blood splattered and he fell backwards. He pulled his right hand away from the trigger, trying to break his fall.

I jumped on his chest, to keep him down and prevent him from getting his finger back on the trigger. The man tried to buck me off, while I brought the haversack back for another sweeping blow. Then I felt him stiffen in surprise.

"You!" he shouted. Then Obie kicked him in the head, knocking him unconscious.

I looked into the picket's face. At first all I noticed was that I had knocked out one of his front teeth. Then I looked at him more closely. Underneath a scraggly, honey-colored beard, I recognized Hawkins. Obie quickly took the rifle from Hawkins' hand.

"How'd he know you, Jed?"

"He's the one whose canteen I put the dead fish in. I don't think he knows my name, but he knows the Cavaliers. One good thing is at least he don't know you."

"Post number three! Report." The voice sounded faintly through the rain.

"We got to get outta here," said Obie frantically. "We'd better run *now*."

"Post number three! Report! Anything the matter?" The voice sounded louder this time. I thought quickly.

"The rain's stoppin'. Now our footprints won't wash away. They'll be able to track us pretty easy. If they catch us, they'll whip us for sure, if they don't kill us instead."

"Sergeant of the guard! Trouble on post three!" The voice sounded more faint, but I knew that was only because it had been directed at someone even further away.

"We got a minute until they get here. Watch him. If he comes to, knock him out again," I directed Obie.

"Why don't we just kill him?" asked Obie, fear in his eyes. "It's us or him. When he wakes up, he'll have the picket on us for sure."

You might think me somewhat innocent, but I was shocked by Obie's suggestion. The idea of killing the helpless, unconscious man repelled me. If I had to kill Hawkins in a fight, I wouldn't hesitate. Cold-blooded murder was something else.

"If we kill him, and we don't get away, we'd be dead for sure," I told him. "Just watch him. And take off your coat. Is your canteen full?" Obie nodded.

I ran back to where I had dropped my overcoat, then brought it and my bucket back to Obie.

"Get yourself back to camp," I ordered Obie. "Hawkins doesn't know you, so whatever happens, keep your mouth shut. Give me the canteen and your overcoat. Where's your bucket?" Obie got the bucket. "Now git!" I said fiercely. Obie ran.

I could hear the pickets coming to check why Hawkins had shouted. I quickly weighted the overcoats with the haversack and uncorked the canteen so it wouldn't float. I waded out to the middle of the creek and held them all under until they sank. I filled both buckets and ran back to Hawkins, who was just coming around.

"Over here!" I shouted. I spilled all the water from one bucket on purpose, then dashed the water from the other bucket into Hawkins' face. Hawkins sputtered and sat up, just as the picket reached us. An infantry sergeant surveyed the scene.

"What in the name of the eternal is going on here?" he demanded loudly.

"Two niggers was runnin' away," yelled Hawkins angrily. "I tried to stop 'em and they attacked me." The sergeant turned to me.

"That so? You're in a heap o' trouble, boy."

"No, Sergeant!" I cringed and pretended to cry. "I'se jest down gettin' water for the horses. Private Hawkins tried to shoot me, sah."

"He's a liar!" Hawkins tried to rush me, but the sergeant held him back.

"Now why would Hawkins want to shoot you, boy?" the sergeant asked, staring intently at my face as I answered.

I told the sergeant of the dead fish in Hawkins' canteen. By the time I finished, the sergeant was grinning and the other pickets were laughing.

"At ease!" the sergeant said loudly, but not too sternly, to the pickets to silence their laughter. He turned to Hawkins. "What gave you to think this boy was tryin' to run away, Hawkins?"

"There were two, not just one!" Hawkins raved. "They were goin' to run, I know it! They was wearin' overcoats. They hit me with somethin' hard. So hard this nigger knocked my tooth out!"

"I did hit Private Hawkins, Sergeant. I hit him with my bucket. I was walking back up the bank after gettin' water for the horses and he says he was goin' to shoot me to get even for the dead fish. I don't want to die, so I hit him with one of the buckets. Look here, sah. When I got the rifle away from him, I splashed water on him to try to wake him up. If I was tryin' to run, I wouldn't have tried to bring him around. And, while he was knocked out, I could've killed him," I concluded quietly.

"He's lyin', Sarge! Lemme at that lyin' nigger." Again Hawkins tried to rush me, but the pickets held him back. The sergeant looked thoughtful.

"I don't see no overcoats, don't see nothin' except them buckets. You're all wet, only one darkie's here and the darkie knows your name. And I do seem to recall a day when your canteen smelled like to somethin' awful, Hawkins. Just like a dead fish.

"Now, as a rule I don't take the word of a darkie over that of a white man, but since the white man is you, Hawkins, I'm seriously considerin' it. Looks to me like you were goin' to get even and shoot him, just like he said. Only he knocked you out, even though you had a rifle and all he had was a bucket.

"I think you made up the story to cover up how a darkie with a bucket trounced you, Hawkins. And he was right. He could've killed you." Hawkins just stared at the sergeant, dumbfounded.

"However, we can't have darkies hittin' white men either, no matter why. Who d'you belong to, boy?"

"Company C, Kentucky Cavalry Squadron, Sergeant."

"Let's pay them a little visit, then." Hawkins started to protest. "Corporal, take over here. Put another man on Hawkins's post.

"Hawkins, you get back to the orderly tent and wait for me there. And I'd better not have any more trouble out of you tonight. Let's go, boy." As I stooped to retrieve the buckets, I saw Hawkins look at me with pure hatred in his face.

"Just let me refill my buckets, Sergeant. The horses'll still need water."

VIII

When the army halted for a few days in Humboldt, Tennessee, an investigation was conducted by a panel of three Confederate officers. I wasn't even allowed in the room as the officers heard testimony, but I could still overhear much of what was said. They heard Hawkins' story and that of the sergeant of the guard. They also had Wade tell them about me and my conduct before the incident. I wasn't asked to tell my side of the story. I just stood in a waiting room, under guard. My ears strained to hear when the colonel in charge of the panel gave their findings in the investigation.

"We find that Private Martin Hawkins exceeded his authority while on picket guard when he attempted to put to death the slave Jedediah, property of Corporal Wade Wentworth," the colonel intoned.

It took a few moments to figure out what he said. I wasn't even aware of how tense I had been until the relief washed over me. Notice there was no mention of my having the right to defend myself. It was not even an issue. As a slave, I had no rights a white man was bound to respect, to use Chief Justice Taney's phrase.

On the other hand, considering that Obie and I had actually attempted to run away, I was elated there was no mention of punishment. I should have known better.

"However, Corporal, this sets a bad example," the colonel told Wade. "We can't have it be known among our servants that one of their number struck a white man and was not punished. Your servant is sentenced to six dozen lashes for servile insurrection. You will put him in chains for the remainder of the march. When we arrive at Corinth, the sentence will be carried out." I was startled by the sound of Wade's hand pounding the table at which the panel sat.

"That's unjust! How could you fault him for defending his own life?" There are no words to describe the gratitude I felt toward Wade right then.

"Perhaps if you had treated your servants more firmly back home, Corporal, this incident might not have occurred," the colonel said sternly.

"Sir, that is my father's property," Wade continued more calmly, "and to put things in another light, one you may understand, by defending himself, Jedediah was defending my father's property. Private Hawkins caused this incident, yet my father is in effect being held liable for the damages. Six dozen lashes will reduce his value by three-quarters, at least." With those words, my gratitude to Wade changed to aversion, but I didn't realize until later that he was only trying to address issues that the panel would accept.

"Whatever the case back home, even though he is your father's property, your servant, and you yourself, are now subject to military discipline. Perhaps you should have taken better care of your father's property by maintaining firmer control. But you're a young man and apt to be careless. And I will say your assertion your father shouldn't suffer a property loss though the fault of another does have an element of validity." The colonel thought for a moment and turned to the other officers. "If you gentlemen concur, we could commute part of the sentence." The other two nodded.

"We do need to set an example, Corporal," the colonel said, almost kindly. "Two dozen lashes to be imposed, with another two dozen suspended, to be imposed on top of any other sentence handed down if another breach of discipline occurs. Authority to carry out the sentence to be given to the commanding officer of the Kentucky Cavalry Squadron. This tribunal will stand down."

I was held under arrest at company headquarters to await the tribunal's written orders authorizing the sentence. First Sergeant Moore detailed a squad to watch me, with a soldier on duty at all times. Obie was allowed to bring me my meals. The first time that Obie came, I could see that he was racked with guilt.

"This thing wasn't your fault," I told Obie softly.

"No talking," said the guard. I mouthed the words without speaking. "Not your fault." Tears came into Obie's eyes. He shook his head and quickly left.

When company headquarters received the orders to carry out the sentence, Brady insisted on telling me himself. This was almost the first time that Brady had spoken to me since we arrived in the camp at Union City the preceding summer.

"There's nothing we can do about the verdict, Jed," Brady spoke softly. I was surprised to see that he felt wretched about the whole thing. "I just wanted you to know we tried and that Wade spoke up for you at the tribunal. I wish there was more to say. We're going to have to put you in irons, Jed."

He motioned to First Sergeant Moore.

"Take charge, First Sergeant." First Sergeant Moore saluted and Brady exited.

"Corporal of the guard!" The corporal marched up with the guard detail.

"Escort the prisoner to squadron headquarters," Moore told him. "In irons." I stood up and was surrounded by the guard detail. They marched me over to a blacksmith, who chained my hands together with a foot-long length of chain, then my feet.

They then marched me over to squadron headquarters. I shuffled along in the leg irons in the center of the little procession, until I stood before Captain Morgan.

"Do you understand the verdict and sentence?" he asked.

"Yes, I understand," I replied, looking him squarely in the eyes and deliberately neglecting to say "sir." Captain Morgan stared at me for a moment, then called for the duty sergeant.

"Chain him to one of the wagons."

I spent the night thinking about the slave whose whipping I had witnessed what seemed ages ago. The next morning, I awoke realizing I had had nightmares, but couldn't remember what they were.

The marching column arrived in Corinth, Mississippi a week later. Corinth was where the western Confederate forces were to gather together into one large army. The first night in Corinth, Wade and Clint came to see me. Both looked very uncomfortable, almost ashamed. Clint spoke first.

"You saved my life during that fight at Belmont," Clint said. "I'm grateful and I'm only sorry I waited this long to tell you."

"I'd do it again, Private Rockwell," I said after a moment, smiling. I meant it, too. Clint looked back, but didn't smile. Wade looked over at Clint.

"Go find out what I told you." Clint said goodnight and left.

"You know, tomorrow's the day, Jed," Wade said in a hushed tone. I only nodded. Wade continued in a falsely hearty voice, "If I ever meet up with that Hawkins again, I'll knock out the front tooth that you left. Or maybe not. If he doesn't have teeth, he wouldn't be able to bite cartridges. Don't want him kicked out of the army now, do we?" I went along with the attempt at humor.

"Oh, no, Corp'ral, we want him just as miserable as we are." Wade tried to laugh, then he looked at me intently.

"Obie's gone." For a second, I must have looked shocked, because I thought Wade meant that Obie had died. Then I realized that he meant Obie had run.

"Gone? You mean run?" Wade evidently misinterpreted my reaction because he just nodded.

"I can see you didn't know a thing about it. Brady said that you probably knew about it but didn't tell us. I said you didn't. I'm glad I was right.

"I guess he ran right after we left Humboldt. He had kept going farther and farther from camp, and staying out longer, but he always came back. One night, he just didn't." Wade stood up to leave.

"I don't know what to say about tomorrow. 'Good luck' sure ain't it. Don't let them see they got you down. Act proud." Wade clapped me on the back, then left.

The hard thing that night was being left alone with my thoughts. Ever since I saw the punishment of the runaway, a whipping had been the stuff of nightmares for me. But I felt strangely at peace. I thought that if Obie made it away, they could give me all six dozen lashes and it would be worth it.

I went to sleep, but no nightmares troubled me that night.

***

I awoke at dawn. I got up and asked to be escorted to the sinks, then came back and got washed. I refused the offer of breakfast. The guards removed the irons and I took off my jacket and shirt.

I wrapped a blanket around my shoulders, because I didn't want to get cold while I waited. If I was cold, I might shiver, and I didn't want anyone watching to think I was afraid.

Of course, I was afraid, but I remembered Wade's last words when he left. "Act proud." I repeated it over and over like a prayer.

A short while later, the guards came and escorted me to the field where an upright post stood. I could see a hundred or so servants standing in a semi-circle, where they could all see the post. A line of cavalrymen armed with shotguns was drawn up, facing them. A little further away, I could see a knot of officers, Captain Morgan in front. I quickly looked for Wade and Brady, but couldn't make out either of them.

The escort halted at the post. A first sergeant with a very loud voice read the charges and the sentence. He stressed that, as a measure of clemency, four dozen lashes had been suspended. He nodded to a corporal, who approached to pull the blanket from my shoulders. Before he reached me, I shrugged off the blanket and stepped over to the post. All the while, I kept repeating to myself, "Act proud."

One of the regimental surgeons gave me a cursory examination and pronounced me medically able to undergo the punishment. He then motioned to the corporal to strap a wide belt of thick leather around my torso to protect my kidneys.

"Required by army regulations," he mumbled. Soldiers were sometimes flogged, but regulations limited the number of strokes. Slaves, on the other hand, could be whipped to death, and some were.

Without being prodded, I held my hands up to be tied to the post. When he finished tying my hands, the corporal put a thick piece of leather between my teeth. Men had been known to bite off their tongues when the pain got too bad.

The first sergeant gave a quiet order. A thickset soldier in shirtsleeves stepped up to the post, holding a short, nine-tailed whip. The first sergeant gave another order, and a drummer beat a low, ominous tattoo. I hunched my shoulders and awaited the first stroke.

The lash snaked across my back, as the first sergeant exclaimed, "One!"

I felt the blow, but almost a second elapsed before I felt the pain. In spite of myself, I jumped. My senses now heightened by pain, I heard the whip tearing through the air before it again snapped on my skin.

"Two!"

"Three!"

I know it was just my imagination, but I thought I could feel my skin pucker and rise up into welts. The lash struck again.

"Four!" I could feel blood bubble up from the welts.

"Five!" My lips curled back away from my teeth, while my teeth bit into the leather pad.

"Six!"

"Seven!" The admonition to "act proud" streamed through my mind. I concentrated on it to keep from thinking about the searing pain on my back, until the lash snapped again and it was driven from my mind.

"Eight!" Blood wasn't bubbling, it was spouting.

"Nine!" Now I thought I could feel drops of blood coalesce into streams, coursing down my back. My skin crawled, anticipating the next stroke.

"Ten!"

"Eleven!" My teeth sawed into the pad in my mouth, and I tasted the salty flavor of the leather.

"Twelve!" It was half over, but that meant nothing. It was just *half* over.

"Thirteen!"

"Fourteen!" I was amazed that, even through the fire in my back, I could feel the pain in my jaws from clenching my teeth on the leather.

"Fifteen!"

"Sixteen!" I loved the pain in my jaws because it was a only dull ache, compared to the fire that was again propelled across my back.

"Seventeen!"

"Eighteen!" My imagination kept trying to picture what my back now looked like while at the same time, another part of my mind kept trying to push the picture away.

"Nineteen!"

"Twenty!" I felt like my entire being now consisted of only two things: my seared back and my mind, which had only one thought, "Act proud."

"Twenty-one!"

"Act proud!" I said to myself.

"Twenty-two!"

"Act proud!" I screamed at myself.

"Twenty-three!"

"Act proud!" I roared at myself.

"Twenty-four!"

I didn't know it was over until I realized that the drum roll had ceased. I straightened up and opened my mouth to let the leather fall. It cleaved to my jaws and my mouth was too dry to spit it out.

I could feel my hands being untied from the post. Now the admonition to "Act proud" was focused on not falling once I was untied.

When my hands were free, I slowly lowered my arms. I then realized how stupid I had been: I should have taken the piece of leather from my mouth before letting my hand down to my side. I felt like it would require an effort beyond by capability to simply raise my hand to my lips. The commands were sent from my brain. For a second, I thought there had been a rebellion by my arm, but my hand made the journey to my mouth. I removed the wad of leather.

Slowly, my other senses came back. My back hurt but gradually, with the realization that the pain would get no worse, I relaxed. I was now sure I could stand it.

I felt hands remove the leather belt from around my waist and that a man had come up on each side of me to help keep me upright. I shook them off. With my head held up proudly and without help, I strutted over to the surgeon's shed.

***

"How's he comin' along today, Doc?" Wade asked the surgeon.

I had spent just over two weeks lying prone on a cot, with a greasy poultice smeared on my back. Every day, except when he was on patrol, Wade came to the infirmary to check on me. Patrols were less frequent, now that Nathan Bedford Forrest had arrived with his regiment of Tennessee cavalry to help with that duty. Wade would read to me from the newspaper sometimes, or just tell me what was going on around the camp.

"He's almost healed." The surgeon spoke in his most "professional-sounding" voice. "He's young and strong, and that helped. While he had some severe lacerations and the whipping covered a wide area on his back, it didn't go too deep and none of his skin was actually excised."

"What's that mean, Doc?" Wade questioned.

"None of his skin was flayed, cut away from his body by the lash," returned the surgeon. "A couple of pretty deep lacerations in places, but there was no damage to the underlying muscles. He still has a few scabs, but almost everything else is already scarred over. It will never be pretty to look at, but all in all, I'd say your boy was lucky."

I wasn't just lucky. Clint had told me that Wade was concerned that the lash in the hands of a strong man could strip both skin and muscle, even in a dozen strokes, so that an onlooker could see the backbone and ribs. The night before the whipping, Wade had sent Clint to find the soldier detailed to wield the lash. Wade had given the soldier a United States five-dollar gold piece and a jug of Kentucky bourbon to make sure that I wouldn't be whipped too severely.

"Don't ever tell him I told you, Jed. He doesn't want you to know what he did, but I thought you should," Clint had told me.

In one way I was grateful to Wade and in another way I resented him for bribing the soldier with the whip. I had faced my demon and come out with credit but, in a way, his interference had ruined it by making it less of an ordeal.

"There's a rumor going around that we're moving north again soon. Think he'll be able to come back to duty by the time we move?" Wade inquired.

"I'll release him in a day or two," said the surgeon. "But don't give him any strenuous work, or the scabs might still open up."

The next day, I left the infirmary. When I got back to the squad area, the cavalrymen were in a state of repressed excitement. Nathan Bedford Forrest, as the ranking cavalry officer, was paying a courtesy visit to the Kentucky Cavalry Squadron and they wanted everything to look its best.

"You'all hear about Forrest?" Wade asked the squad. "How he escaped from Fort Donelson the night before it fell? Just flat out refused to be part of the surrender. Took his cavalry and any infantry that wanted to go, and swam the river. Can you imagine swimming a river in the middle of February?"

"The man's worth his weight in wildcats, that's for sure," agreed Clint.

"There's talk he's being considered for promotion to brigadier general," Henry threw in.

A little while later, I could hear cheering. The men were applauding the arrival of Colonel Forrest. He was escorted by a small swarm of mounted officers. I studied the man at the center of all the attention.

Two things about Nathan Bedford Forrest just leaped out on seeing him. First, he was a born horseman. Only the most experienced jockeys rode a horse like Forrest did.

The other thing was his eyes. They were dark and opaque as black marbles. I thought I had never seen a man who looked so much like a killer. For a brief moment, his eyes rested on me and I knew how a mouse must feel when caught in the glance of snake.

"Would you care to say a few words to the men, Colonel Forrest?" Captain Ballard asked politely. Forrest stopped his horse and looked around.

"There's really not much to say. We're goin' to move against the Yankees again soon. We're goin' back to war, and war means fightin'. And fightin' means killin'. That's about all there is to say on the subject."

The men cheered once more as Forrest rode on to the next company. Of course, if I was prescient and knew of Fort Pillow and the night riders then, I would have done my best to kill Forrest right there, even if I myself was slain in the attempt.[15]

Two days later, I followed the squad, riding one of the spare mounts and leading two others that weren't saddled. One of the spare mounts carried a bag of oats, some extra ammunition and Wade's LeMat carbine.

The rest of the company was strung out ahead of and behind on the road that led back to Corinth, Mississippi. The cavalry was spread out, screening a column of 16,000 Confederate infantry. We were headed north. General Johnston had resumed his bid to win the war in the West for the Confederacy.

Following the cavalry were 3rd Corps, about 7,000 men under Major General William Hardee, then came 1st Corps, 9,000 men commanded by the general who the Cavaliers had served under at Columbus, Major General the Right Reverend Leonidas Polk.

About three and a half miles away to our right, 2nd Corps and the Reserve Corps, another 20,000 infantry, moved up a parallel road. They were all supposed to come together at a place called Mickey's Crossroads and get into attack formation. A Yankee army was backed up against the Tennessee River at Pittsburg Landing, about seven miles from Mickey's.

The Yankees at Pittsburgh Landing were commanded by U. S. Grant, the old adversary at Belmont. He had been promoted to Major General for capturing Forts Henry and Donelson. His army was about the same size as the Southern army marching to attack him. The Confederates had to defeat Grant before an even bigger Yankee army under General Buell could come to his aid.

Captain Ballard, on the road about twenty yards ahead, called a halt. The infantry units that were supposed to be on the road behind us were nowhere to be seen. He called for the company officers. Brady and First Sergeant Moore rode up from the rear of the column. Brady said hello to Wade as he passed.

The officers had a short conference on horseback, then First Sergeant Moore rode back down the line, collecting the squad leaders, including Wade, as he went. They had a short conference. When Wade rode back, he told the squad to gather around.

"Captain Ballard will wait here for the infantry to catch up. We'll go forward with first and second squads to find out exactly where the Yankees are. Brady, I mean, Lieutenant Wentworth will command, with First Sergeant Moore as second-in-command.

"Jed, for now, you come with us with the spare mounts. If anybody loses his horse, even somebody from another squad, give him one of the spares. You might have to give away the pack horse and I don't want the LeMat misplaced, so put it together now and keep it with you.

"We know that the Yankees are about six or seven miles up ahead, somewhere. We need to try and find 'em, so we can tell General Hardee. The Lieutenant will probably split the squads once we get closer."

"Advance guard, move out!" called Brady from up ahead.

"Column of twos," Wade ordered. "Walk march, trot!" We trotted up the road behind the first two squads. I brought up the rear with the spare mounts. I carried Wade's carbine, but had not had time to attach the stock to the barrel.

About ten minutes later, we passed a crossroads. A few hundred yards beyond the crossroads, we came to a stream, where Brady called a halt.

"We'll split up here. First and second squads will scout along this road, but stay off the road itself. First squad, go to the left of the road and second squad, go to the right. Third squad, go back to the crossroads we just passed and scout along the road that veers off to the east. Keep to the right of the road. The Tennessee River should be off to the northeast and Owl Creek is off to the west.

"If you don't find anything by sundown, meet back at the crossroads. If you do find the Yankees, get back there immediately. Wait for the other squads to come in, if you can. If you're pursued by cavalry, try to shake the pursuit so the Yankees don't know where the main army is. Above all, make sure you get the information back to Captain Ballard or Captain Morgan. If you have to, go right to General Hardee. First Sergeant Moore will wait back at the crossroads. Jed, you leave the two spare mounts there with the First Sergeant.

"I'll be on the left with first squad. Remember, we're not looking for a fight, just information. We don't even want the Yankees to know we're here yet. Tomorrow, if all goes well, they'll find out the hard way."

The squads split up. Wade trotted alongside First Sergeant Moore, followed by the squad. When we got back to the crossroads, I dismounted and tied the two spare mounts to a tree.

"See you in a couple of hours, Pres," Wade said to Moore. Then he led the squad off the right side of the road. We waded the horses across another shallow stream. A few hundred yards beyond the stream was a clearing. Wade halted the squad inside the treeline at the edge of the clearing and had the men dismount.

"Henry and I will go check out the other side of that open space," Wade told the squad. "Clint, you're in charge until I get back. If I'm not back in a half-hour, take command and keep tryin' to find the Yankees. It's a good bet they'll be somewhere out that way." Wade pointed across the clearing.

"Henry, follow me, but stay about ten yards behind. If I stop, come up alongside me about twenty yards to my right, then stay even with me. If you see anything, try to let me know, but if you can't, just get back here. Give your carbine to Jed and just draw your pistol." Wade and Henry crouched down and moved into the clearing.

Clint spaced the remaining members of the squad at the edge of the treeline to watch the clearing. He told me to move back about twenty yards with the men's horses.

I went back and tied the horses to trees. They nickered softly to one another, but the sound wasn't even audible at the edge of the woods. With nothing else to do, I began to think.

I reviewed the plan to run away that I had conceived while laying in the infirmary, waiting for my back to heal. I had resolved to make another attempt after I heard that Obie had made it away.

I knew one of the reasons Obie had run so he wouldn't have to watch me endure the punishment. I knew that he felt guilty and ashamed that I had taken all the blame on myself. I would have given anything to have been able to tell him that he shouldn't feel guilty, that I didn't blame him for anything. I wanted him to know that I was glad that he had gotten away. Most of all, I wished that Obie and I were back together, but I realized that I'd probably never see him again.

Thinking of friendship shifted my thoughts to Wade. I was grateful to Wade for speaking up for me at the tribunal, and for bribing the soldier with the whip. I liked Wade and supposed he also liked me. For that matter, I liked every man in the squad, and every man was friendly to me. But being friendly was not the same as being friends.

Even with Wade, as much as we liked each other, I could never be a friend, not a real friend. Wade was as good a master as I could have hoped for, but in the end, he was still a master. He was a product of his upbringing and his society, which said that master and slave, white and colored, could never be equal. Without equality, there could never be true friendship, any more than friendship existed, at rock bottom, between a man and his horse, or a boy and his dog.

Before I followed Wade into the army, I wasn't happy to be a slave, but I wasn't unhappy. I just endured it, because I never even considered that I would be anything but. I desired nothing more exalted than to be a horse trainer or jockey. I contented myself with my lot.

Now I had seen and done things I never dreamed of before leaving the farm. Like many young men, I had wondered if I were a coward, but my the way I bore up under the whip told me that I could conquer fear. I had been in battle. Even if I hadn't fought, I had acquitted myself well. Under fire, I had rescued Clint and won the admiration of the men in the squad. However, like I told Obie, these people were not our people.

What I had seen and done had made me feel too much self-worth to ever go back to being a slave, at least not in spirit. I knew this attitude couldn't be concealed forever, and that it could get me killed. If there was anything white folks feared, it was a colored who refused to be inferior. That was why I had to run.

I reckoned the best time to run would be during the confusion, the distraction, the disorganization that would exist during a battle. The present flow of events indicated that time was not far off.

My musing was interrupted by the return of Wade and Henry.

"There are some Yankee pickets on the other side of this clearing," Wade said when the squad had gathered around. "We smelled their coffee before we saw them."

"Smelled like real coffee, not blackened peanuts," interjected Henry.

"I couldn't see more than six or seven," continued Wade. "They're in the woods and it sounded like there's a creek or stream a little ways behind 'em. I think we could ride around to the right and go across the clearing without being seen. We could get into the streambed and come up behind them before they even know we're there.

"You follow me. We'll go in single file through the trees until we're wide of 'em. When I stop, come up on line to my right. Then we'll go hell bent for leather across the clearing. Don't stop until we get to the stream. File in behind me. Draw your pistols but don't fire unless you have to. The fewer Yankees who know about us, the better. Mount up. Jed, watch the clearing. When we move out, you stay here."

I watched the clearing while the squad filed after Wade. They disappeared among the trees. About a minute later, I could see them galloping across the clearing, then they vanished into the far treeline. I was left alone with a horse and Henry's carbine and Wade's LeMat. The idea that I should run right now ran through my mind.

I knew that it would be difficult. Behind me was the Confederate army. In front of me, I knew not where exactly, was the Yankee army. I knew that they'd have pickets out and realized just how easy it would be to be shot by a nervous Yankee picket mistaking me for a Confederate.

"Despite the danger, it's still the surest way," I said firmly.

Action on my decision was suspended by the sound of gunfire echoing across the clearing. In a few seconds, it was replaced by dead silence.

A minute later, the Rosser brothers trotted their horses back across the clearing, pistols drawn. In front of them, hands up in the air, ran seven Yankee soldiers. The Rossers were yelling at them to run faster.

The Yankees got into the treeline and Rob told them to stop. He covered them with his pistol while Charlie waved back across the clearing. Seconds later, Wade, Henry, Dandy and Clint galloped back across the clearing.

"Get 'em moving," Wade told Charlie. "There's a lot of yellin' goin' on back there. Somebody's callin' out the guard. I'm sure we're goin' to be followed."

Charlie and Rob herded the Yankees back toward Confederate lines. I mounted and waited with the four soldiers, who were watching the far treeline.

"We'll give Charlie and Rob a few more minutes to get clear with those prisoners," Wade said, "then we'll follow."

A few minutes later, as we withdrew from the treeline, I could hear a large number of men crashing through the underbrush on the far side of the clearing. We rode away before the Yankees came in sight. We caught up to Charlie, Rob and the Yankees at the fork where First Sergeant Moore waited with the spare mounts.

Brady galloped up followed by the other two squads. He looked down at the prisoners.

"What unit are you with?" Brady asked them. The prisoners looked dejected. They had not expected Confederates to be anywhere closer than Corinth, so they were profoundly shocked to have been attacked and ashamed to have been taken prisoner so easily.

"Fifty-third Ohio," one of them finally replied sullenly, "in Sherman's division."[16]

"There's some skirmishers followin' us, Lieutenant," Wade told his brother. Brady nodded.

"First Sergeant, take first squad and get the prisoners back to the company. When you get there, tell Captain Ballard what's going on. The Yankees following us might blunder back down this road, which we don't want. I'm going to set up a screen with second and third squads to the right of the road, behind the stream. Try to get back with some help before the Yankees reach us."

"Yes, sir," Moore nodded, then spoke to the corporal in charge of first squad. "Have the Yankees mount up, three to a horse. We'll go faster that way."

"Ain't you afraid they'll get away?" asked Rob.

"If we can't catch three men ridin' bareback on one horse, we ain't cavalrymen. Besides," Moore continued, looking meaningfully at the Yankees, "we don't have to catch 'em, we can just shoot them if they try to escape." When the Yankees were mounted, they rode off.

Brady led the two squads back up the road. When we came to the stream that we had crossed earlier, Brady had the soldiers dismount and take up firing positions. Since Wade and Henry had scouted the area before, Brady had them stay mounted and sent them forward as vedettes.

"Unless you can't avoid it, don't shoot. Just get back here and let us know they're coming, so we keep some element of surprise." Wade nodded and he and Henry rode off.

After about a quarter-hour had gone by, Wade and Henry galloped back. Wade stopped in front of Brady to report.

"Infantry skirmishers, about a company, are in the woods and comin' this way. I figure they'll reach here in about five minutes."

"Good work, Corporal. Rejoin your squad." Brady and Wade both gave mocking smiles at the formality. Wade and Henry dismounted near me and tied their horses. I handed each of them their carbines.

A sound of galloping hooves came from behind. It was Captain Ballard leading the Cavaliers up the road. Brady told him the situation.

I stood about ten yards behind the firing line, straining to catch sight of the enemy. I could hear snapping underbrush and the shouted commands, "Keep in line! Watch your dress!" It sounded about two hundred yards away.

"Some infantry reinforcements are coming up the road behind us at the double-quick. They'll be here in about five minutes," Captain Ballard told Brady. "Deploy the men in line. We should be able to hold off the Yankees until they get here. We want to keep the Yankees as far away as possible, so we'll open fire as soon as they're in sight." Within minutes, blue-coated soldiers could be seen through the woods.

"Fire!" Captain Ballard commanded. The cavalrymen opened fire with their carbines, then drew their pistols and continued to fire. The Yankees barely returned fire before they disappeared back into the woods.

"I never expected dismounted cavalry to drive infantry away so easily," Brady said, half amazed.

"Maybe they're workin' their way around our flank," rejoined Wade.

"It doesn't sound like it," answered Brady as Wade stiffened, then turned around.

"It wasn't us they were afraid of, it was them." Wade pointed back down the road, where a column of gray-clad infantry was quick-marching.

Captain Ballard briefed the colonel of the leading regiment on what had taken place. When he finished, Brady rode over to him.

"Jon, we'd better get some men mounted and form another screen to our front," Brady suggested. "After this little squabble, the Yankees'll probably be back for a reconnaissance."

"I think you're right. Tell James to take squads four, five and six out around where Wade's men picked up those Yankee prisoners. Give them the same general orders as you had." Brady moved off to find Lieutenant Butler.

Dusk fell and with it came a cold, driving rain. Leaving the vedettes in position, the rest of the company mounted and rode back to the rear.

IX

I was jolted awake just after dark by the sound of gunfire.

"That sounded a fair distance away," commented Rob sagely.

"Just about where the vedettes are supposed to be," rejoined Wade with a worried air. We all waited anxiously for about ten minutes.

"Sounds like riders comin'," Rob said at the sound of galloping hoofbeats.

"Hold your fire," Wade said. In the dark, his voice sounded louder than it was. "They're probably ours."

They were ours. It was Lieutenant Butler leading the vedettes back. I could see that only about half the number of men sent out were coming back in. With the other men, I crowded in to hear the report that Butler was making to Captain Ballard and Brady.

"I was with sixth squad. We were just getting close enough to them to see what they were doing when we heard the sound of firing off to our left, where fourth and fifth squads were. So we hightailed it back to the rally point. Corporal Jenkins came in with two men from fourth squad and three from fifth. He said that they had been attacked by Yankee cavalry, who surrounded them before most of them could get away. I don't know if any men were killed or wounded, but I don't think so. I think they were all captured."

"How many did we lose?" asked the Captain.

"Ten."

"Tarnation! The chance for a surprise attack is long gone. The Yankees are going to be ready and waiting. I'd hate to be a doughboy today. We'd better let the General know. Brady, find General Hardee, since we're attached to his corps, and tell him the situation," Captain Ballard ordered. Brady called for his horse, mounted and rode off.

Wade and the squad sat around, trying to figure out who the captured men might be. I drifted off to sleep again.

In the half light of false dawn, before the sun really came up over the horizon, the sound of gunfire again jarred me awake. The men, in some confusion, groped for their weapons and tugged on their boots. At least the rain had stopped.

"Sounds like a whole company skirmish line," Rob said.

"Yeah, but it's in our rear," rejoined Charlie worriedly. "Do you think the Yankees got around us during the night?" We all stood in confusion, not knowing whether to watch to the front or rear, until the corporal of last night's guard ran up to Brady.

"It's the infantry, sir! Our infantry! Some of those dolts are huntin' breakfast and others figure their powder's damp from the rain. Instead of drawin' the cartridges out like their supposed to, they're just shootin' them out."

"Well, definiately no chance for surprise now," said Brady. "Even if they didn't after last night, the Yankees know we're here now and can probably figure out in what kind of strength, without even sending out scouts." Brady dismissed the corporal.

The edge of the sun was now over the horizon. Along with the songs of the larks came the rebel yell. The infantrymen were just shouting for the heck of it. They were not even close to being in position to launch an attack.

I watched the squads detailed for vedette mount up. A little while later, First Sergeant Moore came around to alert the squad leaders to have the men fall in for a company formation. The company fell into a square formation facing in. The top side of the square was open except for Captain Ballard, First Lieutenant Wentworth and First Sergeant Moore. First Sergeant Moore told them to stand at ease, then Captain Ballard spoke.

"The infantry from Bragg's Second Corps are still not in position to launch an attack. Those are the gentlemen whose shooting and yelling so considerately awoke us this morning." The men laughed, then Ballard continued.

"Captain Morgan and the rest of the squadron have been ordered to guard the left flank, over near Owl Creek. Since we are already here, and have vedettes already deployed, we'll remain here behind the center, under Colonel Gardner.[17] After our vedettes come back in, we are to secure the rear and act as the provost guard in this area.

"Securing the rear means we are to ensure that the enemy does not get around behind us without warning to attack us from the rear. If the enemy breaks through our line, we are to do all we can to contain the breakthrough until infantry can counterattack.

"Provost guard means we take charge of any prisoners and escort them away from the battle area. We also stop any of our men who get it in their heads to skedaddle. There may be more than a few.

"Understand that, unlike you, most of the infantry have not yet 'seen the elephant.' For that reason, you are apt to see a lot of shirkers and a half dozen unwounded men 'escorting' each wounded man to the field hospital. When that happens, gather them up. We'll establish a place to collect them. When we get enough, we'll escort them back up to the firing line and turn them over to command of an infantry officer.

"There is one final item that, even though this might not be the most expedient time, I in all honor should make known. We in this company consider ourselves to be gentlemen volunteers in the service of the Provisional Army of the Confederate States. We joined with the explicit understanding that our term of enlistment would expire in no more than one year, sooner if the war concluded before then." Wry laughter answered the last point.

"Well, that is now changed. Last week, on the twenty-ninth of March, the Congress enacted legislation which will involuntarily extend the enlistments of all one year volunteers to three years." There was an angry murmur in the ranks.

"Such high-handedness is what we're fightin' against," a voice shouted.

"Quiet!" bellowed First Sergeant Moore.

"Men, I know that there are serious questions of propriety and legality here," Captain Ballard told the troops. "We can decide what our response is later. Right now, you're still soldiers, legally within your agreed-upon term of enlistment. There's a battle to fight. Get your weapons, horses and equipment ready. First Sergeant! Have the men mount!"

"Get your horses and mount up!" bawled Moore. "Then form up in column of twos on the road, in squad order." The men got their equipment and weapons, mounted and formed as ordered. Then we waited and waited some more. It began to appear that the earliest attack wouldn't take place until well past noon. Finally, orders were passed to dismount.

I sat behind Wade, as the squad relaxed around a small fire where peanut coffee boiled. We had lazed away the whole day.

We could see the infantry still moving up in a seemingly endless column. They were probably from Bragg's 2nd Corps because the color bearers carried the Stars and Bars or state flags. The regiments in Hardee's 3rd Corps had blue and white regimental flags.

"I wonder when they'll all finally get here," said Henry. "Waitin's startin' to get on my nerves."

"After the shootin' gets started, I know I won't begrudge any nice, quiet waitin' time," rejoined Charlie.

"Waiting for this battle is one thing," interjected Clint. "We aren't goin' to leave right before a battle. But the Confederacy has no right to make us stay around after two more months are up."

"What're you goin' to do? Quit?" Rob asked sarcastically.

"No, I'm not going to quit!" retorted Clint. "But the reason we joined is to fight against this kind of tyranny. Lincoln has no right to force the states to remain in the Union. They joined it freely and they should be able to leave freely."

"So you're going to say that since we joined up freely, we should be able to leave the army when we want?" Dandy interrupted. "That's no way to fight a war."

"That's not what I'm saying at all!" said Clint hotly. "We shouldn't come and go as we please, because we did sign up for a year. What I'm saying is that after a year, if I don't choose to re-enlist, I am legally a private citizen once more. That's what it said in effect on our enlistment papers. We have a compact with the government. A government that doesn't keep its word is just like the damn Yankees, it isn't honorable."

"I'd re-enlist anyway," Henry said with conviction. "I'm not leaving this fight until it's won. The thing is, I wouldn't leave somebody else to fight my fight."

"I see Clint's point, though," Charlie threw in. "Whether you re-enlist or leave, it should be your decision. It's a matter of principle."

"That's right, it's a matter of principle," Clint quickly agreed. "We're free men who freely joined. The Confederacy can't hold us against our will. We're not a bunch of darkies who can just be kept in bondage." Everyone fell silent. Clint sheepishly looked over his shoulder at me, no doubt in that moment recalling who had saved his life at Belmont. "Sorry, Jed," he mumbled.

"No offense taken," I said quietly. I knew that the squad still didn't know how to treat me. I was a part of the squad, yet, I wasn't. I knew that they could never let me be one of them even if they had wanted to.

I didn't dwell on these feelings. Like many slaves, I had acquired the skill of being able to mask emotions. The slave's skill went beyond just keeping a blank look so anger and resentment wouldn't show on his face. To keep powerlessness from wilting his own spirit, a slave was able to also suppress his actual feelings. It lessened the emotional pain.

That night, in the dark, I overheard Wade talking to Brady.

"He's as much a part of the squad as any of us. He deserves to be free."

"I agree that Jed's a good servant, but he's not a part of your squad," Brady answered. "You have to see that. We're all equals, military rank aside. If you say Jed is one of us, then our whole social system is wrong."

"Well, maybe it is wrong, maybe not," Wade retorted. "Brady, I agree that most coloreds still need to be ordered around to get them to do anything useful. Most of them need us to care for them because they don't have the capacity to take care of themselves. It's not necessarily their fault. In Africa, I guess all they had to do to be able to eat was pluck fruit from the trees.

"But Jed's a special case. He stood with us at Belmont, and he saved Clint's life. I'm not saying he's our equal, but he deserves to be free." Brady was silent for a long moment.

"We can't legally free him. He belongs to Father. We can write him, asking for Jed's freedom. I have no doubt that father will grant it if we both ask. Do you want to write the letter, or shall I?" Wade smiled.

"You write it. Things always sound more sensible coming from you. I'll get some paper."

After hearing that, I don't know how much I was able to sleep that night. I must have slept, because the next morning I was roused by the stirring of Confederate infantrymen. They had slept, in attack formation, between us and the Yankees. Now they got up and walked away from us, into the woods.

After we woke, everybody began to grumble about breakfast. Almost no one had anything to eat. "Don't worry," said Wade, "I hear the Yankees came well supplied. We'll just drive them off and eat *their* breakfast." Wade turned to me. "Mornin', Jed. Got any water?"

"No, Corp'ral, I sure don't. Want me to go find some?"

"No, never mind. I don't know where you'd go to look for some nearby anyway."

Suddenly, we heard the sound of the rebel yell and shooting on a massive scale. The Confederate infantry had finally made their attack against Grant's army. Incredibly, even though part of Hardee's 3rd Corps had been attacked by a three-company Yankee patrol early that morning, the Confederate attack still seemed to be a great surprise to the Yankees.

The sounds receded very quickly, as if the battle were moving away from us. That meant the Yankees were being pushed back. We mounted up quickly and moved forward to keep pace with the advance. As usual, I followed with a couple of spare mounts and Wade's carbine. I wondered why Wade had bought the thing, since he never seemed to carry it.

As the company moved forward, a few infantrymen came back from the direction the charge had gone. Almost all were wounded. Already the backflow of battle was beginning.

Occasionally a wounded man, especially those with leg wounds, would be supported by an unwounded partner. Once in a while, a man bleeding from the head or chest would be carried to the rear by two or three uninjured men. Except for the most seriously injured, they seemed to be in excellent spirits, exclaiming at how easily they had put the Yankees to flight.

Yankee prisoners began to appear in small groups, escorted by infantry with slung rifles. The Yankees had been stripped of their equipment, except for a few who still had haversacks or canteens. Most of them slouched along, some with their hands in their pockets, and they avoided looking their captors, or each other, in the eye. They all stayed quiet except for one prisoner.

"You secesh should fight fair," he pugnaciously proclaimed. "It's a cowardly trick to attack men in their own camp early on a Sunday morning. Ain't you heathens ever heard of keepin' the Lord's day holy?"

The Confederate infantrymen guarding the prisoners almost caroused. One was busy eating an entire pie by himself. Another munched apples, rotating them as his teeth worked like a buzz-saw, then tossing the cores carelessly away. Several Confederates had almost new Yankee brogans hung around their necks by the laces, waiting to discard their own broken-down shoes. As they turned their prisoners over to the Cavaliers, they described in rich detail the treasure troves of food, drink and supplies that had been discovered in the Yankee tents.

Captain Ballard sent a half-squad further to the rear with the prisoners, while the rest of the company advanced to catch up to the rear edge of the infantry line.

Before long, we came to a cluster of tents, with a United States flag trailing down onto the damp ground from a broken pole. A few dead Confederates were scattered here and there among the tents.

Live Confederates were among the tents also. Some were still scrounging food. One was rolling his spare underwear and some personal belongings into a blanket he had just pulled out of a tent. Another, fantastically, was lounging on a cot, reading letters.

Just beyond the tents was an orderly row of Yankees, shot down as they had tried to form a firing line to stop the Confederate advance. A smear of blue spread from the ruined firing line back into the woods behind them.

I dismounted and walked over to the prostrate forms. It was clear how much of a surprise the attack was, for hardly any of the Yankees had managed to get their equipment on. I reached down and shook the canteens of the few who had them. I pulled off the corpses any canteens that had water in them and got four partially filled canteens that way.

"I found us some water, Corp'ral." I held the canteens out to Wade.

"Did you get these the same way you got us the ammunition at Belmont?" Wade asked. The question sounded like an accusation in my ears.

"Yes, Corp'ral. I figured they don't need it anymore." Wade must have realized then the way I had taken his statement.

"You're right, they don't," Wade said. "Back at Belmont, I was a little squeamish, I guess. Now I'm not at all finicky about where it came from. War sure does change a man's values, doesn't it?" Wade took the canteens and gave one back to me. "You need a drink, too." Then Wade shared the water with the rest of the squad.

"Get as many of them up onto the spare mounts as you can," Brady ordered me, indicating the wounded soldiers, Yankee and Confederate, sitting and laying all around us, unable to get to the field hospital by themselves. "Get the most severely wounded first, but not those wounded so severely that they will probably be dead anyway. Our boys first, of course, but also the Yankees. Be ready to go when we send back our next passel of prisoners." I listened and thought quickly.

"Sir, somebody might wonder about a colored riding a fine horse and leading two others. What if somebody back there tries to take the horses from me?"

Brady considered for a moment. "Good point. I'll write a note stating you're transporting the horses under orders from me."

I led one of the spare mounts over to where a wounded Confederate, barely more than a boy, lay on his back, seeming to stare up at the sky. The left side of the boy's uniform looked like somebody soaked it in a tub full of blood. He looked about my age or maybe a year older, at most, and probably lied about his age to get into the army.

I stood over him and the young soldier's gaze shifted slightly to focus on me. He seemed to be trying to talk. I knelt on the ground beside him and put my ear to the boy's lips.

"Water," I heard faintly. I didn't have any more water in the canteen I took from the dead Yankee, but the soldier had his own canteen. I shook it and felt water sloshing around inside it as the boy groaned.

I guiltily put the canteen back down. I didn't want to cause the boy any more agony, so I took out my clasp knife and cut the strap of the canteen. I pulled it clear of the young soldier's body, uncorked it and trickled some water slowly into his mouth. The boy seemed to smile with his eyes.

I corked the canteen and put it down. I pulled the boy's good right arm over my shoulders and got his left arm behind my back. With a grunt from me and a groan from him, we got upright.

I half dragged, half carried him over to the spare mount and, as gently as I could, hoisted the young soldier onto its back. The boy couldn't stay upright, but sank forward onto the horse's neck.

I led the horse over to another Confederate, sitting up on the ground. He seemed almost cheerful, in spite of the fact his right thigh looked like it had been chewed by a large, very hungry dog.

"I'm goin' to try and get you up on this horse," I told him.

"Okay, boy. I think I can stand on my good leg, so if you'll just help me up, I think I can manage." The cheerful soldier reached up both of his hands and braced with his good leg. I grasped his hands and backed away, slowly pulling the soldier up until he balanced on his one foot. Without letting go, I shifted around until I was next to the man, who leaned on me while he hopped over to the horse.

The soldier leaned against the horse's side while I boosted the man up. With a grunt of pain, the man threw his bloody leg over the horse's rump and settled in behind the young soldier, then reached forward to keep him steady on the horse.

"I'll get a few more on the other horses, then we'll go back to the surgeon," I told him. The cheerful soldier nodded.

"This should keep you out of trouble with any busybodies in the rear," Brady said, handing me the note. I took it and looked at it. I don't know why, for at the time I didn't know how to read.

"Thank you, sir." I carefully folded the note and put it in my pocket.

I got two more wounded aboard the second horse and another onto the last horse.

"We got enough prisoners to go back," a corporal shouted. "Hurry up and get the last of the wounded, Jed." I looked at the corporal for a second, wondering how the man knew my name, until I recognized Porter Lawliss behind a new, still scraggly beard.

"Just one more, Corp'ral." I led the horse to a Confederate infantry sergeant. A noticeable feature of the sergeant's appearance was how unnaturally pale he was and the size of the hole in his chest. With a start, I realized he was dying and would never make it back to the field hospital.

The sergeant appeared to notice the change in my expression and a look of real fear clouded his face. With a feeling of enormous guilt, I quickly moved away. I felt like crying.

I quickly got a wounded Yankee up onto the last horse. His eyes were bright with anxiety, and he refused to take his hand away from the side of his neck. A slow but steady flow of blood ran through his fingers and down his arm, where it dripped slowly from the elbow of his jacket.

I walked with the reins of a horse in each hand. On the second horse, the cheerful soldier held the boy with the badly wounded shoulder with one hand and trailed the reins of the third horse with his other hand.

We could barely keep up with Lawliss and his walking prisoners, although they slouched slowly along, much like the first prisoners I had seen. I was afraid that if we went too fast, the wounded would be pitched off their horses. I simply followed Lawliss, until I bumped into the back of the man's horse. He had stopped to give me some new orders.

"Look for a green cloth up in a tree. Sometimes the surgeons tie their sashes up in trees to mark where they are. You could also look for a stack of drums. Sometimes the drummers and other musicians act as stretcher-bearers. We should be back along in about a quarter-hour." Lawliss and his squad hurried on with the prisoners.

I continued on, watching for a green sash in the trees or a pile of drums, but could see neither. But I caught sight of some wounded men and followed them. They led us to a field hospital. I stopped the horses at the edge of a circle of wounded men.

Medical orderlies were carrying the wounded into a small stand of trees. Other medical orderlies were carrying things out. Some were bandaged men, who were laid out under the trees. Others were bloody but not bandaged, dead, who were laid out in an ever-widening row. Still other things were smaller, also bloody, and dropped in a pile near the heap of dead. I almost vomited. Corporal Lawliss should have told me to look for a pile, not of drums, but of amputated arms and legs.

I got the wounded off the horses as gently as I could. When I helped the cheerful soldier down, the young soldier slid off the far side of the horse and fell heavily to the ground. I was outraged at myself for letting the wounded boy fall and ran over to help him.

There was no need. He was already dead. His face was almost as gray as his homespun jacket. He had bled to death.

I collected the horses and left the area of the field hospital as quickly as I could. I moved carefully to avoid bumping into the wounded men that congregated there and returned to where Lawliss had left me.

I had no idea how much time had gone by, but I didn't see Corporal Lawliss. While I waited, I thought about the promise of freedom I had overheard the previous night. I hoped Brady was right, that Mr. Wentworth would free me as soon as the request reached him.

I estimated that it would take a week for the letter to reach Kentucky and another week for Mr. Wentworth's reply. Some legal documents might be necessary, so leave another week for that, and throw in another week for things to go wrong.

My heart beat faster as I realized that, in less than one more month, I might be free, maybe even before my sixteenth birthday sometime around the end of the month.

I felt a great deal of gratitude to Wade for insisting that Brady attempt to persuade their father to grant my freedom. I wondered what had given Wade the moral courage required, given their upbringing, to even broach the subject with his brother and their father.

When I was sure I had waited long enough, I swung up into the saddle and gathered the leads of the spare horses. Without further thought, I turned my back to the sound of the firing and nudged my horse forward.

I was running away.

X

My biggest problem was that I didn't know where to go. I would have liked to have just gone over to the Yankee army, but I was unlikely to get there alive. I couldn't just cross between the lines of the two battling armies. If I wasn't shot in the back by a Confederate, I'd probably be shot in the chest by a Yankee. In either case, my being shot was as likely to be the result of sheer bad luck as someone on either side shooting specifically at me. The sheer number of bullets moving in both directions rendered such an approach almost absurd.

I couldn't just sit tight, in hiding, and wait for the tide of battle to flow past. The course the battle was taking, with the Yankees being driven back towards the river, further away from me, indicated I had only one real choice. I had to ride back through the rear area of the Confederate army, which meant I had to pick a direction.

I could go south on the Corinth road. I knew that the army was still likely to have resupply wagons coming up from the base in Corinth, as well as wagons filled with wounded going back. The Corinth road was probably the quickest way to get away from the main army, but I was likely to be seen. On the other hand, I had the orders signed by Brady to explain my presence on the road with the horses.

I could also strike out cross-country to the west. There was less chance of being stopped, but if I was stopped, it would be harder to explain what I was doing. Somebody with nothing to hide would stick to the road.

I had almost decided to take the Corinth road, when I recalled that in his speech to the company, Captain Ballard had said that the rest of the Kentucky Cavalry Squadron was off to the west, on the left flank of the army. If I was stopped while heading west, I could claim that I was simply taking the mounts to them.

I decided to take the Corinth road for a short way, to get away from the battle area in the shortest time before heading west. The area was thick with reinforcements moving to the battle, and wounded, prisoners and shirkers moving away, so I shouldn't be too noticeable.

Having made the decision, I boldly walked the horses out on to the road. As regiments of infantry marched up the road to reinforce the successful attack, I kept the horses over to the verge. Four or five regiments went by, but no one asked me what I was doing there.

After I traveled for about twenty minutes, the road crossed a stream. I pulled off the road and dismounted to let the horses drink. I drank too, and filled my canteen. When the horses had finished drinking, I let them graze for a while on the tender but sparse spring grass.

After a while, I returned to the road, but still stayed well to the side. Infantry regiments continued to pass by, going north. Every so often, in response to shouts from behind, the infantrymen scurried to the sides of the road to let cannons and caissons thunder by. During one such halt, an infantry lieutenant accosted me.

"What're you doing here, boy?" he demanded gruffly. I forced myself not to look afraid. Of course, I still took off my hat and looked down.

"Just doin' what the lieutenant told me to do, sah."

"And what might that be?" The infantry lieutenant was now staring at me, suspicion plain on his face.

"Takin' these horses to the squadron, sah. They're remounts."

"What squadron is that?"

"The Kentucky Cavalry, sah. They're over by Owl Creek."

"Are you lost, boy? Owl Creek's over that way, to the west. You're going south."

"I suppose I was a bit astray then, sah. Thank you'all for pointin' the way." I turned away from the lieutenant and, before he could say anything else, quickly led the horses off in the direction he had pointed.

The infantry were called back onto the road to resume their march, and I breathed a little easier when I heard them moving away.

I slowly continued in the direction that the infantry officer had pointed, occasionally looking back at the road until that regiment was out of sight. There was another regiment behind the first, and just in case some of those men had seen me with the officer, I kept on going west.

When I was sure that the trees blocked me from the view of anyone in that second regiment, I cut back to the southeast to pick up the road again. I really wanted to go west, but I didn't want to do it so early that I risked actually running into the Kentucky Cavalry.

When I got back on the road, the last of the infantry was going by. They were followed by three regimental supply wagons, then a four gun battery thundered around the bend. I heard them before I saw them and had time to get the horses out of the way. After they went by, I resumed leading the horses south on the road.

As I walked along, I constantly looked up and down the road. I didn't want to be surprised. I came to hate bends in the road because I couldn't see who might be coming around them. I listened hard though. It seemed that nothing else was on the road. I began to relax.

Up ahead about two hundred yards, I saw another bend. I strained to hear if someone was coming around it, but from two hundred yards away, the only things I would have been able to hear were an artillery battery or galloping cavalrymen. My nerves tightened a bit, for as I watched, four men on slowly walking horses came around the bend.

I shot a quick glance to the side of the road, looking for a way to avoid them. When I looked back, the leader was pointing my way. They had seen me. I would just have to keep going. Turning now would only arouse suspicion.

Behind the horsemen, a wagon swung into sight from around the bend, followed by another. As the horsemen approached, wagons continued to come around the bend.

I pulled the horses to the side of the road, hoping the horsemen would just pass. The leader, a captain, motioned for the convoy of wagons to continue up the road, then with a sergeant, he rode over and stopped in front of me.

"Just where do you think you're going, boy?" the captain asked, not casually but not suspiciously either.

I took off my hat and looked down at the ground. I had been rehearsing a story ever since I had been seen by the horsemen. I didn't want to mention Owl Creek, in case the man knew where it was.

"Tryin' to find the Reserve Corps, sah. The lieutenant said they'd be along this road. He said if I didn't see them, to just go left on the road and I'd catch 'em sooner or later. That's what I'm doin', sah."

"Where'd you come from?"

"Up yonder where the battle's bein' fought, sah." I pointed back up the road.

"Was your unit on the left or the right?"

"Don't know, sir. Guess we were in the middle, because there were other soldiers on both sides of us." The captain started to look confused.

"What unit were you with?"

"Kentucky Cavalry Squadron, sah."

"Who's your commanding officer?"

"Captain Ballard, sir."

"I don't know him. If he's a captain, he probably commands a company. What's the squadron commander's name?" His tone had become a bit sharp, so I thought I'd better not play dumb too far.

"Captain Morgan, sah."

"Did your captain give you any orders, anything in writing, to authorize you to be riding around alone?"

"The lieutenant did, sah." I reached into my pocket and pulled out the note Brady had given me. The captain read it.

"This looks to be in order." He handed the note back. "So why are you so far from where you should be?"

"Cap'n," the sergeant chimed in, "ask him if he knows his left from his right." Then, without waiting, to me he said, "Boy, hold up your right hand." I hesitated, trying to look confused, then deliberately held up my left hand. The captain and the sergeant both chuckled.

"See, just as I figured. He don't know his right from his left," the sergeant said.

"Boy, come with us," said the captain. "We'll get you going where you need to go." My heart sank, but I had no choice. I swung up into the saddle and followed the two Confederates. We soon caught up to the slow-moving wagons.

"You say you've been up this road, boy. Any place to water the horses along here?" the captain questioned.

"Yes, sah. Not too far, less than a half-hour, I think, even as fast as these wagons go." I dropped back behind the other two mounted men and rode in silence.

About a half-hour later, we came to the stream. The captain motioned the wagon train off the road over to the stream so the animals could drink. I let my horses drink again also.

"We might as well stop so the men can eat," the captain told the sergeant. "But get the wagons to the other side of the stream first."

The sergeant and the two privates led the wagons to the other side of the stream. They pulled off to the side of the road and the teamsters got down off the wagon boxes. Some of the teamsters started to build small fires and put cans of water to boil for coffee. The others lined up at the rear of one wagon, where the sergeant handed out salt pork, hard biscuits, peanut coffee and sugar.

I looked at the food hungrily, not having had anything to eat since a little breakfast the previous day. The sergeant looked over at me.

"Hey, boy! You get anythin' to eat lately?" I jogged over.

"No, Sergeant. The lieutenant said as soon as we captured the Yankee camp, we'd all feast on their soft bread and beefsteaks." The sergeant laughed.

"Well, I guess they'll get the cavalry to believe anythin'. But, if you're goin' to be with the army, stay with the commissary. We don't get no glory, but we rarely go hungry either." Some of the teamsters heard this and laughed. "Here's some grub, boy." The sergeant gave me a chunk of salt pork, some corn bread and a biscuit.

"Thank you, Sergeant." I resisted the impulse to just wolf down the food. I walked over to a tree and sat under it. I pulled out my clasp knife and cut a slice off the salt pork. I tried to cut the biscuit, but it was too hard. I glanced around at the teamsters. Most of them just smashed their biscuits up and soaked the bits in coffee. I ate a slice of salt pork and the corn bread and put the biscuit and the rest of the pork into the pocket of my jacket. As I did, the sergeant yelled for the teamsters to get back on the wagons.

I rode with the commissary wagons back past the place I had started from that morning. We began to see dead men all around, most of them in blue coats. We also began to see wounded men in wagons, going south along the road we were coming up.

A bit further on, we passed a log cabin, where a smaller road cut across the road we were following. The cabin was done up to look like a church, with a weathered sign in front.

"Shiloh Meeting House," the captain read. "A name from the Bible. Do you know what 'Shiloh' means, Sergeant? I'm pretty sure it means 'place of peace.' I think the Almighty sometimes has a morbid sense of humor."

Today, instead of a congregation, wounded men dressed in gray and blue were sprawled on every open space between the trees. I quickly looked away before I could see the inevitable pile of sawn-off arms and legs. One of the two privates on horseback noticed my squeamishness.

"What's the matter, boy? Spooked by the sight of a little blood?"

Just then, the rattle of rifle-fire, which I had been hearing so long I longer noticed it, was overlaid by the boom of cannon, a battery or even two, firing together. After a few seconds, the booming climbed to a sustained roar.

"Must be fifty, sixty guns," I commented out loud. The private sneered at me again.

"You can tell that from all the battles you been in, huh, boy?" I looked at him steadily.

"No, this is only my second one, after Belmont. How many have you been in?" The private looked chagrined. He turned away and kept quiet.

We rode another mile and during that entire time, the cannonade had not lessened in intensity one bit.

"See the fork in the road we're comin' to, boy?" the sergeant asked me after dropping back alongside. "We'll be goin' right, while you take the left fork." I remembered to pretend not to know right from left.

"Which way's that, Sergeant?" The sergeant pointed.

"You go that way. You should find your people somewhere that way." I nodded.

"Now you be careful, boy."

"I will, Sergeant. You'all be careful, too. And thanks for the food."

"Don't worry," the sergeant called back. "We're not fixin' to get anywhere close to where the fightin's goin' on." He waved.

I turned at the fork, resisting the impulse to turn around to see if the teamsters were watching. I wanted to get off the road before anyone else saw me. As I rode, the cannonade off to the right seemed to get louder, while the rifle fire to the front seemed to fade.

As soon as I was sure I could no longer be seen from the main road, I turned left into the woods. The afternoon sun was starting to dip low in the sky, and I headed straight for it. I was finally going west, about four hours after I had started out. After all that time unaccounted for, there was no way I could return to the company.

To spare the horse, I dismounted. I didn't want her to stumble or trip on the rough ground among the trees. I also wanted the horses as fresh as possible, in case I was pursued and had to make a run for it. I wished I had some oats for the horses, to help them keep up their strength. They weren't used to eating just grass.

The trees thinned out as the land began to slope downhill. A little over a mile away, I could see a wide stream and supposed that it was Owl Creek. I hoped that by going south along its bank, I could avoid the Kentucky Cavalry. I'd cross the creek as soon as I could find a ford, figuring that, once I was on the other side, the chance of pursuit diminished to almost nothing.

Off to the left ran another road. It looked inviting. I wondered whether to chance it, but having lost four hours already by being caught on one road, decided against it. I led the horses down the slope toward the creek.

I reached it about a half-hour later. The creek was wider than most streams in the area and it flowed swiftly because of the recent rains. I stood on the bank, trying to decide whether to should chance swimming across with the horses. I wasn't worried about the width of the creek or the depth of the water. The problem was the current looked too swift to control all three horses at once. The horses, or me for that matter, might be swept downstream. I hoped for a ford or a bridge nearby, because I didn't want to abandon any of the horses if I could help it.

I quickly realized that a ford or bridge was most likely to be found where the road crossed Owl Creek. I stood for a few moments, weighing the risks, then reluctantly made up my mind to follow the bank of the creek south toward the road. I thought I might get lucky and find a ford before long.

Before I started out, I took Wade's LeMat carbine out of the bundle it had been carried in and checked the cartridges to see if they were wet from the rain the previous night. They were probably damp, so I carefully drew the cartridges from the cylinder, then inspected them to make sure I hadn't torn any of them when drawing them out.

I inventoried my ammunition and found there were four boxes of forty-four caliber ammunition, with six cartridges in each box. I also had six buckshot charges. I could reload the LeMat four times with what I had in boxes and what I had just drawn.

I attached the stock to the barrel and loaded fresh cartridges. I put the damp ones in the empty box to dry out and repacked the boxes in the saddle bags.

After pivoting the LeMat's pin so the buckshot barrel would fire first, I loosely wound a blanket around it. I tied the bundle behind my saddle, making sure I could reach into the rolled blanket and withdraw the carbine quickly. As I started out for the road and the expected bridge, I noticed that the cannons had stopped firing.

I led the horses along the bank as the creek meandered. Once, where there was a sharp bend, I simply went straight and soon picked up the creek bank again. After about a mile and a half, the creek bank changed to dense undergrowth and I figured I was within a half-mile of the road.

I decided to wait until it was dark to find the bridge, so I walked the horses back to the last clearing we had passed. I unsaddled the horses, took the bits out of their mouths, hobbled their front legs and turned them loose to graze.

I sat down under a tree at the edge of the clearing, with the blanket-wrapped carbine close at hand, took the salt pork and hard biscuit out of my pocket and began to eat. The biscuit was too hard, so I ate the salt pork. As I ate, I could still hear the clamor of battle, although it now sounded faint and far away.

The next thing I knew, I was snapped awake by the neighing of the horses. I didn't even realize I had fallen asleep.

I turned toward the sound and saw a Confederate soldier trying to catch a horse. Another soldier, with a pistol stuck in his belt, stood over me, scowling down from beneath a blue-trimmed forage cap. He nudged me with his foot.

"Ya'll in charge o' these heah horses, boy? Get up and put saddles on 'em, now!" To emphasize his command, the man put his hand on the butt of his pistol.

"Got but one saddle. Who're you, sah?" I asked nervously. My first thought was I had been caught by provosts. I resisted the impulse to reach for the carbine, but was considering reaching for the orders Brady had written when I suddenly realized the two men weren't provosts at all. They were deserters.

"Never mind who we are, boy! Get that horse saddled," the soldier snarled. "And round up the others. We goin' to take 'em all."

The other soldier had given up trying to catch the horse and walked over. He was armed with only a bayonet, still stuck in the scabbard on his belt.

"Lem, he got any food?" asked the soldier with the bayonet as he drew near. Lem kept his hand on his pistol-butt as he spoke.

"You hear Calvin, boy? Got any food?"

"Just this biscuit." I handed the biscuit to Lem, then got up, slowly. Lem took it and began trying to gnaw it. Calvin grabbed for the biscuit himself.

"Hey, gimme some!"

"Can I go with you'all, sah?" I asked quietly. I really didn't want to go with the two soldiers, but I didn't want to be left stranded. Calvin laughed.

"What d' we need ya'll for? Hard enough the two of us runnin' away, keepin' outta sight o' the damned provosts. Just do what ya'll been told and saddle that horse." I bent down to pick up the saddle.

"Sah, will you leave me just one of the horses? I won't tell anybody I seen you'all." Lem stood up and drew his pistol.

"Ya'll ain't careful, ya'll ain't goin t' tell nobody nothin' ever again. Now get a move on, boy."

I knew I'd have to get away from the two deserters, or drive them away. I shrugged and carried the saddle past them, towards the horses. Lem watched me pass, then put the pistol back in his belt.

I squatted down with my back to the two deserters and put the saddle on the ground quietly. I put my hand inside the rolled up blanket and, with a quick movement, withdrew the carbine. With the carbine held ready, I quickly turned to face them.

The two deserters were kneeling on the ground with their backs to me, fighting over the biscuit.

"Dammit, Calvin! Ya'll ate almost the whole thing," Lem shouted. Any reply Calvin was about to make was preempted by the sound of the carbine being cocked. The deserters started to turn toward me.

"Don't turn around! Just put your hands up!" I shouted, hoping I didn''t sound as scared as I was.

Lem raised his left hand as he got to his feet, reaching for the butt of his pistol with his right. He spun around to face me, raising the pistol and reaching with his thumb to cock the hammer back, all in one fluid movement.

I almost balked at shooting the man, but pulled the trigger just in time. The sixty-caliber buckshot blasted into Lem's midsection, flinging him back down on the ground. The gun flew from his hand. Calvin was up in a flash, running away.

I quickly pivoted the hammer and aimed the carbine at Calvin's back. For some reason, I just watched Calvin until he was out of sight, then lowered the carbine. I slowly became aware that Lem was screaming.

I looked down at him. Blood soaked the bottom of his jacket and the top of his pants. The buckshot had torn open his belly. I could see a twisted, blood-slimed intestine peeking out through the hole.

I dropped the carbine and vomited up salt pork. Then I began to cry, grief-stricken at the horrible damage I had done to the man's body.

"Why'd you'all do that?" I shouted at the dying man, who was now sobbing. "I didn't want to hurt you. Why'd you'all do that?" In reply, Lem stopped sobbing and he stiffened. Then his eyes glazed over and he went limp.

Looking at the dead man, I was horrified. I knew I had to get away from the spot. I thrust Lem's pistol into my belt, picked up the LeMat and took Lem's forage cap.

I'm surprised that, given my state of mind, I took the cap. Unlike my slouch hat, a forage cap was a soldier's hat. I figured that it would help me deceive anyone I encountered in the dark by making me look more like a soldier.

I calmed myself down so I wouldn't spook the horses. After much fumbling, I got one saddled. I put my slouch hat into the saddlebag, put the forage cap on my head and mounted. I rode straight down to the road and turned right, praying I'd come to a bridge soon.

XI

Through the darkness, I saw a large building off to the right of the road. Just beyond it loomed the bridge over Owl Creek. I stopped my horse in the middle of the road so I could scrutinize the bridge, but I couldn't make out anything suspicious. The bridge seemed to be totally unguarded.

The only sounds were two distant explosions, shells from heavy guns. The explosions had gone on about every quarter hour just about from the time the rifle fire had stopped for the night. Sometimes, I could see the fuse from a shell trailing sparks through the night sky.

I took a deep breath and walked my horse slowly toward the bridge, trailing the two spare mounts. I jumped, startled at the loudness of the mare's hooves when she stepped up onto the bridge's planks. I was sure the racket all three horses made would surely bring the entire Confederate army down on me.

After what seemed to be hours, the horses' hoofs clopped softly into the dirt of the road on the other side of the river. For the first time since I left the wounded at the field hospital, I relaxed a little.

With the sudden release from stress came unbidden thoughts about the past few hours. I couldn't put out of my mind the sight of Lem's bloody insides bursting through his jacket, and how he had screamed, loud and long. I couldn't believe I had hurt a man so terribly, and I wished I could undo what had been done, that I could take back that blast of buckshot.

But even if I could redo that moment, what could I have done differently? Lem and Calvin were undoubtedly planning to kill me. They certainly wouldn't have left a witness to put the provosts on their trail. At the very least, they were going to take my horses. Without horses, the odds against me successfully running to freedom would have been formidable, if not almost hopeless.

It was at that moment I decided that my life and my freedom were as valuable as life and freedom were to any man. After a lifetime of living with the notion, I consciously rejected from that moment the assumption that I was a less worthy being. To defend myself, I knew I would kill if I had to. The proof was there: I had done just that. I wouldn't go looking for those situations, but I wouldn't shrink from them either.

I have the same right to life and freedom as any man. I will never let any man take freedom from me again. I'm worth something, if only to myself.

Having accepted that, the only thing I would have done differently during the confrontation is I would have tried to give Lem an easier death. I hated causing the man such suffering. Next time, I would aim for the chest or the head. It sounded brutal, but the sight of the field hospital convinced me that a swift and painless death was a mercy.

A muffled sound forcibly reminded me I wasn't safe just yet. I pulled back on the reins and strained to discover the source of the sound over the horses' fidgeting and nickering.

A vague fear pricked my consciousness, but if an ambush had been set, it would have sprung by now. I was just starting to believe I had imagined the sound, when one of the spare horses began to stamp its hooves fretfully.

The stab of fear returned. I transferred the reins of the spare mounts to my left hand and raised the carbine with my right. With the stock held steady under my arm, I pointed the muzzle off into the darkness.

"Who's there?" I whispered loudly, waited a moment, then whispered again, "Come on out with your hands up. I've got a gun." Nobody answered, so I eased my horse off the road toward where the sound had come.

A flash of lightning split the night and in the bluish white light I clearly saw three faces, two huddled together as if they were hugging each other. The eyes in the faces widened in fear as they stared at me. I stiffened in surprise.

"You're colored!" I said loudly and lowered the carbine. Just then, a pair of hands seized my arm in a powerful grip, forcing the muzzle of the carbine straight up into the sky.

I threw the reins out of my left hand and balled it into a fist and punched across and down, trying to hit the person who gripped me. The lightning flash had dazzled me so much, I couldn't see where to punch. My fist barely made contact with something hard, which I guessed was the man's skull. I drew back my fist for another punch as lightning flashed again. The man who held me had the blackest face I had ever seen.

Must be an African, I thought irrelevantly as his hands levered me back out of the saddle.

I had been thrown from horses before and knew how to take a fall. I got in position so that I wouldn't land on my head or break my neck, and let myself be pulled down. I sensed that the African, if that's what he was, seemed momentarily surprised. He probably expected me to try to keep my seat in the saddle.

As I went down, I lashed at the man's face with my foot, but he easily avoided the clumsy kick. When I hit the ground, my pistol slid from my belt. I cursed myself for forgetting I had it.

The African shifted his grip to twist my arm up behind me and with a grunt of pain, I let go of the carbine. In that instant, he seemed to let his guard down a hair, so I tried to bring my knee up sharply into his groin. He seemed to have anticipated such a move, and my knee collided only with his thigh.

The man's face was right in from of me, so I butted with my head and heard him grunt as the thin skin of his eyebrow split bloodily. As I tried to butt him again, he suddenly let go of my arm and chopped the edge of his hand into the side of my neck where it met the bottom of my skull.

My head swam. I fought to keep from blacking out. A girl's voice shrilly screamed.

"He's one of us! Don't hit him!" Another flat-handed chop thumped against the base of my skull.

"Samson, don't hurt him!"

"Too late. Samson's already gone and done it," I tried to say, but the words just wouldn't come.

***

I felt like I was at the bottom of a dark river, trying to get to the top. I clawed and kicked my way up, and finally broke the surface. It was odd how my face still felt wet.

"He's comin' round," a voice said, vaguely like the shouting girl's voice but not as shrill, and sounding more gentle. I opened my eyes and raised my head at the same time. What a mistake! Waves of nausea and dizziness washed over me. I closed my eyes and lay back down.

"Don't move," said the gentle voice, "Just lie there for a little while and you'll feel better." I felt the wetness leave my face, and then return. I guessed a wet cloth was being pressed against my forehead.

"What about my head?" This voice was deep, gruff and certainly not gentle.

"Your bleedin's stopped, hasn't it?" returned the gentle voice. "Now you hush up and let me take care o' this one."

I chanced opening my eyes again. Everything was a bit blurred, but with an effort, I forced my eyes to focus. It was dark, except when lightning flashed.

In the sharply flickering light, I made out the speaker with the gentle voice to be a mature woman, not a girl. Around her eyes and the corners of her mouth, her skin was lined with fine wrinkles. Then the wrinkles were obliterated by her smile.

"Feelin' better, child?" she asked sweetly.

"Yes, ma'am," I replied. I was lying. In truth, I felt like I had been run over by a six-horse team pulling a caisson.

"I reckon he's goin' to be all right," the woman told the small group gathered around.

"Delighted to hear it," said the gruff voice sarcastically. The speaker was the African, nursing the cut over his eye. He had been called Samson by the girl.

"But who is he, Mama?" said another feminine voice. "He can't be a soldier, so who is he?"

This was the girl. She resembled the older woman so much I knew they must be mother and daughter. Instead of her mother's laugh lines, the girl's forehead was all scrunched up, as if she constantly reasoned through perplexing problems.

"You ain't a soldier, are you, child?" I began to notice how the mother's voice had a deep richness where her daughter's was thin and reedy by comparison.

"No, ma'am."

"Do you ever say anythin' besides 'yes, ma'am' and 'no, ma'am'?" she laughed.

"Yes, ma'am," I replied and then felt foolish. I was trying to think of something to add, when Samson growled.

"I hate to end all this pleasantness, but it's nigh on to ten o'clock from what I can see. We have to get movin'." Samson's speech sounded like he came from the Deep South but some words were spoken the way I supposed they spoke in the North and the whole was overlaid with an accent I couldn't place at all. I wondered if my presumption was correct, that Samson really was from Africa.

You have to understand that, even in 1862, Africans were rare in this country. Two things accounted for this. The trade in African slaves had been outlawed by the United States and many European governments and the ban was enforced, by the British navy especially. Secondly, the rate of natural increase among the slaves made the importation of Africans superfluous, and uneconomical, given the uncertainty of getting a slaver through the naval patrols.

But Africans, especially males, were highly prized by some masters. They were usually recognizable as such, being of darker hue than most of us. I'll leave it to you, as a journalist, to describe how, without offending the sensibilities of your readers, masters forcing their attentions on their female slaves mixed white blood with ours.

"Can you'all move now, child?" the woman asked. I almost said "Yes, ma'am" but only nodded instead and got to my feet.

Besides the woman and her daughter, and the glowering Samson, there were four other people. A colored man with black hair salted with white turned around from where he was keeping lookout.

"Name's Marcus," he introduced himself, and then turned back to lookout.

"I'm Belle and this here's my daughter Effie," the woman said, as she put her arm around the girl.

"My name is Ophelia," the girl said, somewhat impatiently. "Missy Lorene named me after a tragic princess in a story."

"That's my son Josh and that there's Lucinda and her baby, Ella." Belle pointed to a boy who looked to be about ten and young woman of about twenty holding an infant. "Ella's who gave us away with her fussin' and all. And over there's Lucinda's man, Abner." I turned around to see man in his twenties, watching the road behind us. "And you already met Samson," she said with a twinkle of mischief. I nodded to them all at once.

"My name's Jedediah, but most people just call me Jed. You'all didn't lose the horses, did you?"

"No, your horses are right over there. Abner tied them to some trees," Belle told me. "Jedediah, do you'all want to join up with us? We can sure use a man who can fight like you."

I was flattered that she had referred to me, twice now, as a man. But I wasn't sure that Belle's smile was friendly or mocking me for having lost the fight with Samson. In the darkness, she couldn't have noticed the embarrassed look that must have flitted across my face, but she added hastily, "Not many men ever drew blood on Samson."

"Hardly a man alive," said Samson, nastily emphasizing the last word. "Now, let's get movin'. You comin' or not?"

"Where you'all goin'?"

"North, to freedom," Belle replied simply.

"I'll come. We can let the children and the women ride the spare horses.

But I want my carbine back. One of you'all can keep the pistol, but the carbine's mine."

"The carbine's the long gun?" asked Samson. I nodded, then realized, in the dark, the man probably couldn't see me. I was about to say yes, when Samson handed me the carbine. He must have had eyes like a cat.

"We need to hurry and get them horses movin'," said Marcus.

A cold drizzle started to fall as I got the horses. I picked Josh up and put him on the back of one of the unsaddled horses. When I went to hoist Effie up behind Josh, she turned away abruptly.

"I can walk," she declared.

Lucinda handed her baby to Belle so Abner could lift her onto the unsaddled horse's back. She sat sideways on the horse, with both her feet dangling down the horse's left flank.

"You all right up there?" Abner asked her.

"I'll manage," Lucinda replied, her voice tight.

"Don't worry, this horse is gentle," I reassured her. "Just try not to pull her mane. You'all can walk alongside and hold her on." Abner put his arm around Lucinda's waist as Belle handed up the baby.

"You'all goin' to ride?" I asked Belle.

"No, Jedediah. I can walk better'n I can ride," she said, moving to stand beside the horse that carried Josh.

"Who knows which way we're goin'?" I asked the group.

"I'm the guide," replied Marcus. "We were goin' north to Ill'nois, then we heard the Yankee army crossed the river into Kentucky. Now we hear the Yankee army's in Tennessee, along the river, so we're makin' for there."

"The Yankee army's down here, but the Confederate army's between us and them," I told them. "They're fightin' a big battle. When I left, it looked like the Yankees were losin'. I reckon it'd be better to head for Kentucky still.

"If you'all can ride, you could take the saddle horse and scout out the way and we could follow."

"I can ride, and so can Samson." I handed Marcus the reins and he swung up easily into the saddle.

"Better take the pistol," I said. "Deserters might be around, or some other trouble." Samson handed Marcus the pistol and he tucked it through his belt. Flicking the end of the reins on the horse's rump, Marcus rode off in the darkness ahead.

As soon as he was gone, I regretted not having remembered to get my slouch hat out of the saddle bag to keep the rain off. I remembered the forage cap and searched for it on the ground. I found it and was about to put it on, when I noticed Josh's head was bare.

"Bend down," I told Josh and put the cap on his head. Even in the dim light, I could see Josh looked delighted. Belle looked at him sternly for a moment.

"Thank you," Josh at last remembered to say.

We filed into the darkness in the direction that Marcus had gone. Belle, with Effie beside her, led Josh's horse. Abner held Lucinda with one hand and the horse's headstall with the other. Samson walked last in the file, watching out to make sure we weren't being followed. They let me lead the way.

Around midnight, the cold drizzle turned into a downpour. When lightning flashed, I would see the others suddenly thrown into sharp relief and then fade back into invisibility. But the storm was a godsend. It would keep anyone who didn't absolutely need to be outdoors inside and so lessen the chance of discovery and pursuit. At the same time, I was concerned for the women and children, especially little Ella. I walked back to Samson.

"Should we try to find shelter from the storm?" I asked.

"A little rain ain't goin' to hurt you."

"I didn't mean for me, I meant…"

"I know what you meant," Samson laughed. "Don't worry. We've all been through worse than this."

I still felt so embarrassed, I just tucked the carbine under my arm so the cartridges would stay as dry as possible and trudged on. For the tenth time, I wished I had my slouch hat to keep the rain off my face.

The squishy, regular sound of hoofbeats on soggy ground came from the darkness ahead, heading our way. I pointed the LeMat up the road and hoped it was Marcus, not the least because if it was, I could retrieve my hat from the saddlebag.

It was Marcus who rode out of the rain and murk ahead, reining the horse to a halt just in front of me. He leaned from the saddle to make himself heard.

"A few hundred yards further is the road that leads north to Purdy. I wisht I could see the stars, so we wouldn't have to use the road. I don't like usin' a road, but I don't think too many people will be on it tonight. But, come dawn, we'd better get back to travelin' overland."

"We need to rest the horses,' I told him. "If you're goin' to keep scoutin', it'd be good idea to change horses. And before I forget, hold the horse still." I unbuckled the saddlebag and pulled out my hat. I shook some rainwater off my hair and clapped the hat on. I immediately felt better, even though the hat was soaked through within a minute.

Marcus dismounted. Abner went to take over as rear lookout while Samson came forward.

"Want me to take over ridin' scout?" he asked Marcus.

"Do you know this stretch of road?"

"Not as good as you, but I know it. You're startin' to look tired," replied Samson.

"I can handle it till we get through Purdy," Marcus decided. "Jed, please put the saddle on whichever horse you want me to use now." I handed the LeMat to Samson and unsaddled the horse Marcus had ridden. I went to the horse carrying Josh.

"We need to switch horses," I told Belle as I lifted Josh off. "This one's probably the freshest we have. I'll put Josh back up on this one. He's so small and light, I don't think he'll strain her." I quickly put the saddle on the fresh horse. Marcus mounted up and rode back into the rain ahead.

When I went to lift Josh onto the horse, he backed away.

"The horse is tired. I'll walk."

"You all don't need to walk. The horse will hardly notice you're up there."

"I'll walk," Josh said with a hint of anger in his voice. "I'm not a baby." I guess I had embarrassed the boy and sought to make amends.

"I didn't say you were a baby. In fact, why don't you all take charge of leadin' this horse?" Josh straightened up to his full height.

"I'll take good care of him."

"I know you will. But it's a her, not a him."

"How can you tell?" Josh frowned. Now it was my turn to be embarrassed.

"I just can, that's all. If you really want to know, ask your Ma," I said and turned hurriedly away. I sought out Samson.

"Want me to take over rear lookout?" Samson shook his head.

"You're doin' fine up front. Better get movin', though."

Abner moved back over to lead the horse Lucinda and Ella were aboard. The march resumed.

The rain had turned the surface of the road into a gooey mud that threatened in some places to suck the shoes right off our feet. Even with boots, I found the going hard. I led the little procession over to the side of the road, where grass grew and the going was a little easier.

The rain finally stopped just before dawn. Walking through the mud had made us all bone-weary and we went slowly. We had still not passed through Purdy when the sky began to lighten.

From up ahead, I could make out Marcus, riding in from scouting out the town. Samson, Abner and I gathered around Marcus as he dismounted.

"We're still about two miles from town," Marcus reported. "People will start to stir soon. We need t' get through to the other side this mornin' cause there's no good place to hide on this side of town.

"The problem is, a group like us is goin' to attract too much attention goin through town. We should've been through before sunrise. I don't know how we're goin' to get through now." I kind of felt like I was to blame, since I had led the night's march.

"It was really hard goin' because of the mud. We went as fast as we could."

"Nobody's blamin' you, Jed," said Samson. "Travelin' with young ones, you can't expect to go as fast as with just adults. They should've planned for that." I wondered who "they" were, but didn't ask. After thinking for a minute, I spoke.

"If we don't look like we come from afar and don't try to go through town all at once, we could make it.

"Yesterday had to be Sunday. I remember a Yankee sayin' what a dirty trick it was for the rebs to attack on a Sunday mornin'. So today is Monday, market day. Lucinda could take Josh and the baby and pretend to be goin' to market. Same with Belle and Effie."

"What about us?" asked Abner. "White folks see colored men they ain't seen before, with no chains or overseer, they ain't goin' to sit still for it without askin' questions. And they sure ain't goin' to think we own these horses."

"I've got a paper to explain the horses," I replied. "I could just lead them through town and show the paper if I'm stopped. As long as folks see what they expect to see, they won't get suspicious. You'all do what the white folks expect, fetch and carry. Just look like you'all are workin'. When you get near town, pick up something heavy and carry it. The thing is, if you'all tote the same thing, go through town together so you look like a work gang.

"Lucinda will go with Josh and the baby first, then the men go. Start carryin' as soon as you can, even if you'all have to carry a fence rail all the way to town. Then Belle and Effie. I'll wait until you're in town, then come through with the horses.

"With any luck at all, they'll be busy noticin' me and you'all can get through. Marcus, give me the pistol. Get started."

The men just looked at me without moving, then they looked at each other. Abner plainly didn't want to leave Lucinda to travel with just Josh and Ella. Belle nudged Lucinda.

"Abner, I'll see you on the other side o' Purdy," Lucinda told him. "And don't even look at me in town. We better get started. Gimme your hand, child," Lucinda said to Josh.

"Wait." I took the Confederate forage cap off Josh's head and replaced it with my slouch hat. "It'd be easier to explain me wearin' it." Belle kissed Lucinda's cheek and gave Josh such a hug that it's a wonder she didn't drive the breath from the boy. As they started out, I noticed tears on Belle's cheeks.

"Don't worry. They'll get through all right," I told Belle. She nodded, without looking at me.

"It's a good plan you came up with, Jedediah. Please the Almighty, it'll work."

It took almost a quarter-hour for the slow-moving Lucinda to be lost to sight in the morning haze. When she was out of sight, the men started. They moved much faster than Lucinda and when they were lost to view, I turned to Belle and Effie.

"Try not to catch up to 'em. It'll be easier for Josh if he doesn't have to try hard to not notice you. Time to go." Belle hugged me. I felt awkward, not knowing whether to hug back or not, though I wanted to.

"You'all be careful," she told me. I don't know what we'd do without you." Effie stared at me kind of strangely, then Belle grabbed her hand and pulled her off down the road.

I just stood in the road for a while, remembering how Belle's hug had felt and trying to remember my mother.

XII

I estimated that it would take Belle and Effie a little less than an hour to cover the two miles to town. I planned to reach town just as they entered it. It would give me a chance to check on them and I'd be in position to start a disturbance if it became necessary to divert attention away from any of them.

I detached the LeMat's stock and hid it in the blanket-roll which I tied behind my saddle. I stuffed the pistol down into the bottom of a saddlebag. I changed horses, putting the saddle on the horse that Lucinda had ridden. Then I just waited.

When I figured that about three-quarters of an hour had gone by since Belle had left with Effie, I put on the Confederate forage cap, checked the written orders to make sure the paper wasn't soaked and mounted up. At a brisk trot, I led the two spare horses towards Purdy.

I entered the town with the horses slowed to a fast walk. I didn't want to attract attention, but I didn't want to look like I was sneaking around either. Expecting to be stopped and questioned at any moment, my nerves were wound tight, but so far I had received only a few curious glances from passersby.

I caught sight of Belle and Effie in front of me, walking slowly up the town's main street. I caught up to them and was careful not to look at them as I went past.

In the center of town, a few farmers were unloading baskets of storage potatoes, squash, beets and turnips from their wagons. Fruits and vegetables in jars were also displayed as it was too early in the season for fresh.

I took one look and my stomach began to rumble, reminding me I hadn't eaten anything since the day before but the chunk of salt pork, and I had vomited most of that. I had no money and nothing that I could trade without arousing suspicion, so I just closed my mind to the thought of food and rode on.

"Hey, you! Stop!" The words were shouted from somewhere behind me. I resisted the impulse to stop and turn around.

"Stop!" came the voice once again. This time I stopped and turned around.

A farmer who had ridden in with squash and pumpkins to sell was shaking his fist at a wagon driving away. The farmer was standing over some smashed pumpkins. The driver of the other wagon had run over them. I tried not to breathe my sigh of relief too audibly.

I got apprehensive again as I saw Belle and Effie walk up to the angry farmer and stop to talk. There was nothing I could do, so I turned and continued through town.

I had almost reached the outskirts of town, when a man wearing a dark suit slowly walked into the road in front and motioned for me to stop. As I slowed down, the man put his hands on his hips, pulling back his coat to reveal a star-shaped badge pinned to his vest. More impressive was the Navy Colt he wore in a holster.

"Come on down off that horse, boy," he said. I slid out of the saddle. Instead of taking off the forage cap, I saluted the way soldiers did.

"Mornin', sah," I said cheerfully. "Are you'all the town sheriff?"

"I'm Sheriff Ames, boy." Sheriff Ames looked at me narrowly. "Why're you askin'? And what're you doin' with them there horses?"

"My lieutenant said to always check in with the sheriff or somebody in authority, sah. As I went through a town." I spoke quickly, hoping to bewilder Sheriff Ames. "He, that's Lieutenant Wentworth, sah, he said it'd save lots of trouble. These horses belong to him and to Corp'ral Wentworth, his brother. They're part of the Mercer Cavaliers, that's Company C of the Kentucky Cavalry Squadron. They just come out of a big fight with the Yankees on the Tennessee River and …"

"Quiet, boy!" Sheriff Ames interrupted. "Where are you goin' with the horses? And give me a short answer," the sheriff added hastily.

"I'm goin' back up to Kentucky. They sent me 'cause they said it'd be easier for me to get by the Yankees. I'm supposed to go back to the farm and have the master gather more horses. Then I'm to take the new horses back to the army. The Army of Tennessee, that is."

"Got anything to prove what you told me?"

"Yes, sah. Got a paper right here." I reached into my pocket and took out the orders, then unfolded it and held it out. Sheriff Ames took the paper. As he stood reading it, I saw Belle and Effie walk quickly past, holding pieces of broken pumpkin.

"Looks all right, boy," Sheriff Ames said, handing back the paper. "But why didn't you just stop at my office? There's a big sign out front."

"Can't read, sah," I said, refolding the paper and putting it back in my pocket. "Thank you, Sheriff. Good mornin' to you'all, sir." I saluted again and mounted. Sheriff Ames watched me as I rode past him and I felt his eyes on me until I was out of his sight.

Just outside of town, I nudged the horses up to a trot and rode past Belle and Effie. I didn't even glance at them and no sign of recognition crossed their faces, either.

After I had covered about two miles, it occurred to me that I didn't know how I was supposed to find the others again. I was wondering what to do when I saw a small fluttering movement from a tree up ahead, just to the left of the road. When I got closer, I saw that the fluttering was caused by a small branch shifting in the breeze. It had been carefully broken up from the bottom so it was held by a thin strip of bark.

I saw a grove of trees about a half mile off to the side of the road. Checking to make sure I wasn't being watched, I rode toward the treeline. I was in among the trees and had ridden right past Samson before I noticed him.

"Where're Belle and Effie?" Samson asked.

"They're way behind. Now that I know where you are, I'll go back and get 'em." I started to turn the horses, but Samson took hold of the bridle.

"You stay here. They'll find us. If you go back on the road, you'll stick out like a sore thumb." Samson looked steadily at me, until I finally nodded.

"Go get somethin' to eat. We managed to grab some potatoes. Marcus and Abner found some deadfall, so we can make a fire without too much smoke." Samson motioned for me to take the horses deeper into the woods.

I found the others sitting by a small clear brook. Marcus had made a small fire and had potatoes roasting on sticks. Abner was sitting with Lucinda and baby Ella. Josh was helping Marcus with the potatoes. Marcus and Josh glanced up at me.

"Any trouble?" asked Marcus.

"No. The sheriff stopped me, but I showed him my orders," I replied as I dismounted. "Belle and Effie are about a half-hour behind. I said I'd go get 'em, but Samson said to stay here. Should I take the horses and go get 'em?"

"No, stay here. Belle and Effie will know how to find us. They've been doin' this for almost six weeks now, ever since we left Louisiana. They'll know what to do," Marcus repeated, looking a little worried, but he turned back to cooking the potatoes.

I unsaddled the horse I had ridden and took out the bit. Then I led all three horses a little way downstream and let them drink. I drank from the brook myself and refilled the canteen. Instead of just turning the horses out to graze,

I asked Marcus for a few potatoes.

"In a few minutes. They ain't quite done yet."

"Id like three of 'em raw, if you can spare 'em. For the horses."

"Take them," he replied. "I didn't know horses ate potatoes."

"I don't know if they will, but they aren't used to eating just grass and we don't have oats for 'em. I guess they'll eat a potato just like an apple, if they're hungry enough."

I pulled out my clasp knife and cut a raw potato in half. I held it on my outstretched palm in front of a horse's nose. The horse sniffed it, then with its teeth, picked the potato off my palm. I fed each horse a potato apiece, then hobbled their front legs and turned them loose to graze on the spring grass.

"Potatoes're ready," Marcus announced. I picked two potatoes on sticks from the edge of the fire.

"I'll take one to Samson," I said and walked back to where Samson remained on lookout. I thought I walked quietly, but Samson was turned my way when I saw him.

"Breakfast," I said, holding out a potato. I wanted to show I had no hard feelings about the fight. For some reason, I wanted Samson to like me.

"Thanks," he said, taking the potato off the stick as he turned back to watch the road. He broke open the potato to let it cool.

"Marcus said you'all came from Louisiana."

"Yep," Samson grunted.

"Pick cotton?" I persisted, still trying to get Samson talking.

"No, cut cane, on a plantation near Baton Rouge," Samson said without taking his eyes from the road.

"Cut cane?"

"Sugar cane." After what seemed like a long while, he asked, "You?"

"Horse farm in Kentucky. Masters joined the Confederate army and I got taken with 'em. Ran away yesterday during a big battle. I mean, I didn't run because of the battle," I added hurriedly, "it just seemed like a good time to get away." I stopped, noticing that Samson seemed to be laughing softly.

"Don't worry," he said. "After our little how-do-you-do last night, I didn't think you'd have been running from the battle." Samson ruefully fingered the cut over his eye.

"Sorry about that. I didn't know who you'all were. Almost thought you were provosts."

"Provosts?" asked Samson.

"Soldiers that keep order in the army and prevent desertion. That's army talk for runnin' away. Did you'all walk all the way from Louisiana?" I knew that Louisiana was so far south that it bordered the ocean, but didn't know just how far it really was. I wondered if Obie had passed the band, going south to join the navy.

"Yes, we did walk all the way. Probably a bit over five hundred miles. We started the middle of February. It doesn't get cold down there like it does up here. There were ten of us when we started, not counting Marcus and me. Marcus is a conductor for the Underground Railroad, and I'm in trainin', learnin' the route.

"One of our 'passengers' we call 'em, one of our passengers was killed. She got swept away crossing a river and drowned. Another was captured by slave-catchers and led away with a iron collar around his neck." I noticed a funny look came into Samson's eyes when he said "iron collar."

"Two others got separated when we ran away from another bunch of slave-catchers. They might've got caught, or killed." After a pause, Samson continued, "They might even have gotten away. We just don't know."

"You're from the Underground Railroad?" I said with some admiration. "How far does it go?"

"Before the war, all the way to Canada. That's a country north of the United States. Slavery isn't allowed there. Now, I guess we just have to get North or to where the Yankee army is." Samson looked over at me for a moment, then looked back at the road.

"The Underground Railroad has helped thousands of us escape. This is Marcus's fourteenth trip as a conductor, or guide. It's my fourth. The best conductor is a woman. They call her 'Moses,' like in the Bible.[18] Others, includin' white people, keep houses called stations where we can rest in safety during the trip.

"So a lot of people help us, but we each have to take that first step on the road to freedom. Before we can be free, we have to realize that we were never slaves. I don't mean that the master doesn't own your body, because he does. But you're not a slave if you don't let him own your spirit."

"I know what you mean. The night before I ran, my master told his brother that I should be freed."

"And still you ran? Why?" I tried to formulate an answer.

"Freedom can't be given by the master and it can't be earned by the slave, for they never had the right to make us slaves in the first place."

"That's a great insight for one who was born into slavery." Samson's statement both mystified me and kind of embarrassed me, so I changed the subject.

"My friend Obie said if the Yankees win, we'd all be free. But when Wade, my master, when he read me the newspaper, it sounded like the Yankees're fightin' for the old country the way it was. I hope they win and all, but what if things just go back to the old way? The white folks ain't goin' to keep fightin' this war just for us."

"We have friends who are trying to get the Yankee government to agree that if they win, we'll all go free."

"Right now it sure don't look like the Yankees are winnin'," I commented morosely. "At least they weren't in the battle I left."

"I hope the war goes on for a while. So long that the Yankee army needs help, so much help they'd let us be soldiers. Once we're soldiers, there's no goin' back to slaves." Samson got a faraway look in his eyes. "That happened to me once, but not ever again," said Samson fiercely.

"What happened once?" I asked. Samson started, apparently not aware that he had said the last part out loud. He looked quickly at me and then looked away. Suddenly he pointed.

"Here they come! Go tell Marcus that Belle and Effie are comin' in."

I looked toward where Samson had pointed and saw Belle and Effie hurrying toward us. They still carried the pieces of smashed pumpkin. Instead of going to tell Marcus, I went out to help them.

"You'all made it! You're safe," I hugged Belle and took her load of pumpkin. Effie looked at me like she expected something, then she frowned as I led them back among the trees. Samson stayed on watch.

When we reached the little camp, I put down the pumpkin and helped Belle sit down. Josh ran over to hug his mother and sister, and they hugged him back.

I got Belle a potato and then ran to get the canteen. I offered the canteen to Belle. She took it gratefully, then handed it to Effie to drink first.

"Thank you, I'll get my own water. And my own potato," Effie said stiffly, then walked down to the brook, leaving me wondering what her problem was. I turned back to Belle, to see her regarding me speculatively. She said nothing but just took a drink from the canteen.

Abner went to replace Samson as lookout. Marcus told everyone to rest, and told me to take the last watch. Our journey would resume at sunset.

I was awakened by Marcus late in the afternoon.

"Time for your watch," he said. "Wake me when you see the sun halfway below the horizon."

I got up and took post as lookout. There was little to see. As it got closer to sunset, the sky got cloudy. It looked like there would be rain again that night.

I had to estimate when to get Marcus up, because it got so cloudy that I couldn't see the sun. When Marcus was up, he woke Abner and told him to take lookout while I got the horses ready to travel.

After letting them drink at the brook, I saddled one horse and put the remains of the sack of potatoes on another. I was about to lift Josh onto the last horse's bare back when Marcus stopped me.

"Are the horses starting to get worn out, Jed?" he asked.

"They're a bit tired, but they ain't worn out."

"We'll need to change the scout horse a lot. Nobody rides tonight but the scout. Samson, take the pistol and mount up. I'll carry the carbine, if it's all right with Jed."

"It's all right with me."

"Jed, you'll lead the horses. Get the carbine from the horse before Samson goes off. Abner, take rear lookout." Marcus gave Samson some final instructions, then Samson mounted up and rode off.

Before we started off, I remembered to give Josh back the forage cap and I put on my slouch hat. As I did, it started to rain.

The night seemed to pass uneventfully. Belle, Effie and Lucinda took turns carrying the baby. Marcus, walking at the head of the column, seemed to be ever alert.

I was worried about Josh being tired, but he seemed to be in good shape. Actually, I was probably the person in the group who was least used to walking long distances. I hadn't walked very far during my whole time with the Cavaliers.

We walked all night, about a quarter-mile off to the side of the road. From time to time, Samson rode back to report to Marcus. When he rode in after midnight, I switched the saddle to the fresh horse.

Finally, just as dawn was breaking, the rain stopped. Our little band walked into a stand of trees where Samson stood waiting.

After taking care of the horses, I ate a potato, then went to sleep. Abner shook me awake. It seemed like only a few minutes since I had fallen asleep, but the sun was high in the sky.

"When the sun is directly over that tree over there, wake Marcus for the last watch." Abner went to sleep while I took post as lookout. When the sun was over the tree, I walked to the sleeping figures and woke Marcus.

I thought I would have trouble getting back to sleep, but the next thing I was aware of was Marcus shaking me awake. It was dusk.

I got the horses ready to travel, while Marcus again assigned us men to our positions. Marcus was scout, Samson led the band, Abner was rear lookout, and I led the unsaddled horses. The women and children would again walk.

"Tonight, if we're lucky, we'll make it to the station," Marcus told us. We were all looking forward to a day or two of rest.

As we started out, it began to rain, just like the previous two nights. But tonight, the temperature dropped, and the rain quickly turned to sleet. A stiff wind blew the sleet right into our faces, making it hard to see. I was concerned for Josh and Ella. Leading the horses, I hurried to catch up to Samson.

"I think we should let Lucinda ride with the baby, and Josh, too." I had to shout to be heard over the howling wind.

"No. What if a horse slips on the ice? They'll have a better chance walking. But call Abner up here. I don't think we'll need a rear lookout tonight. Have Abner lead one horse while you take the other. Use the horses as a windbreak and put the women and children between 'em."

I hung back to tell Abner, then we did as Samson had told me. Samson walked behind everyone, not as rear lookout, but to make sure nobody dropped out.

Marcus came back, looking half frozen. His eyelashes were crusted with sleet. For a long time, he rubbed his face with his hands, trying to get the blood circulating again. I checked the horse, but she seemed to be all right. Finally, Marcus warmed up enough to speak.

"We're only about three miles from the station. But it will take us about three hours to get there in this weather." To raise our spirits, he reminded us, "Food, shelter, the warmth of a fire and a few days rest are waiting for us there. We've got to keep moving." Marcus turned to get back on the horse, but Samson stopped him.

"I'll ride scout for a while. You try to thaw out. Huddle behind the horses with the others." Marcus looked like he would protest, then just nodded.

"Don't get too far out in front. Twenty rods should do. When you get too cold, come on back." Samson mounted and rode slowly out ahead.

Hailstones, some as large as quail's eggs, began to fall with the sleet. Lucinda nestled closer to the horses and leaned forward over Ella, trying to protect her from the hail. Being close to the horses was dangerous as they occasionally slipped on the round hailstones.

I faintly heard a horse neighing up ahead. It sounded like it was hurt. I looked at Marcus, who appeared to have also heard.

"Stay here, Jed," he ordered. "We'll all get there together. It's too dangerous for you to be off by yourself in this storm."

We struggled on through the hailstorm. The neighing of the horse grew louder, but more infrequent. After a few minutes, we arrived at where I thought the horse would be, but could see nothing.

Marcus and I went cautiously forward. The horse neighed again, sounding like it was right in front of us. I was walking in front and almost slid down the bank of a small creek. I caught myself in time, then dropped to one knee as I strained to see through the sleet and hail.

The bank was steep, almost vertical, but it was only about ten feet deep. At the bottom, where the water still flowed among some rocks, lay the horse. Even from the top of the bank, I could see she had broken a leg. Samson lay pinned under the horse, not moving.

I looked up and down the bank, to see if it was less steep somewhere else. I got up and walked up and down a short way in both directions, but the banks were just as steep and they seemed to get deeper so I went back to where the horse had slipped.

"Abner, take the headstall off the horse," I commanded, as I began to do the same with the other horse. I unstrapped all the pieces of bridle we had, than began to buckle and tie them together into a long strip of leather. When I was done, I had a strip that looked long enough to reach Samson.

"Tie this around a tree. A small tree, so it'll still be long enough to reach," I told Marcus and Abner. "I'll slide down and tie this around Samson. You'all pull him up, then throw it back down and pull me up."

"Be careful, Jed," Marcus cautioned. "Be really careful you don't get kicked by the horse."

"I'll be real careful." Just before I went over the edge, I noticed Effie looking at me, anxiety on her face.

I slid down the bank, only stopping when I skidded into the horse. She neighed shrilly.

"Sorry, girl," I said guiltily. I was sorry, not just for having slid into the injured horse, but for having placed her in a situation where she could get hurt like this. Above all, I was sorry for what I now had to do.

I pulled the pistol out of the saddlebag, and trying not to think, I quickly cocked it, held it against the horse's head and pulled the trigger.

The sound of the shot roared, even above the storm, and echoed into the night. Silence returned. The horse lay still.

I quickly pulled Samson out from under the horse. Even though he was half unconscious, Samson groaned. I quickly checked him, but could feel no broken bones. Then I tied the harness around Samson's body, under his arms.

"Pull him up," I yelled. Samson was slowly pulled up the bank.

I put the pistol back in the saddlebag and took the saddle and headstall from the dead horse. The rope was thrown back down and I quickly tied them to it to be hauled back up. The second time the rope was thrown back down, I tied it around myself.

"Pull!" As I was hauled up, I looked at the dead horse with tears in my eyes. I had never before lost a horse placed in my care.

When I got to the top, Samson was already conscious, but both his ankles were badly sprained. I strapped the saddle on another horse, then Abner and I struggled to put Samson into the saddle as gently as possible.

We started off once again. After about an hour, the hail and sleet tapered off and finally stopped. Everyone felt revived simply by not having to fight the storm anymore.

Toward dawn, we saw the faint glow from the lights of the station and hurried toward it.

XIII

I sat next to the bed where Samson lay, both ankles bandaged, reading a newspaper that was only a few weeks old. The cut that I had given him looked to be healing nicely, although it was plain that Samson would always have a scar.

I sat on the floor, cleaning the carbine. I had taken the cartridges out of the carbine and the pistol, and the spare cartridges out of their boxes. They were set around the room so the warmth would leach the dampness from them.

I sat thinking about when Marcus and I had carried Samson into the house and brought him into the bedroom. When we peeled off his wet clothes, I saw that two letters, "MJ," had been crudely branded into the skin of Samson's back.

Sitting there with Samson, I wanted to ask about the brand, and about what Samson had meant when he had talked about not going back to being a slave, and about how it had happened to him once. But no matter how much I wanted to, I didn't dare ask outright. Instead, I tried to open a conservation by asking if he was from Africa. Samson turned and stared at me for a moment, then turned away.

"Yes, I'm from Africa, a country called Dahomey." I waited for Samson to continue, but for a long time, he stayed silent. I wondered if I had overstepped my bounds by asking, when Samson continued.

"My real name is Ma'ina, son of Ka'ita. Whites want you to believe that in Africa, we live in the trees like monkeys, or that we are as simple as children, or that we are savages, but we aren't any of these things.

"We are different nations, some friendly with others, others not so friendly. We travel and trade with each other. We exchange embassies and make war. Some men are kings and other men want to be kings. Great kingdoms have come and gone, and others are rising to greatness.

"Dahomey is one of the great kingdoms, even though it is small in size, because it has great wealth. It also has one of the best armies in Africa, the equal to even the Zulu of the south. The Asante to the west, themselves formidable fighters, have learned of our prowess to their cost.

"My father was a soldier, a general of King Gezo's. Throughout my youth, I was trained to be a warrior, learning how to wrestle and fight with spear, sword, bow and musket. I lived for the day that I would be able to take my place in the army at my father's side.

"My father had a rival, one of the king's councilors. The rival got people to swear that my father was plotting to betray King Gezo. He told the king that my father would attack the palace and raise himself to the throne.

"King Gezo was as suspicious a man as has ever been born, but even he didn't really believe that my father would do that. He knew my father to be an honorable man.

"But the councilor had sent my father a message that rebels were attackin' the palace. My father, as a loyal general would do, raced to the palace with the warriors of his own bodyguard, ready to battle what they believed were rebels. The king's guards had been alerted to expect an attack by men they were told were rebels.

"As soon as he reached the palace, my father knew he had been tricked. The only troops there were *Fanti Nyekplehhentoh*, royal guard razor women. In Dahomey, the royal guard are all women. It is felt that women will be more loyal because a woman could never herself be king. But they're as fierce as any man, and before my father could explain, they attacked.

"My father's men were outnumbered and they were all killed. My father died knowin' he had been deceived and betrayed.

"As a traitor, my father's property now belonged to the king. Since I was still a boy, I was part of that property. With an iron collar around my neck, I was marched to the ocean coast. There I was sold to slave traders. I was seventeen years old.[19]

"I was put into a cage with many other people. There were many other full cages around us. One day, we were branded with the initials of a ship's name, the *Mary James*.

"After that, we were taken from the cage and put into canoes and boats. We were taken out to the ship and put inside it, away from the sunlight and fresh air, chained lying side by side on a shelf. We were fed there, we lay in own filth there, and many of us died there.

"We were only allowed up in the fresh air and sun every second or third day. They made us dance so our muscles didn't get weak. While we danced, they watched us with guns in their hands. There was even a cannon aimed at us. They were afraid that we would take over the ship.

"In spite of the warships sent to stop the slave trade, it went on. Sometimes, when a slaver was pursued, the crew would throw the slaves overboard, still in chains. I was told that the reason was, if there were no slaves aboard, the navy couldn't prove the crime." He paused, then said bitterly, "I suppose we were lucky that no warships came near our ship.

"When we got to America, some of us had to be painted with tar to hide where our skin had worn away so we could be sold as 'prime goods.' One by one, we were stripped and put on the block. White men screamed and yelled, biddin' to see who would own us. You have no idea of the feelin' you have standing on the block. It happened six years ago, but I remember it like it was yesterday.

"I'll never forget the fear, fear of the unknown. But I had been trained as a warrior and knew how to keep my fears in check. Far worse than the fear was the humiliation of it all. I thought that no man had the right to sell me like I was an animal, but I was wrong. Sell me they did.

"I was sold to a planter in Louisiana. All day, we would hoe and weed fields of sugar cane. When it was harvest time, we worked as long as there was light, every day. We cut, baled and carried great bundles of stalks. The older slaves and the women and children would cut the stalks into pieces and toss them in huge cauldrons to boil the cane down into sugar. Then we filled and carried hundred-pound bags of sugar to the warehouses. Men, strong men, sometimes died in the heat. Weak hearts or lungs, I guess.

"But one day I had a chance to run and I did. I was given shelter by an old white woman. She ran a station for the Underground Railroad. Only by luck did I find her. She sheltered me until a conductor came through. I thanked her for her kindness and courage but I never knew her name. I wasn't told, so that if I was recaptured, I wouldn't be able to tell.

"We went north, all the way to Boston. Abolitionists gave me shelter and food and sent me to school. Thanks to them, I can read and write. Now, to pay it back, I'll be a conductor myself and help others escape."

For a long time, I didn't say a word, because I didn't know what to say. Finally, almost to change the subject, I asked, "Will you teach me how to read and write?" Samson looked at me and smiled.

"You saved my life, so I'll do better than that. I'll teach you to read, write and wrestle." I just nodded. I wasn't just happy about what Samson said he would teach me, I was more happy about the prospect of he and I becoming friends. To keep the conversation going, I asked him what the news stories were about.

"The newspaper says that in Kansas the governor is enlistin' colored men into the militia, to fight for the Union," Samson told me. "He doesn't really care that the Yankee government doesn't allow it and that they want him to put the coloreds back out of the army."

As soon as I heard the news, my heart leaped. All at the same time, I felt I could jump up and run all the way to Kansas to be able to enlist, and felt sad that Obie was not there to go with me, and felt afraid that I wouldn't be able to measure up as a soldier. Almost instantly, I knew that I could be a soldier, if Samson stood and fought at my side.

"Samson, would you go to Kansas to enlist if you had the chance? If you did, I'd go with you."

Before he could answer, we were interrupted by knocking on the door. Without waiting for an invitation, Effie barged into the room. She didn't even look at me as she spoke to Samson sweetly.

"Are you feelin' any better this mornin', Samson? I got so worried when we couldn't find you in the hailstorm! Thank goodness you're all right. Jedediah, doesn't Samson look all right to you? I'll bet you're back on your feet in no time, a strong man like you. Why, Samson..."

"Effie!" Samson interrupted. "Could you please tell Marcus that I'd like to talk to him?"

"Why, of course, Samson. I'll be right back along with him," replied Effie. "Won't be a minute." She flounced out of the room, leaving the door open. I watched the whole exchange in bewilderment.

"Is she always this strange?" I asked Samson.

"Only when she's around you, Jed," replied Samson.

"Me? What did I ever do to her?" I was truly puzzled. Samson laid the pieces of the pistol aside and regarded me for a moment.

"You really don't know, do you?" he laughed. "You turned her head." Samson saw I still had a blank look on my face. "She's sweet on you, Jed."

"Sweet on me? You mean she likes me? How d'you know, Sam? Did she tell you that?"

"Jed, you don't have to be around women too long to figure it out, without them tellin'. She's sure actin' like she's sweet on you."

"She is? It looks like she's purposely ignorin' me."

"Exactly. She's actin' strange because maybe she doesn't want you to know it—yet. Maybe she doesn't even know it herself, but..." Samson's voice trailed off as footsteps approached. Marcus came into the room, followed by Effie.

"What did you want to see me about, Samson?"

"I just wanted to talk about when we could get back on the road north, that's all," Samson replied.

I began cleaning the pistol, not listening as the two men talked. I was thinking about what Samson had told him about Effie being sweet on me. I had never given much thought to women, other than Belle. Not that Effie was a woman, I thought, she was still a girl.

I liked doing things for Belle. I got it into my head that Belle was about the same age my mother might be, if she hadn't died. I know Belle wasn't my mother, but I hoped, deep down, that Belle might have enough of a mother's love and understanding left over to share with me. Up until then, I didn't really give much more thought to being an orphan than I had being a slave. Again, I used that slave ability to suppress emotion.

I understand now that's why I tried to be helpful, and treated Josh like a younger brother and ignored Effie like she was a younger sister. It wasn't fraud, it was because I was driven by a need for family, to belong.

I looked up to see Effie looking at me. She hurriedly looked away, got up and left the room. I wanted to follow her, to ask her how she felt about me, but I knew that, unlike asking Samson about his past, I'd never get up the courage to ask how her she felt. I just sat and watched her go, then finished cleaning the pistol.

***

The following night, our band of runaways left the relative safety and comfort of the station-house.

The old white woman who ran the station gave us a little money and enough food for three or four days. Although we had more than a hundred miles to go before we reached Paducah, the next station was only about forty miles away, just north of Lexington, Tennessee.

As we took leave of the old woman, I felt my thanks were stilted and inadequate, that I could never convey the gratitude I felt for keeping her lonely, dangerous vigil. The woman just smiled, hugged me and wished me good luck, then turned to say goodbye to Lucinda and baby Ella. As was usual in the Underground Railroad, she never revealed her name, but she did teach me what is meant by the trite phrase "unsung hero."

Abner and I carried the food in sacks. Samson had offered to take the sacks on the horse, but I told him that now that there were only two horses, they had enough to do carrying him and Marcus.

As I walked along, I mulled over Samson's news of colored soldiers in the Kansas militia. I didn't know exactly how far Kansas was, but recalled Wade saying that it lay just west of Missouri. When the company had fought the battle at Belmont, we had been in Missouri. I had just resolved to ask Samson again if he would consider going to Kansas to join the militia, when Effie fell into step beside me.

I was a little annoyed with her for again interrupting my thoughts about becoming a soldier. Glancing over at her, I waited for her to say something, but she was looking down, watching where she put her feet. I was just about to ask her what she wanted, when she finally broke the silence.

"Do you need any help with the sack, Jedediah?" Again, she just rubbed me the wrong way. I was certainly capable of carrying a sack. Just as I was about to tell her a curt no, I realized that she was only trying to start a conversation.

"No, thanks. It ain't that heavy. After another day of us eatin' like we do, it won't be heavy at all." She gave a little laugh.

"You do say the funniest things." I didn't think it was all that funny, but I smiled back at her. She looked into my eyes and the smile left her face.

"I think you were very brave to slide down that icy gully to rescue Samson," she said.

"I don't know about that. There wasn't time to think about nothin'. I just did what needed to be done at the time."

"Didn't it make you sad to shoot your horse?"

"It was better for her. You can't set a horse's leg so you've got to shoot it, so it don't suffer." I was surprised at how defensive I felt, like I had to prove to her that I wouldn't just shoot a horse for no good reason. At the same time, I was getting more annoyed. I had cared for that mare since before the battle of Belmont.

"Samson said that you were in a battle and you saved the life of one of the rebel soldiers. That was also a brave thing to do," Effie said breathlessly. "But why did you save a rebel? Aren't they our enemy?"

I had never thought of any of the Cavaliers as the enemy. The only person in the whole Confederate army I ever thought of as an "enemy" was Hawkins. I thought maybe I should also consider Lem, the soldier I had shot, an enemy, but I tried not to think of the shooting at all.

"Just because some men are Confederates don't mean they're the enemy. Now, some are our enemy just cause we're colored, but I hear some Yankees hate us, too. They think that the war started because of us."

"But you would fight if we were in danger, wouldn't you? I think it would be romantic, to have someone fight for me." Effie looked at me dreamily. "Just like a knight from the olden days." I didn't know what "romantic" meant exactly but, from just the way she said it, it didn't sound like something worth killing or dying for.

"Romantic! You don't know what you're talkin' about. There's nothin' 'romantic' about fightin'," I said vehemently. "You just don't want to die, and you're willin' to kill to stay alive." Effie looked as though I had struck her. Her look quickly changed to acute embarrassment.

"You don't have to be so mean. If you don't like me, just say so." Effie stomped off to the head of the file. For the rest of the march, she was careful to stay away from everyone.

I hadn't meant to hurt her feelings, but visions had sprung into my mind: the rebel boy bleeding to death on my horse; the sergeant reading his impending death from the look on my face; and, worst of all because I had caused it, Lem sobbing and trying to hold his torn belly together.

I quickly ran through all the reasons why shooting Lem had been the only thing I could do. Then, I realized that I would do the same to anyone who threatened our little band. I wasn't about to pretend that fighting wasn't a grim and terrible thing to have to do, but I knew that I would fight against anyone who threatened my newfound friends, just as I would join the army in Kansas, to fight to win freedom for colored people.

"She's young." Belle came up from behind and walked next to me. "Her head is a little laden with some silly notions. It's not really her fault." I didn't know what to say. I was embarrassed that Belle would think I would have hurt Effie's feelings deliberately.

"The plantation we lived on was so big, the next plantation house was miles away. Effie was chosen to be a companion to Miss Lorene, the master's daughter. Lorene's the one who renamed her 'Ophelia.' Since she was young, Effie's spent more time around white girls than colored.

"White girls whose daddies own plantations seem to be raised to act delicate and helpless. They get ideas like 'romance' and 'ardor' put into their heads so there's no room left for sensible things. Effie's havin' to outgrow that kind of nonsense." Belle paused.

"But one of the most sensible things she's ever done is settin' her cap for you, Jedediah. You are one fine young man." Belle smiled.

I wasn't sure I wanted to be the object of a young girl's affections, especially not Effie's. Around her, I wasn't quite shy, but I did feel kind of clumsy, as if my hands and feet were too large for the rest of me.

For the next three days, until we reached the next station, Effie seemed to keep her distance from me. She didn't really ignore me. For example, if I spoke to her, she answered, but in curt, clipped sentences. At the same time, I noticed her looking at me whenever she thought I wasn't looking at her. I kind of wished she would go back to acting the way she used to, but I didn't know what to do or say to get things back the way they were.

By the time we arrived at the station, Samson's ankles had healed to the point where he could walk without much pain. The cut I had given him had faded to a scar that split his right eyebrow neatly into two almost equal segments.

Our first day at the station, I began my first reading and writing lesson. Samson used a newspaper as a textbook. After about an hour, Effie knocked and asked if she could join us. Samson invited her in.

Since she could already read and write a little, Effie alternated between student and assistant teacher. She sat next to me, sometimes helping me, sometimes learning the same thing I was. Gradually, during the course of the morning, the awkwardness between us began to go away.

After the reading and writing lesson, Samson took me outside to begin to teach me to wrestle.

"In America, many men know how to use rifles and pistols. Some men can use knives. A few, mostly in the South, know how to fight with swords.

"But very few are those who can fight without weapons, barehanded. Mostly they flail at each other with balled fists, or get in close to each other and try to gouge each other's eyes out, or bite and scratch. Some even use their heads as clubs." I squirmed and Samson laughed at my discomfiture.

"To be good at barehanded fightin', you need to learn to use a man's own force against him. One way is to make the force go where it can't hurt you, or can even hurt him. Try to knock me down." I hesitated.

"Come on," Samson urged. "You won't hurt me. In fact, with my sore ankles, I hope I'm quick enough to keep from hurtin' you."

I tensed, then ran to drive my shoulder into Samson's midsection. Just as I reached him, I felt a gentle push. I went sprawling into the spongy turf, unbalanced by my own momentum.

"Try again," Samson ordered. I stayed on one knee for a moment, pretending to have had the wind knocked out of me. Without standing up, I launched myself at Samson, trying to tackle him at the waist to drag him down.

I felt a small thump on the back of my neck and another across my shins. I had the fleeting impression that the ground and the sky had decided to switch places. Then I skidded to a stop, lying on my back, staring at the sky.

I heard a small, muffled laugh and looked over and saw Effie holding her hands to her mouth, trying not to laugh again.

I knew I looked ridiculous and the thought made me angry. I now understood what Samson had meant about using a man's force against him. I liked Samson, but I was determined to knock him down.

I climbed to my feet and approached Samson slowly. Samson just stood with his knees bent slightly, weight thrust forward. I approached to within arm's length of Samson and also stood, knees slightly bent. I figured whatever he was doing must be right.

Suddenly, a loud, savage yell erupted from Samson. I felt a pang of fear that made me unable to move for a split-second. Then I felt my right arm grasped at the wrist and shoulder and a shoulder thrust against my chest. For a moment, I was on Samson's back, but the pressure in his shoulder forced me to continue over, feet in the air. As I was thrown to the ground, I hooked my right hand under Samson's left armpit, trying to use his momentum against him.

Samson twisted his body a little and, instead of sailing over my shoulder as I intended, he landed on top of me, driving the wind out of me. He continued his roll, and came to rest on his back next to me.

"You learn quickly, Jed. Let's stop for a moment." Effie came over to where we lay side-by-side.

"Marcus said to tell you to get some sleep. We're goin' on tonight."

"Thank you, Effie," Samson replied. "We'll come inside in a minute." Effie went back into the house. We got to our feet and Samson clapped me on the back.

"You did well, but there are some things you should remember. Never get angry. When you're angry, you're not in control. You saw how easy it was for me to use your own force against you.

"When you're facing a man you're goin' to fight, look at his eyes. Most men's eyes will tell you when they're goin' to move, and may even tell in what direction. Try to surprise your opponent. Try to move quickly and from an unexpected direction. If you are not fast enough to move before he can react, a shout may also surprise him and make him unable to move for a moment.

"We'll continue both our readin' and writin' lessons and our wrestlin', but right now, let's get some sleep."

That night we left the station, the last station in Tennessee. If all went well, we would be in Kentucky in four days.

XIV

During the day, when we hid in the woods and neither of us was on lookout, Samson continued my lessons in reading, writing and wrestling. Effie almost always joined us for the reading and Josh watched the wrestling with avid interest. Samson often let him practice with us.

Sometime during the fourth night, we crossed into Kentucky. I was surprised we hadn't seen any Yankee soldiers so far, since the Yankee army was south of us.

The following morning, after we had settled into our hiding place for the day, Samson and I scouted the surrounding area. Samson rode the saddled horse, while I rode the other one bareback. Samson carried the pistol, while we left the carbine at the camp with Marcus.

We circled around the camp, about a mile out. We had almost completed the circuit when we heard a shot fired. The sound came from the direction of the camp.

We galloped until we were about a quarter-mile from camp, then slowed to a walk. After a few hundred yards more, we dismounted. Samson drew the pistol.

As quietly as possible, we walked until we were about fifty yards from camp. Through the trees, I could make out two white men on horses holding shotguns. A third had dismounted and was pushing our friends together into a small group. Samson leaned over to whisper in my ear.

"Circle around to your right. Don't get too close to camp. Make sure that those three are the only ones here. I'll do the same thing from the left. I'll meet you on the other side of camp." I nodded and set off, crouched over to avoid being seen.

I scuttled from tree to tree, keeping the big trees between myself and camp. Before I moved, I'd look in all directions to make sure nobody was watching me. After what seemed like an hour, but was probably only a few minutes, I made it to the other side of camp, where Samson already waited. I shook my head at him to indicate that I hadn't seen anyone and he shook his head also. The three white men were alone.

The dismounted man stood over Marcus and Abner, who were lying face down on the ground with their hands behind their backs. The man appeared to be tying their hands with short pieces of rope.

"I'll make some noise and run," I whispered to Samson. "At least one of the mounted men will chase me, maybe both. If two chase me, can you shoot the last man without hittin' any of our friends?"

"He'll probably stand up to look at the two on horses as they start chasing you," Samson replied. "I'll try to get in position so the women and children aren't in the way when I shoot."

"Just stay here. I'll circle around before I run, so when he stands up he'll be off to the side." I picked up a stout piece of deadfall and crawled a few dozen yards further away from camp.

As I slowly got to my feet, I heard a woman cry out. It sounded like Belle. I almost ran back into the camp before I got control of myself and remembered the plan. I swung the branch against the trunk of a tree, making a sharp cracking sound. I stood for a moment to give them time to catch sight of me, then ran directly away from camp. From behind me came a shouted warning to stop.

Without turning, I could hear two sets of hooves coming. Both mounted men were chasing me. I knew they would catch up to me in less than a minute. I prayed that Samson would be able to free our friends before that.

I ducked behind a large tree, crawled forward behind another large tree diagonally to the left, then circled back to a third tree, closer to my pursuers. I listened and could hear the horses slow to a walk, then stop.

"See 'im?" I heard a voice say.

"No," another voice replied. "He ducked behind that big tree yonder, so he can't be far. Go around that way and I'll go over this way. See if we can get around behind 'im and herd 'im back t' the others. He won't get away." They started moving again.

The booming sound of a shotgun being fired came from back at the camp, followed by two other shots, sharper, higher-pitched.

"That was a shotgun and pistols! Stay here. Try t' find him," the first voice said. I heard the sound of hoofbeats racing away and peered around the tree.

A dirty-looking bearded man sat a horse, scanning the woods, only his head and eyes moving. I was tempted to crawl away, but didn't want to turn my back to the man.

I remembered how I had surprised Hawkins by attacking him from an unexpected direction from behind a tree, so I picked up a rock and threw it behind me, off to the right. If the man rode directly after it, it would bring him to the right side of the tree where I hid. To use his gun, he would have to aim across his body and slightly behind himself. I figured it would be a difficult shot and take a second or even two to line up. At least that's what I hoped.

Hardly daring to breathe, I stood with my left shoulder against the tree trunk, listening. The horse clopped forward and sounded like it would pass the tree on the right side.

When I judged the horse was even with the tree, I rushed out, swinging the branch. I hit the horse across its chest. It reared back, hooves pawing the air. The rider fell heavily to the ground and, as he hit, his shotgun flew from his hand.

I dropped the branch and ran to get the shotgun before the man could get up. I almost reached it when the horse ran past, knocking me down.

I got to my hands and knees, trying to stand back up, when the man landed on my back. I rolled and the man fell off. We both regained our feet at the same time.

I looked at the man, then ran away from him, in the direction opposite where the shotgun lay. He immediately chased me.

I ran only a few steps, then suddenly dropped to one knee, crouched over. The running man fell over me and landed on his face. I lunged for him, but he was on his feet in a flash.

I backed away and faced him, focusing on his eyes the way Samson had taught me. His eyes narrowed just a bit, so when he rushed me, I was ready for it. I turned quickly to the side and again dropped to one knee. The bearded man tripped over my outstretched calf.

I sprang to my feet and faced him as he got back up. This time he came slowly, arms reaching. I watched his eyes, then stepped quickly back. The punch went so wide, he almost spun completely around. While he was off-balance, I gave a push against the back of his shoulder and he fell down.

The man hastened to his feet again just as a fusillade of shots sounded. The deep roar of a shotgun mingled with the high snap of pistol shots. He glanced over in the direction of camp.

I instantly lashed out with my foot and swept the man's legs out from under him. I waited until he rolled over onto his hands and knees to get up then leaped on his back. I pulled his wrist up behind his back with one hand and pulled back on his chin with the other, while getting my knee in the small of his back. Now he couldn't move, but I couldn't let go.

I was wondering how long I could hold on and what to do next, when Samson and Marcus ran up, holding shotguns. Samson had the pistol thrust through his belt. I noticed that Marcus' wrists were scraped raw from where he had been tied.

"I got him covered, Jed," said Samson. "You can let him up now." I released the man's chin and wrist and quickly got to my feet. The man stayed stretched out on the ground.

"Get up!" Marcus commanded. The man slowly got to his feet, rubbing his shoulder. His long, bushy beard was flecked with tobacco spittle and he wore a greasy buckskin shirt. He looked at us with undisguised hatred.

"They're slave-catchers, Jed," Marcus continued. "This one's the only one left." The slave-catcher's face suddenly registered alarm.

"What were you doin' aroun' here?" Marcus asked him. The slaver stayed silent. Samson pushed past Marcus.

"If he ain't goin' to be friendly, we might as well part company now. We can't take him with us anyway." Samson made a show of breaking open the shotgun to check that it was loaded, closing it and thumbing back one of the hammers. He stared at the slaver.

"At close range, these make unbelievably big holes. If you don't believe me, you can go take a look at your two friends back there." The cock-sure look on the slaver's face disappeared.

"Us catchers jus' stay a little ways away from where the Yankee army is. Slaves're always comin' through, tryin' t'get t' th' damn Yankees. Wit' most of 'em, the excitement of bein' close makes 'em get careless, like. That's when we catch 'em and return 'em t' their masters for th' reward." He paused. "Get a bigger reward if'n th' goods ain't damaged. Thass why we treated ya'll so nice back thar." Marcus scowled.

"They were tyin' us up so they could rape the women, includin' Effie." He turned to the man. "Are there any more catchers around here?" The man grinned unpleasantly.

"Prob'ly."

"What're we goin' to do with him?" I asked. "We can't take him with us and can't chance him gettin' free to hurt the women." Marcus thought for a moment.

"We could tie him to a tree here. If there are other slavers around, they should find him soon enough."

"Ya'll cain't do that," the man whined. "Ah could starve t' deat' or be e'ten by wild an'muls."

"We can't tie him for another reason," said Samson. "What if he gets loose too soon? A cuss like him'll get every slaver he could find after us."

"Well, let's take him back to camp. We'll decide what to do there," Marcus commanded. "Jed, get his shotgun." With his shotgun, Samson prodded the slave-catcher in the direction of camp.

When we got back to camp, Abner was on lookout with the carbine. Lucinda was sitting with her back to a tree, singing softly to Ella. Belle was standing with her arms around Effie and Josh. Josh had his face buried in his mother's skirts. The two dead slave-catchers were off to one side. Everyone had moved away from them.

When I got closer, I saw that Belle's bottom lip was cut and swollen. The top two buttons of her dress had been torn off. Josh looked up. The left side of his face under his eye was bruised.

I felt rage build up inside me. My experience with war had given me an understanding of the cruelties men could inflict on each other, but violence to helpless women and children was unforgivable.

Before I could react, Abner motioned for us all to be silent and hide. In an instant, I could hear voices in the distance. I quickly quieted our two horses and grabbed the bridle of one of the slave-catchers' horses. The horse, not knowing me, bolted in the direction of the voices, followed by the other slaver's horse.

Everyone's involuntary reaction was to look at the running horses. The slave-catcher took advantage of the momentary lapse to run, shouting in the direction of the voices. Abner raised the carbine, but I pushed it down.

"No! We can't risk the noise. They might be more catchers."

Samson jumped up after the slaver. I leaped aboard the saddled horse and galloped past Samson and into the fleeing man, knocking him down. I reined the horse to a stop and slid from the saddle, blocking the intended route of the slaver's flight.

The slaver reached behind himself and pulled a knife from under his shirt. He gave a nasty laugh as waved the knife at me.

"Ah owe ya'll sumpthin' for hittin' me back there, nigger. Now yore goin' t' get it. I'm goin' t' cut yore heart right out'n yore chest."

I looked into the man's eyes and steeled myself for the attack. I so closely concentrated on my opponent that I was startled when the man fell backwards. Samson had crashed into the man's legs from behind, upending him.

The slaver sprang to his feet, holding the knife, and faced Samson. With a shout, he slashed at Samson.

Samson was crouched, but suddenly he stood straight up as the blade reached him. My heart gave a lurch as the knife appeared to go right through Samson's body.

The fighting men swung toward me and I could see how Samson had caught the man's knife arm under his own left forearm, between his rib cage and upper arm. The knife dangled uselessly half a foot behind him. By pulling his forearm up, Samson was exerting pressure that threatened to break the slaver's arm at the elbow.

The slaver held onto the knife and clawed at Samson's eyes with his left hand. Samson pushed the slaver's hand away with his right and at the same time, gave a small jump upward. I heard an audible crack, then the man screamed. He dropped the knife.

Samson rammed the heel of his hand into the slaver's face, spraying blood from his nose and lips. He was drawing his hand back for another blow when a voice from behind us boomed.

"Halt right there! Nobody move!" Samson let the slaver drop to the ground. Then he actually smiled.

I turned around to see a group of heavily armed horsemen. They all wore blue jackets. It took a few seconds for me to realize they were Yankee cavalry.

***

A day later, I stood in front of three army officers. They were tasked with determining whether charges of murder should be brought against us.

The Union cavalrymen had escorted us to their headquarters. All our weapons were confiscated as "contraband of war." The slavers' horses were also judged to be contraband. An officer decided that my orders from Brady were proof that the horses were Confederate property and therefore also a legitimate wartime capture.

We ourselves were also considered to be contraband. When Marcus demanded to know what that meant, the officer told us that contraband of war was any item that assisted the Confederates' ability to make war. Since slaves did most of the heavy labor in the South, they contributed to the Confederate war effort. When captured, they were considered contraband just like the horses and the weapons.

The officer told us that, as far as the Union army was concerned, we were to be prevented from being returned to our masters, but apart from that we were free to do what we wanted. We weren't legally free, but that was a technicality, as long as we weren't recaptured by the Confederates.

Our joy was short-lived when we were informed that the slave-catcher had insisted that he and his companions had been on a hunting expedition when they had been set upon by us and his two friends murdered.

Then we were separated from each other and held under guard. One by one, we were all called upon to testify what had happened when we were confronted by the slave-catchers. When we testified, none of the others of our band were present.

When I was called, I briefly told about my attempt to draw the catchers away from my friends and the fight with the surviving catcher.

"Then you were not at the campsite when the two men were shot?" The question came from the president of the tribunal, a colonel of infantry.

"No, sir. I wasn't there when the fight happened."

"You say there was a fight. How do we know your companion," he checked some notes, "your companion, Samson, did not just fire first from ambush and murder the two men?"

"Samson had a pistol, sir. The first shot fired was from a shotgun."

"You say that it was a shotgun that fired first," replied a cavalry major. "How can you be certain of that?"

"By the sound, sir. A shotgun sounds different than a pistol." The other officer, a major of artillery, broke in.

"How do you know it wasn't the shotgun barrel on the LeMat carbine?"

"I know that I didn't change the hammer to fire the shotgun barrel, and I don't think Abner knew how, sir. So, if it was fired, it had to be by one of the white men."

"What makes you sure of that?" asked the cavalry major.

"Marcus' and Abner's hands were tied. I saw them on the ground with their hands roped behind their backs."

"The record shows that the carbine had not been fired," said the colonel. He paused and glanced at the two majors. "Any further questions for the witness?" Neither officer spoke. He turned back toward me.

"You are excused. Escort the witness back to the holding area."

An infantryman with a fixed bayonet took me by the arm and led me back to the empty, windowless room where I was being held. The soldier opened the door, motioned me inside, and shut the door behind me. I heard the sound of the key being turned in its lock.

I nervously paced around the room. I never expected such a turn of events and wondered if we had done the right thing to seek out the Yankee army.

My rage against the slave-catcher again flared up, now for falsely accusing us all of murder. At the same time, I was scared. Remember, I grew up in the pre-war South, where a white man's word always counted for more than a colored's, no matter what the circumstances.

After a few hours, I heard the lock turned again and the door opened. The soldier told me to follow and I was brought back before the three officers.

Marcus and Samson were already there. Abner was escorted in half a minute later. I glanced behind and saw Belle, Effie and Josh, minus his Confederate forage cap, standing to one side of a white man in clerical garb. Lucinda, holding Ella, stood on the other side. They all looked nervous.

My attention was brought back to the officers by the sound of a chair pushed back. The colonel stood up.

"It is the opinion of this board of inquiry that the charges alleged against these persons are not supported by the physical evidence presented and the testimony given. This board will not press any charges against them. They are remanded to the supervision of the Reverend Thaddeus Howell, here present. The Reverend Mister Howell is reminded that this supervision requires the voluntary cooperation of these persons. This inquiry is closed."

We were free! I shook hands with Samson, Marcus and Abner. I turned and Effie ran to me, smiling. She threw her arms around me and kissed me. That startled me. I had never been kissed by anyone but my mother.

Apparently, Effie was also startled. After a moment, she drew back. As she looked up at me, I could see a look of surprise on her face, surprise and something else I didn't recognize.

After another moment, our gaze was broken as Josh grabbed my hand and solemnly shook it. When I looked at her again, Effie had turned away, but then Belle caught my eye. I couldn't read the expression on Belle's face, either.

The man in the clerical clothes bustled up.

"Come, come, we have to get you situated," he told us. The cavalry major handed the cleric a wrapped bundle and shook his hand. Marcus carried the bundle and walked beside him as we filed from the room. When we were outside, Marcus made the introductions.

"This is Reverend Howell. He runs this route on the Underground Railroad and has worked for abolition for many years." Marcus introduced each of us to Reverend Howell.

"Reverend Howell also has a school for freedmen and runaways in Cairo, Illinois and an organization t' help runaways find work," Marcus told us.

"He doesn't usually meet passengers himself, but he heard about the board of inquiry and hurried down here from Cairo." Howell nodded at us benignly.

"I needed to make sure that justice was done. We couldn't have people condemned for protecting their lives and their women from ruffians." I was thinking how differently the Confederate tribunal had viewed the same thing when he turned toward me.

"Marcus has told me about your bravery in assisting the escape, young man, and on behalf of our organization, I thank you." I noticed Effie looking at me in open admiration. "Your conduct is such that I would like to offer you a place in our organization, as a conductor. I'm sure you would like to emulate the good work done by Marcus and Samson." I was a bit surprised and said nothing but, after a moment, Samson spoke.

"Reverend, we heard that the Kansas militia is acceptin' colored men. Jed and I have decided to join the army." When he said those words, how my heart soared!

"But you could be of great service to the cause as conductors," the Reverend complained. "Both of you."

"Reverend, I appreciate what you and the society have done for me. But if the Confederacy is defeated, we won't have to run away. We'll be free wherever we are." Howell frowned.

"We don't know that. President Lincoln has resisted the call to end slavery. He has said his only concern is to preserve the Union. I'm afraid there is still a great need for an organization such as ours. Samson, Jedediah, that means we'll need men such as both of you." I spoke up.

"Reverend, I lost my best friend when he ran off to join the Union navy." I noticed the man's look, then added, "I don't mean he was killed. He ran away and I never heard from him again. But before he went, we used to talk about this thing.

"Obie said that if coloreds fight, not just for our own freedom but for the Union, for the whole country, how can they keep us slaves? Fightin' for the Union will free us as sure as anythin' else. To my mind, Obie was right. Some colored men fightin' will free all colored folk. I'm not sayin' you'all should disband the Underground Railway. I'm askin' you'all to help Samson and me get to Kansas, so we can join up." Reverend Howell remained silent for a while, as if considering the merits of what I had said.

"I fear that your confidence may be misplaced, young man, but since you are so sincere in your conviction, I will see what I can do. But before you finally decide, please consider my offer to be conductors. Now, we must go. It's still a long way to Cairo."

We journeyed to Cairo in a wagon driven by Abner. We rode in the wagon bed with some barrels and boxes of supplies. Reverend Howell drove a buggy, accompanied by Marcus.

I started to notice that when we started out each morning, Effie tried to be in a position where she would have to sit near me. She had not mentioned the incident after the conclusion of the inquiry when she had kissed me, and neither did I. I thought about it a lot, though.

I could close my eyes and remember the feel of her lips brushing mine. The softness, the sweetness, the gentle pressure of her breath on my cheek. I knew I liked the memory at the same time that I was vaguely disturbed by what it could mean.

My feelings for Belle were still close to being those of a son. I treated Josh as if he were my younger brother, but I no longer regarded Effie as a younger sister. I wondered if I was in love and whether Effie was in love with me.

I decided to dismiss the whole idea. I still clung to my hope to join the Kansas militia and told myself that being in love would only complicate matters. Besides, I felt it wasn't fair to Effie. What if she waited for me and I was killed?

That last thought let me know I wasn't being honest with myself. Like many youths, I could never see death coming for me. I couldn't even imagine ever growing old.

We had traveled north almost a week when I realized that I had begun to look forward to sitting with Effie in the wagon, listening as she talked. Sometimes she talked about great things, like being free, and sometimes small things, like the roughness of the ride. No matter the subject, I hung on every word.

"This is our last camp, you'll be happy to know," the Reverend announced one evening. "By tomorrow afternoon, we will be in Cairo." I glanced at Effie. She looked at me, then looked away. A look of sadness seemed to cross her face.

Later, after supper, Effie came over to me. She looked up at the night sky.

"Sure is a nice night for a walk," she said. I looked over at Belle, who seemed to be studiously ignoring us. Effie took my hand and led me out of the circle of firelight. We walked in silence for a little while, then Effie stopped and faced me.

"I guess that tomorrow means goodbye, doesn't it?" The thought had never crossed my mind, although it should have.

"It don't have to be," I shrugged.

"You mean you're not goin' to Kansas?" she asked hopefully. I looked away.

"I still want to go. I think the only way to be free is to fight for freedom. That way, a man who wants to take our freedom away has to think whether it's worth the fight to do so."

"I know you feel you must go, Jedediah," she said regretfully, "but I'll miss you. We could never have come this far without you."

"I'll miss you, too, Effie." To break the sudden somberness of the mood, I added lightly, "Or should I call you Ophelia?" Effie's somber mood didn't change.

"It would be easier to part if I knew that I'd see you again someday."

I almost said that of course we would see each other again, but I stopped myself. I knew want she really meant, and I didn't want to make any promises that I couldn't, or wouldn't, keep.

"We could write to each other, now that Sam's taught me how." Effie nodded.

"Of course. We could write." Her voice sounded flat.

"We could write," I repeated. "I'll write to you about the army and you write to me about livin' free in the North. We could tell each other things, like we talked about during the wagon ride. If we write, we could keep bein' friends."

"Yes. We could keep being friends."

Suddenly, Effie was in my arms. How she got there, I didn't know. She pulled my face down to hers and kissed me. Then she turned and started to run.

I caught her by the hand and pulled her back to me. I bent my face down to hers and kissed her gently. I didn't know that the roaring I heard in my ears was my own heart hammering, and my eyes seemed to lose focus. Then we just stood and held each other close for a long time.

In this cynical age we live in now, what with ragtime music and all, you might think it went further than that. I don't know if it was an innocent time, or that it was just we who were innocent, but that's all that happened. It was all that we needed.

When we walked back into camp, nobody asked where we had been.

XV

When we arrived in Cairo, we found the river port bustling with activity. It was a major supply base for the Union armies fighting south into Tennessee and Mississippi.

In short order, Reverend Howell's organization found work in a weaving mill for Belle and Lucinda. Effie would also work there part-time, while she and Josh attended the school run by the organization. Abner volunteered to accompany Marcus to be trained as a conductor for the Underground Railway.

Samson and I were to be deck-hands on a riverboat, *Queen of Cairo*. The boat would take army supplies up the Mississippi River to Jefferson Barracks, Missouri and then up the Missouri River to Fort Leavenworth, Kansas.

Kansas and Missouri had been the scene of bloodshed before secession started the war in 1861. The people of Kansas were firmly committed to keeping slavery from their state, while neighboring Missouri was just as firmly committed to extending slavery. Since the mid-1850s, Kansas "Jayhawkers" and Missouri "Border Ruffians" had committed incidents of savage violence against each other.

Missouri was itself torn in two, with a large segment of the population supporting the Union. The two sides waged a bloody war of bushwhacking and ambush against each other, with no prisoners taken.

Samson and I stood on the wharf to say goodbye to our friends. We had spent the previous two days helping load the *Queen*, and in a few minutes, it would sail upriver with three other supply boats.

"For you and Jed," Reverend Howell said, giving Samson a package. "Food, some clothes and some other things you might need for the journey. Be careful when you open it."

I shook hands with Reverend Howell, Marcus and Abner. I hugged Lucinda and kissed baby Ella.

"I bet when I see her again, she'll be so big I won't even recognize her."

"I bet you'll be so grown up, we won't recognize you," Lucinda replied.

Josh approached me, extending his right hand to shake. I gave it a quick shake, then pulled Josh to me and gave him a hug.

"Take care of your mother and sister." Josh, his eyes moist, nodded solemnly.

"Don't be a hero," Belle hugging me tight. She held me for a long time. "Just do your fair part and come back to us safe and sound, you hear?" She kissed my cheek and I kissed her back.

Before she let me go, Belle pulled Effie over and pushed her into my arms. Then she turned, took Josh by the hand and led everyone else away, over to the end of the wharf.

Samson waved to them, then turned to me.

"I'll see you on the boat."

"I'll write. And I'll come back." The boat's whistle blew and the paddle-wheel began to turn.

"I know you will. I'll wait. Now go." She kissed me then pushed me toward the boat. "And listen to what Mama said. Don't be a hero, Jedediah."

The *Queen* pulled away from the wharf. I leaped aboard, turned and waved to Effie.

I found Samson standing at the rail, waving. Our friends, standing at the end of the wharf, waved back as the boat steamed away. I kept waving even after I could no longer see them.

I followed Samson below-decks to see what was in the package. There was a little food, a couple of extra shirts, a pen and some writing paper, and a primer for Samson to use to help me with my reading and writing. The LeMat carbine, with the stock removed, was also in the package, along with its ammunition.

"It must have been in the bundle the Yankee officer gave the Reverend when we left Tennessee," Samson said.

"No wonder he said to be careful when you opened it."

We didn't have a cabin on the boat. We would sleep on deck in good weather and in the boiler room when the weather was bad. We ate in the boat's galley with the rest of the crew.

The *Queen's* captain and mates ate in a small dining room with the army quartermaster and ordnance officers aboard. There were also some infantrymen aboard as guards for the supplies.

The boats, heavily laden and moving against the spring current, still covered close to two hundred miles a day. Samson and I had little to do until we reached Jefferson Barracks. When the boats docked at Jefferson, we helped unload some of the cargo. Most of the supplies stayed on board, destined to be shipped further west.

The army still maintained a string of forts starting at Independence, Missouri all the way to the Pacific coast. The forts had been built to protect the Oregon and Santa Fe trails from marauding Indians, and they still had to be supplied.

After taking on more wood to fire the boilers, the boats continued north up the Mississippi until they could enter the Missouri River, which would take us west to Kansas.

The soldiers aboard kept mostly to themselves, but we became friendly with two young infantrymen from Indiana. Tom Carter was the older of the two and he had just turned eighteen. Nate North was seventeen. They enjoyed acting like "old soldiers" with me, showing off what they had learned so far in the army.

Samson and I learned the manual of arms and the sequence for loading a rifle. The soldiers described the different formations for marching and fighting.

"Sounds just like what I saw the rebs do," I told them.

In return, Samson let the two young soldiers participate when he instructed me in wrestling. Samson also taught the three of us how to fight with bayonets, both fixed to the end of the rifle and held in the hand.

"Back in Dahomey, the king's guard had muskets, but most other warriors used spears, cleavers and clubs," he told us. "But we were expert in their use. Now, the first thing you should do is sharpen the edges of your bayonets."

"Ain't a need to," replied Tom. "You're just supposed to thrust straight ahead with the point."

"Fightin' with a bayonet is different from fightin' with a spear, especially without a shield," Samson told him. "But if you block and feint and attack from unexpected angles, you get the advantage over your opponent, who gets so worried about what you're goin' to do, he just waits for you to do it." As he spoke, he demonstrated what he was talking about with Tom's rifle, the bayonet still covered in its sheath. Tom tried to follow the intricate movements Samson made, feinting and parrying. Then all our blood ran cold as a savage scream tore from Samson's lungs. Tom must have been stunned momentarily. He stood, frozen, as Samson slashed the bayonet at his throat, stopping just before he touched the skin.

"Tarnation!" yelled Tom. There was a look of real fear in his eyes. Samson put up the bayonet and smiled.

"With a few days of practice, you'll be doin' that same thing."

"You sure know what you're doin' with that," said Nate admiringly. "But what're you learnin' all that for?"

"Jed and I are headin' for Kansas. We heard that the militia there allows coloreds."

"No. I know that coloreds aren't allowed to join up," said Tom with great certainty.

"Ain't you been listenin'?" Nate retorted. "Only the Kansas militia's lettin' 'em. That's why Jed and Sam's goin' to Kansas."

"Well, I don't think that anybody knows whether coloreds would make good soldiers. Lots of men say that wouldn't want a colored regiment in line with 'em. Don't think they'd stand," Tom said self-importantly. "Besides, why'd you want to join up anyhow?"

"Tom, why're you fightin' this war?" Samson asked gently. Tom didn't hesitate.

"To put down the rebellion."

"But why did the South rebel?"

"They said we was treadin' on their rights."

"But what is really the only thing the Southerners do that you don't?" Samson persisted. Tom thought for a moment.

"Own slaves, I guess."[20]

"Right there you see why we coloreds will fight. If the South wins, we'll always be slaves. If the North wins, and we help it to win, at least we'll have a chance for freedom. We'll fight because we have more to gain, and more to lose, than you." Tom was quiet for a long moment.

"I reckon you make a good argument there." I think he wanted to change the subject a bit, so he turned to me.

"You know you got to be eighteen to join up? They make you swear that you're legal age to enlist."

I suddenly remembered the young wounded Confederate at Shiloh who had bled to death before I could get him to the field hospital and how I wondered if he had lied about his age to join the army.

"You'all just turned eighteen," I retorted. "Did you lie to join up?"

"You can't lie to your own gover'ment," said Tom. "It'd be unmoral." Nate looked at Tom, rolled his eyes, then looked back at me.

"What you do, Jed, is get a piece of paper and write the number eighteen on it, see? Then you put it in your shoe. When they ask your age, you're standing with eighteen under your foot. Then you can say, 'I'm over eighteen' and not be lyin', see?" I nodded. I thought it was still lying, but they were soldiers, so it must work.

You're laughing at how ingenuous we were. These days, I suppose if you wanted to join up and you were under age, you'd just walk into the recruiting station and swear you were eighteen anyway. How morals have declined since I was young.

"Can you write, Jed?" Tom asked.

"I can write some."

"Then you better write it now, just so you don't forget to do it. Got any paper?"

"I've got some in my bundle. I'll get it." Carefully, so the pieces of the carbine would not show, I fished around until I pulled out the writing paper. Tom took it and tore off a little piece. He turned to Nate.

"Gimme your pencil."

"Ain't got it with me. It's in my haversack."

"I got a pen in here," I said. I felt around the bottom of the bundle and took out the pen, but I couldn't find the ink bottle.

"Just dump it," Nate said. He grabbed a corner and upended the bundle.

"No, there's ink in…" The stock to the carbine thumped on the deck.

"Jiminy! What the heck's that thing go to?" asked Nate. I looked around, then opened the bundle wider to show them the LeMat.

"Where'd you get that?" asked Tom.

"What kinda gun is that?" asked Nate at the same time.

"It's a LeMat carbine. Belonged to Corp'ral Wentworth."

"Who's he?" asked Nate, fingering the weapon to see how it worked.

"I used to be with him, in the Confederate army. I cooked and took care of the horses for him and his brother."

"And he just let you take this?" asked Tom. I felt a little uncomfortable.

"No, I used to carry it around for him. He had two pistols, so he had me carry the carbine for him. I had it when I ran away."

"Ever shoot anybody with it?" Nate asked half in jest. He and Tom had been in the army for almost a year and neither one of them had even shot at a Confederate, let alone hit one.

"Just once. He had a pistol and was goin' to steal my horses," I said quietly, remembering the day I shot Lem. The two young soldiers looked impressed.

"Was he a reb?" asked Tom, taking the carbine from Nate and aiming it himself.

"Yes, he was a reb."

"Well, it's all right then," said Tom with a note of finality. "I mean, that's what you're gonna join up to do, ain't it? Shoot rebs?"

"I guess so," I said in a subdued voice. All the time I had imagined myself fighting, killing never entered my thoughts. I guess I had forgotten the truth of Forrest's words.

I found the ink bottle and handed it to Tom. Tom handed back the carbine. While I put it away, he took the pen and wrote the number eighteen on the paper.

"Now, when ya go to enlist, just make sure it's at the bottom of your shoe," Tom said importantly.

"Jed, what's your last name?" asked Nate. "When you enlist, you got to tell 'em your family name."

"Slaves don't have family names. We just have first names, like horses or dogs. Families're broken up so often, last names don't have much meanin' for us." There was an uncomfortable silence, but it lasted a mere moment.

"Well, you should pick your own before you go enlist," Tom asserted.

At the time, many freedmen took their master's last name when they were freed, but that didn't seem right to me. I thought for a moment about myself, what I had done since being taken from the farm, with the Cavaliers, and the Underground Railroad. I remembered telling myself, on the road that first night after I ran away, how I was worth something, if only to myself.

"Worth. My last name is Worth," I told them proudly. "That's the name I'll use when I enlist. Jedediah Worth." Nate clapped me on the back.

"Sounds like a good name to me, Private Worth."

XVI

The days passed slowly as the boats continued upriver and spring faded into early summer. We had little work to do except helping to toss wood into the firebox of the boat's steam engine.

The easy routine was disrupted early one morning by a scraping sound along the *Queen's* hull, a shudder that I could feel right through the deck. The boat came to a stop, with the deck canted to port a few degrees. The vibration of the engine ceased for about thirty seconds then started again. Samson and I ran out on deck to see what had happened.

In the half light just before dawn we could see that the boat had apparently strayed too close to the southern bank of the river and had run aground on a mudbar. Off the stern, the boat's paddle rotated in reverse, slapping futilely at the water in an effort to pull her off.

The captains of the other three boats hailed through their speaking trumpets, and the captain of the *Queen* shouted something in reply. The captain went back into the wheelhouse and about ten seconds later, the paddle stopped.

One of the other boats backed water and cautiously approached. A sailor on the deck of the boat threw a line to our deck. A sailor caught it, then looped it around a bollard .

One of the mates told me and the other deckhands to go help with the line. A sailor got us in a file, ready to pull.

"Now, heave!" he shouted. We pulled and a heavy rope that had been tied to the line went over the side of the other boat into the water. "Heave!" shouted the sailor again and again until we had pulled the rope over to the *Queen*. The sailor tied it around the bollard, then shouted to the mate.

The mate shouted to the captain and the paddle wheel again churned the water as the other boat tried to pull us off the mudbar. She shuddered as her engine strained, but the suction of the mud was too great. Finally, the captain gave the order to stop engines and the paddlewheel again ceased rotating. The mate had a gangplank run out to the bank.

"All right!" he shouted. "You men start unloading the cargo."

The deckhands, sailors and most of the soldiers went below to begin bringing up the cargo. A corporal and four soldiers with rifles went a few hundred yards beyond the bank to stand guard, while one of the boat's officers scanned the horizon with a telescope. One by one, the other boats came alongside the *Queen* and ran out a plank to transfer some deckhands and soldiers to help with the unloading.

After about an hour of unloading, I had just dropped another box on the riverbank and was starting back up the gangplank, when the officer on watch with the telescope called out.

"Deck ho! Horsemen on the south bank. Appears to be three or four of them." I looked back and could see a small cloud of dust about three miles off.

"You men, get out on the bank! With rifles and ammunition, now!" a gray-haired sergeant ordered in a loud voice. The soldiers hurried back aboard to get their rifles and cartridge pouches.

"Sergeant Barry, there are only three of them and they're miles away," I heard a young second lieutenant say to the sergeant. "The men would be more useful if they continued unloading." The sergeant frowned.

"Yes, sir, Lieutenant Edwards. But I think that a show of force now might convince whoever that bunch is scoutin' for to leave us alone."

Before the young officer could reply, Sergeant Barry ordered the men to get in among the crates and barrels with their rifles. Lieutenant Edwards shook his head and walked beyond the pile of crates.

"Form a line on me!" he shouted to the soldiers. Sergeant Barry went over to protest, but Lieutenant Edwards spoke first. "If we're going to have a show of force, we should do it correctly, Sergeant."

"Yes, sir. But there's no need to give 'em an exact count of how many men we have. Hide the men among the crates and the rebs will know that there's more than a few, but they won't know how many exactly." Lieutenant Edwards turned away, but didn't order the men to take cover. After a minute, the mate with the telescope shouted again.

"They're goin' away." Lieutenant Edwards smiled and was about to say something to Sergeant Barry, but the Sergeant turned away.

"Stack arms!" he shouted. "Right where you are. Then get back to work." The soldiers, three or four at a time, leaned their rifles against each other, forming pyramids. Then they took off their cartridge pouches and hung them from the stacked rifles. They filed back aboard the riverboat and continued unloading cargo.

"Continue unloading, you men," the mate shouted to us deckhands.

About a half-hour later, the mate told us all to stand clear of the gangplank. The paddle wheel rotated again, while the rope between the *Queen* and the other boat went taut. After a half-minute, our boat lurched backward and the gangplank dropped into the water. She was free of the mudbar.

One of the other boats, using a lead line, had sounded the bottom of the river and found a deep spot close to the bank about a hundred yards upriver. Hands retrieved her gangplank and she steamed to the spot. Then we began the exhausting task of reloading the cargo.

After another hour's work, barely a third of the cargo had been reloaded. Deckhands and soldiers were exhausted. Sergeant Barry conferred with the mate.

"All right, break for the noon meal," he ordered. The soldiers immediately crowded into line to be first to the galley. While the soldiers ate and rested, so did the deckhands. The officer with the telescope continued to watch the horizon.

I got a plate of food and sat with Samson with my legs dangling off the gangplank. I felt good to be off my feet. Most of the soldiers ignored us, but the irrepressible Nate stopped by.

"Think them horsemen were rebs?" he asked. Without waiting for an answer, he continued, "The Sarge thinks they were probably bushwhackers. He says if we hurry up, we could be outta here before they have a chance to gather together."

Bushwhackers weren't regular soldiers. Many of them were little more than outlaws, using the war as an excuse to pillage, rob and settle old scores with their neighbors. Because they weren't usually together in large bands, it would take them a while to assemble enough men to attack the riverboats.

Before we could comment, the mate called us back to work. The call was echoed by Sergeant Barry a minute later. Soldiers and deckhands resumed the tedious job of reloading the cargo.

After another hour, we had just over half of the cargo reloaded. My hands were raw from splinters and nails in the crates and my muscles were sore. I had never worked this hard on the farm.

"Manure's a lot lighter than what's in these barrels," I told Samson ruefully and he laughed.

"Deck ho!" called the lookout. "Dust cloud on the horizon. Probably horsemen approaching."

"Can you tell how many?" Sergeant Barry shouted up to the lookout.

"Not yet!" the lookout replied.

"All right, grab your rifles and your cartridge boxes!" Sergeant Barry loudly ordered the soldiers. I saw Nate and Tom scrambling towards the stacked rifles, then I ran below to get the LeMat.

"Better be careful, they might not like a colored with a gun," Samson told me as I reappeared on deck. By now, I could see horsemen trotting toward us, but because of the dust they raised, I couldn't tell how many there were.

"I don't think they'll mind when that bunch gets closer," I replied, then heard Sergeant Barry raise his voice.

"It'd be better if we got behind the crates, sir. Especially as most of our men ain't never been in a fight before."

"Keep the men in line, Sergeant," Lieutenant Edwards said crisply. "We'll do things just like you would have done them in Mexico. As you are so fond of reminding me."

"They're bushwhackers, sir, not lancers. They ain't even gonna have no sabers. They're gonna use pistols and shotguns, maybe a few carbines. And we don't have smoothbores. We can open up long before they're close enough to return fire."

"Volley fire, on my order, Sergeant." Sergeant Barry stared at the lieutenant for a long moment, then shrugged.

"Form a line to my left. Two ranks. Make sure you're loaded," he yelled. The thirty-four soldiers hurried into two ranks checking to make sure they were loaded with powder and ball, with caps on the nipples. Two or three bit into cartridges and loaded.

The *Queen* lurched as she began to back off the bank. Samson and I were still standing at the rail. I tapped Samson.

"Let's go." We both leaped over the rail onto the bank as the boats backed toward the far bank. We ran forward to stand just behind the double line of soldiers.

The horsemen had stopped about six hundred yards away. There appeared to be about sixty of them. Most wore gray or butternut brown, with some dressed in civilian clothes. The Sergeant had been right: most seemed to carry shotguns and carbines.

A thick skein of oily black smoke curled up over the mass of horsemen, then separated into a dozen separate smoke trails. They had stopped to light torches to set fire to the supplies and, if possible, the boats. Once the torches were lit, unlike trained cavalry, they made no attempt to get into formation. They just cantered toward the line of soldiers.

I glanced at Sergeant Barry, who appeared to be counting down the range.

On one hand, rifles were accurate to almost four hundred yards. If they fired early, they could possibly reload and get another volley off before the horsemen were upon them. On the other hand, most soldiers were not very good shots. They received very little target practice and almost no training in how to estimate range, the distance to a target, and windage, the wind causing a bullet to drift laterally. Windage normally wouldn't matter with a target as wide as a line of cavalry or infantry but in those days, rifles had a tendency to "loft" the bullet instead of it following a "flat" path, unlike the Krags we had later or the Springfields the army has now.

"When you get the order to aim, aim low!" the Sergeant shouted. "Aim for the horses." He glanced at Lieutenant Edwards. "If they aim for the horses, they might hit somethin'," he said, almost apologetically. "I'd suggest waiting until they're about two hundred yards away, then firin' by rank, sir. That way, we'll get a few hits and slow 'em down so the men'll have time to reload." The Lieutenant's only response was to snort derisively.

By then, the bushwhackers, who were a little closer than three hundred yards away, broke into a gallop.

I had seen charging cavalry before, but from the side, looking on. Watching them ride headlong right at me, I felt fear claw at my innards, insisting I run. I felt my vision seem to get fuzzy at the edges, while things in front sharpened to an intense clarity. I seemed to be looking through a gray tunnel.

Puffs of dirty gray smoke appeared at random in the mass of charging horsemen, before the sound of the shots reached us. Most of the bullets must have gone wide, because none of the soldiers seemed to be hurt, but my urge to run grew stronger than ever. Sergeant Barry must have noticed the same feeling ripple through the ranks of soldiers.

"Stand fast!" he shouted. "Hold your fire."

"Ready!" Lieutenant Edwards shouted in a high, quavering voice. Both ranks quickly raised their rifles. Sergeant Barry started to shout "No" but his voice was drowned out by the officer yelling "Fire!" A ragged volley sounded. Both ranks had fired simultaneously.

I looked quickly at the charging mass to see the effect, before the choking cloud of powder smoke obscured my view. Not more than two horses went down, lost quickly in the mass.

This seemed to provoke a new spate of shooting by the bushwhackers. Only one of our men went down, though. It was Lieutenant Edwards, shot through the thigh. His blood pumped out and was sucked up by the parched ground.

"Carry 'im to the rear," Sergeant Barry ordered. Two men quickly moved to pick up the groaning officer and take him away. The Sergeant walked behind the two ranks of soldiers.

"The lieutenant's down, so take your orders from me. Reload, quickly now! Don't a man of you shoot till I give you the word. These things shoot high, so aim low. Aim for the horses, like I told you before. We're gonna fire in two ranks. Remember, wait for my order."

Soldiers quickly bit cartridges open, poured the powder down the barrel, then pressed the paper wrapped bullets into the muzzles. The ramrods made a scraping noise as they were withdrawn from the pipes under the barrels. The movements were strangely rhythmic as the charges were rammed down, but then the rhythm was lost a little as one soldier, hunched over while ramming, suddenly straightened up before falling forward onto his face. Sergeant Barry shot him a quick look of concern but I guess he saw that the man was beyond help. His face set into a mask of indifference as he continued to walk up and down behind the two ranks. Preston Moore had had that same look at Belmont, and I suppose I've had that same look on my own face at times these past thirty years. As a non-comm, you're always concerned about your men, but in time of crisis, your concern is for the living. You know you'll have plenty of time for the dead when the danger is past. It sounds harsh, but it helps you keep your living men alive.

"Everybody loaded? Good! Front rank only! Kneel. Remember, aim low. Aim at the horses." The Sergeant glanced up at the charging horsemen. When they were within two hundred yards, he shouted, "Ready! Aim! Front rank only, dammit!" as a few men in the rear rank raised their rifles. "Fire!"

A horseman toppled backwards over his horse and another cartwheeled out of the saddle onto his face as his horse collapsed. It looked like two or three other horses went down with their riders.

The Sergeant again calmly walked behind the second rank. He was almost knocked over by a soldier, who seemed to be suddenly picked up off his feet and thrown backwards.

"Rear rank, two steps forward, march. You're now the front rank. Rear rank, reload. Front rank, aim!"

A few horsemen, now just over a hundred yards away, tried to turn out of the line of fire. Sergeant Barry bellowed, "Fire!"

Again flame, followed instantly by blinding smoke, leaped out from the line to pluck five or six horsemen from their saddles.

"Rear rank, stand fast and finish reloading, quickly now. Front rank, get back among the crates and reload. Move!"

The men who had just fired ran back the few yards to position themselves among the crates and barrels of supplies. One dropped on all fours, then stretched out and lay still on the ground. One or two of the rear rank soldiers turned to follow the front rank, but were roughly pushed back into line by Sergeant Barry. I was again reminded of Preston Moore at Belmont and wondered if manhandling men to keep them in the firing line was a duty of all sergeants.

A soldier dropped his rifle and clutched his arm. Samson ran forward to pick up the rifle and help him to the rear.

Now the horsemen looked very close. I had to keep telling myself not to run.

"Ready! Aim!" Sergeant Barry yelled. This time I raised my carbine and thumbed back the hammer.

"Fire! Now get back to the crates and reload. Move!"

Without waiting to see the effects of the volley, I turned to run back to the crates. I was knocked off my feet and dropped my carbine. On my left leg, a soldier lay moaning. I rolled the man off, got to my feet and picked up my carbine. Then I stooped down to drag the wounded man back to the crates. It was Tom.

I got a hand under Tom's arm and pulled. He was loose-limbed and deadweight and I hardly budged him. I was wondering whether to drop the LeMat and pick him up, when another soldier ran back to help. It was Nate.

"Jed! I'll get one side. You get the other." I hunched under Tom's arm and straightened up. Nate and I half-carried, half-dragged Tom toward the crates.

We were about ten yards away when I heard a thunder of hoofbeats behind us. In front of us, among the crates, I heard Sergeant Barry yell, "Aim!"

"Get down!" I yelled to Nate and dropped to the ground with Tom.

"Fire!" I winced as bullets cracked overhead. I felt the vibration through the ground as horses and men crashed to earth.

"Let's go!" I cried to Nate. As we dragged Tom upright, a bullet snapped past my ear and raised a puff of dust in front of me. I turned to see two horsemen, no more than thirty yards away, riding straight for us.

I dropped Tom and stepped clear, thumbing back the hammer of the LeMat, and aimed. A horseman filled my vision. I recalled Sergeant Barry's words and switched my aiming point to his horse. I squeezed the trigger and the carbine bucked in my hands.

A dot of red appeared on the horse's chest. The stricken horse reared back and fell against the other horse. Both riders spilled into the dirt.

I thumbed back the hammer again as one of the riders got to his knees and aimed a pistol at me. He fired, but missed and was thumbing back his hammer again when I fired. Again, the carbine jerked in my hands, and the horseman was knocked backwards. I didn't see him get up.

I went back to help Nate with Tom, hoping that the other fallen horseman wasn't going to pop up with a pistol also. I had just reached Nate when the man fired from behind his dead horse. I flinched as dirt exploded in front of me, stinging my eyes. I tried to ignore it as I thumbed back the hammer again and fired. I missed, but the shot must have been close as the horseman stayed sheltered behind the horse. I didn't know what to do as more horsemen filled my vision.

Another soldier ran out from behind the crates. Nate told the soldier to help him with Tom. I stayed behind to cover them from the bushwhackers. I thumbed the hammer back and fired three times in quick succession, aiming at the horses. Two horses went down. One fell on top of his rider, who didn't move again. The other horse fell forward onto its chest, throwing his rider over his neck. I stood frozen in fright as it seemed the man would cartwheel right into me, but he came to a halt a few yards away. Both his arms stuck out at odd angles and he screamed.

I glanced behind me, my vision obscured by smoke, smoke from the gunfire and from burning wood for a few of the crates had caught fire. The two soldiers had almost reached the relative safety of the crates with the unconscious Tom.

Some bushwhackers continued after them. I sidestepped back a few yards, knelt and aimed at another horse. I squeezed the trigger and felt the now-familiar punch against my shoulder. The horse crashed sideways, pinning its rider to the ground. My thoughts again flashed back to the battle of Belmont, when I had saved Clinton Rockwell from the same situation.

Nate, Tom and the third soldier finally reached the pile of crates, so I turned and ran. Bullets continued to snap overhead, occasionally spilling a rider to earth or snatching a foot soldier backward.

I was about five yards from the crates when just ahead I saw a red spot suddenly appear in a soldier's forehead, an instant before the man fell backwards and out of sight. I turned again to find my vision was filled with the sight of a galloping horse. I barely had time to dive out of the horse's path as an unseen bullet plucked the rider out of the saddle.

I rolled to my feet and, looking over my shoulder, sidestepped to the rear.

I jumped behind the crate and landed on the soldier who had been shot in the head. I popped back up to aim, when a bullet hit the crate right in front of me. A long, jagged wood splinter snapped up and hit me over the right eye.

I dropped back behind the crate as everything went pink. Blood flowed down so that I couldn't see. Desperately, I wiped at my eyes, trying to clear my vision.

A horseman rode past the crate, then jerked hard on the reins, trying to turn the horse as he noticed me. I pointed the carbine and fired without really aiming. The rider arched back so far I thought he'd break in two before he went out of the saddle. His body landed on the far side of his horse, which kept on running.

Another horseman came around the other side of the crate, followed by yet another. I aimed and fired at the first one, but then the hammer clicked down on an empty chamber. As I froze in horror, the horseman was blasted back out of his saddle.

I almost didn't register the sight of the second man riding past me, firing his pistol first at me, then at someone behind me.

I turned to see the horse rear as Samson stabbed a bayonet into the rider's side. The wounded rider slumped over his horse's neck and rode back into the smoke.

Samson joined me behind the crate. I started to pivot the firing pin at the tip of the LeMat's hammer to fire the buckshot, then a vision of Lem clutching his blood-soaked belly filled my mind. I can't explain why, in that moment, shooting the enemy with buckshot was so different from shooting them with bullets, but the memory of Lem's death just wouldn't go away.

I dropped the LeMat and picked up a fallen soldier's rifle, checking to make sure it was loaded. It had powder and ball, but the percussion cap had fallen off. I fished inside the dead man's pouch for a cap and put it on.

Samson and I looked for attacking horsemen, but they were all riding away. Slowly, we straightened up from behind the crate and looked around. Everywhere I looked seemed covered with fallen horses, dead men and burning boxes. My feeling of looking through a tunnel, which I hadn't noticed during the fight, went away. Only when it started to fade did I notice it again.

"All right, men," a voice shouted. I recognized it as Sergeant Barry's. "You done good. It don't look like they'll be back." The soldiers gave a ragged cheer.

"First thing is tend to the wounded," Sergeant Barry continued. "You men, get the boats to throw you some buckets. We got to put these fires out."

Sergeant Barry walked around to check his men. He stopped near Samson and me.

"You! You the one that helped save Carter?" I nodded.

"Well, you done real good. Better get over to the doc's and get your head taken care of." The Sergeant moved off.

I had forgotten the gash in my forehead. Now that the Sergeant had mentioned it, I could feel a dull throbbing going through my head. Samson looked at my forehead and gently wiped the blood away, then smiled.

"Looks like you'll have a scar just like the one you gave me. Let's go see if Tom's all right."

I looked around and saw Nate kneeling on the ground. He held Tom in his arms, talking softly. I ran over, followed by Samson.

"How is he?" Samson asked. Nate looked up. It seemed to take him a moment to recognize us.

"What happened to you?" he asked me. Without waiting for an answer, he said, "Tom's bleedin' a lot."

There was a wet stain around the jagged tear on Tom's dark jacket, just over his belt. His breathing was rapid but shallow. Samson knelt down and gently undid Tom's belt and unbuttoned his jacket.

"Jed, you got your knife?" he asked. I quickly got out my clasp knife, opened the blade and handed it to Samson.

Samson slit Tom's shirt open. When he peeled it away, I could see a hole in Tom's left side, just under his ribs. Samson rolled Tom over slightly, and we could see a slightly smaller hole in his back.

"It went right through him from behind," Samson said. "It's good it didn't hit bone and that we don't have to cut the ball out. Jed, before they put all these fires out, boil me some water and see if you can find some blankets. Nate, see if you can find some material for bandages." Nate looked at Samson quizzically.

"Ain't we gonna take him to the doc's?"

"We will, but we'll help him first," Samson replied. "The doc might not get to him for awhile if there are men more severely wounded." Nate wriggled out from under Tom, then jumped up to look for bandages.

I cut a canteen off a dead Union soldier and brought it back to Samson. I forgot about the blankets.

Samson had put Tom up on a crate and cut away his shirt and jacket. He rolled Tom so he was halfway on his side, and then went over to a burning crate. He held the blade of the knife in the flames until it turned a dull red.

He walked quickly back over to Tom. Nate came back with the bandages.

"Hold him still," Samson commanded. He gently scraped the edges of the small wound with the hot knife. Tom stirred a little and moaned. There was a smell like meat burning and a small puff of steam rose up.

I bent quickly, so I wouldn't have to watch, and gathered some wood and lit from a burning splinter from a crate.

"The biggest problem with a wound is when it festers," Samson explained to Nate and me. "Then, you could get mortified flesh and blood poisoning. You have to clean the wounds out. In Dahomey, during warrior training, we were taught that little bugs, so small you can't see 'em, make wounds fester. You have to kill the bugs with heat and then keep 'em away by keeping it real clean."

Nate and I looked at each other, clearly thinking Samson was a little strange in his beliefs, but neither of us said a word. You have to remember that this was almost a decade before the French doctor Pasteur discovered germs.

Samson put some of the bandage cloth into the water, which was now boiling. He left it to boil for a little while, then fished the cloth out with a stick. He held it and let it cool off after putting more bandage in the boiling water. He bathed Tom's wounds with the boiled cloth.

Samson took the other bandage cloth out of the water and let it cool. He pressed it up against the wounds, then held it in place by tying the rest of the cloth around Tom's body.

"We got to move him. Careful, so you don't open up the wounds," Samson told us. As gently as we could, we picked Tom up and carried him to the boat.

XVII

The *Queen of Cairo*, along with the other three supply boats, steamed towards the wharves at Kansas City two days after the fight with the bushwhackers. Some of the supplies had been destroyed and eight soldiers had been killed. Five more had been wounded, Tom and Lieutenant Edwards among them. Fourteen dead rebs had been counted on the field. Six, all wounded, had been captured and placed under guard after their wounds had been treated.

Tom didn't regain consciousness until the day after the fight. When Samson and I came to visit him, Tom looked stiff and ill at ease. Nate had told him how I had fought off the bushwhackers so they could drag him to safety, and how Samson had doctored him.

"I would like to express my deepest gratitude to you both for saving my life," he said formally, but very weakly. "If they're all like the two of you, I think coloreds'll make real good soldiers." Tom looked really embarrassed.

"How long did you rehearse that speech?" Samson asked jokingly.

"Only a few times," he laughed.

"He couldn't tell you any of this before," Nate chimed in, "because the doc had given him too much laudanum." We laughed again and kind of kept it going longer than the jest really deserved, trying to all feel comfortable with each other again.

A day later, we said goodbye to Nate and Tom. The boats had docked at Kansas City and the guards were to be replaced by a detail from Jefferson Barracks. Tom was still not able to get up, so we gathered in the boat's sick ward. Samson took Tom's hand and shook it.

"Goodbye, Tom. I hope we meet again someday."

"Me, too, Sam. Don't do anythin' like jumpin' in front of no bullets like I did and maybe we will. Take care of yourself, Jed. I know the both of you will make outstandin' soldiers."

"Thanks a lot for teachin' us how to use the stickers," Nate told Samson, referring to the bayonets. "After that last fight, I hope I never have to use what you taught me." Nate solemnly shook Samson's hand.

"Nate," I asked, "when you get back to Cairo, could you see this gets delivered to the Reverend Howell's school for colored folk?" Nate took the letter.

"To Effie? If I get a chance, I'll deliver it to her myself." Nate put his arm around my shoulders and clapped me on the back. "Now, even though you'll be a fine soldier, you take care of yourself. You already didn't listen to Effie's maw when she told you not to be a hero."

Samson and I helped unload the supplies that were to be left at Kansas City. Most of the supplies stayed aboard the boats, which continued up the Missouri River.

When we arrived at Fort Leavenworth, the easternmost fort guarding the Oregon Trail, Samson and I spent most of a day helping to completely empty the boats. The supplies would be sent to the western forts by wagon train, while the boats steamed back downriver to Cairo.

Samson and I picked up our bundles and went up on deck, to be paid off by the *Queen's* purser. For the first time in my life, I had money. It felt odd. I was very conscious of it in my pocket as Samson and I walked down the gangplank.

We asked a passing soldier if he knew where the recruiting office for the Kansas militia was. He directed us to a shed near the stone gate of the fort. We walked up the bluff overlooking the river.

"'Enlistments'," Samson read. "This is the place. Last chance to back out, Jed. We can still be conductors on the Underground."

"Is that what you want to do, Sam?"

"No. I just wanted to make sure this is still what you want to do."

"It is." I remembered about having to be of legal age to enlist. I walked away from the recruiting office, sat down and took off my boot. I put the paper with the number 18 in the boot and put it back on. "There, now I'm ready to join up."

We walked into the office. A sergeant sat behind a desk. Before we could speak, the sergeant asked, "You boys here to join the colored regiment?"

"Yes, Sergeant," Samson answered for both of us, then he asked, "Is there a whole regiment?"

"Not yet, but there will be. Like the general said, you coloreds can't have white men fight for you while you stay at home. Are you contrabands?"

"We've escaped and come and fight," Samson replied. "Is this where we join up? And who is the general you talked about?"

"The general is Senator Lane. He was personal friends with John Brown and was commissioned a brigadier general at the personal insistence of Abraham Lincoln. He plans to enlist four white regiments and two colored and turn 'em loose in Missouri to stamp out bushwhackers.

"The War Department hasn't authorized enlisting coloreds as soldiers, so you'll have to join officially as laborers. But the general is going to have you fight, just as soon as you're trained and have rifles. To enlist you, I need to know your name, how old you are and where you're from."

"I go by Samson Miner." The sergeant wrote Samson's name in the roll book.

"And how old are you?"

"Twenty-three. I was born in Dahomey."

"I'm guessing that ain't in Georgia," the sergeant joked.

"Dahomey is in Africa."

"Thought you were darker than most home-grown coloreds. What state was your master in?"

"Louisiana." The sergeant entered it into the roll book and then wrote it all out on Samson's enlistment papers.

"You'll get your papers after you've been sworn in by the Captain," the sergeant told him, then he turned to me.

"How about you, son?"

"Jedediah Worth from Kentucky and I'm over eighteen," I said all in one breath.

"Jedediah Worth, age eighteen, Kentucky." As he said eighteen, the sergeant looked up at me with a slight smirk, as if he knew I was lying about my age.

"We'll have to wait till Captain Williams comes back to officially swear you in. Make your mark here." Samson and I took the pen in turn and signed our names.

"Well, I'll be," said the sergeant. "Contrabands who can write. You can help me here in the recruiting office until the captain gets back. Should be in a couple of days. He's up north, recruiting."

We were told to go to a small camp behind the fort. Almost one hundred colored men were already there, mostly coloreds escaped from Arkansas and Missouri. A number of the men were not exactly volunteers, but seemed to have been forced into service. Many of them were afraid of what would happen to the families they left behind, still others feared they would be ill-used by white officers. Some others had been literally stolen from their masters. But most of the men seemed to regard enlistment as a unique opportunity to advance the cause of their freedom.

During the day, while we helped the recruiting sergeant, the other men did menial chores and hard labor around the fort. They cared for the cavalry horses and cooked for and cleaned up after the white soldiers. In the late afternoons and evenings, we all drilled under the command of white sergeants from the fort.

Because Samson and I already knew the manual of arms, we were detailed to help teach individual drill to the "remedial squad," the men who were having trouble learning the movements.

After two days, Captain Williams returned with another dozen recruits. The sergeants paraded us for the swearing in. Captain Williams had us raise our right hands and repeat the oath to defend the Constitution against all enemies and to obey the orders of superiors. The oath completed, I lowered my hand. I was now officially Private Worth.

Our first order of business was to march south along the river, almost back to Kansas City. A training camp had been established at Wyandotte. It took us two days to march the twenty-six miles. Samson and I were better off than most of the men. Our escape had made us more used to marching than many of our fellows, although the past several weeks aboard the riverboat had made us a little soft.

Abe and Joe, two runaways from a cotton plantation in Arkansas, sang work songs as we marched. Learning the songs kept my mind off the dull monotony of marching.

Our training camp was called Camp Jim Lane. One company of men was already at the camp. Almost half of them had been enlisted in September of 1861, almost a whole year prior.

When we reached camp, the men were divided into squads, or "comrades in battle," as Hardee's tactics manual called it. This was the same Hardee the Cavaliers had served under at Shiloh. The squads contained eight men each, instead of the four prescribed in the manual, because the officers felt not enough of us were suited to be non-commisioned officers.

Samson and I were assigned to the same squad, along with Abe and Joe, the singers and four other men. We were issued a wedge tent, which we all shared for sleeping and stowing our equipment and clothes. Almost the only private property in the tent was my LeMat carbine.

The crowded conditions seemed to bother me more than the others. I had grown up sleeping by myself in the loft over the stable, while most of the men had lived in small slave cabins on cotton and cane plantations. Eight men crammed into the tent with their weapons and equipment, all trying to dress or clean equipment at the same time made it seem like the tent would burst at the seams. Sometimes I wished I was back over the stable, where I could be alone when I wanted.

Within a week, enough men had been recruited to fill two companies. A third company of eighty men marched in to enlist together. I thought some of them appeared uncommon, with coarse hair and coppery skins. I finally realized they had Indian blood.[21]

We soon had enough companies to be organized into a battalion. Captain Williams, who had administered the oath to make us soldiers, had been promoted to colonel and placed in command. Most of the men recruited the previous fall were designated Company A. A few of them were promoted to sergeant and put in charge of platoons in other companies. The group with whom Samson and I had marched from Fort Leavenworth was designated as part of Company B, and our squad became the Third Squad of the First Platoon.

A short time later, we were issued uniforms. The dark blue four-button fatigue coats and forage caps were the same as those issued to white soldiers but we received gray trousers instead of the light blue pants that most Union soldiers wore.

Robert, the only freedman in the squad, was delighted to receive his uniform.

"Wear it proudly," he admonished the rest of us. "For now we all are clothed as free men and if we do not dishonor our uniforms, we shall be free."

With the uniform, I was also given a pair of heavy shoes, the kind infantry wore. I had worn boots as long as I could remember, so the shoes took some getting used to. One of my squadmates, Charles, a quiet, almost shy young man of about twenty, had to teach me how to tie my shoelaces.

A few days later, we received our weapons, Model 1841 Rifles. In uniform and holding the rifle that had just been issued me, even though I had already fought a battle, for the first time I felt like a soldier.

I didn't realize it then, but the Model 1841 rifle we had been issued was the one used by the Mississippi regiment when their one volley broke the Mexican cavalry charge, so they were known as "Mississippi Rifles."

We were also issued socket bayonets. I didn't think anything of it at the time, but later I learned that when the Model 1841 was re-bored to take the larger minie bullets, most were fitted with saber bayonets. Saber bayonets were more expensive than the socket type, and for a long time I thought that we had been deliberately given inferior equipment. Later, at Petersburg, when talking to one of Berdan's Sharpshooters, I learned that many of them preferred socket bayonets for they were lighter and made it easier to hold the rifle steady while aiming. I guess Colonel Williams got us cheaper bayonets for a reason.

Back at the tent, Rufus, a sullen man who also bore scars from having been whipped, turned to me and smiled for the first time, but it was a smile without humor.

"Now let them try t' whip us, hey, Jed?" he said raising his new rifle. Noah, just a year older than me, turned to Rufus.

"Got sumpthin' there for yore friends in Missouri do you?"

"Ain't got no friends in Missouri," Rufus replied. "And this sure is better'n a whip. Just teach me how t' use it. I already know who t' use it on, by God." Caleb, normally a mild man, whirled around.

"The good book says, 'Thou shalt not take the name of the Lord your God in vain.' God will not smile on this endeavor if you blaspheme, Rufus." Rufus opened his mouth to say something back, but just ducked into the tent, muttering.

"All the men here an' I got t' get hooked up wit' a damn preacher."

"I heard that! Do not swear, Rufus," boomed Caleb.

The ensuing days passed a lot like those I remembered from the Confederate training camp at Union City the previous summer. The men drilled in company formations, movements and tactics, including skirmishing.

I recalled how at Belmont, Yankee skirmishers, moving from tree to tree, had fought in two-man teams, one loading while the other fired. I thought I would pair up with Samson as my partner, but Samson was promoted to be our squad's corporal. Instead, my partner was Robert, the freedman.

Abe and Joe were paired, as were the shy Charles and Noah, the jokester. The final pairing almost seemed like a joke in itself: the serene, God-fearing Caleb with the angry, profane Rufus.

Since Samson, as corporal, had made the pairings, I asked him why he'd put Caleb and Rufus together. Samson smiled.

"Back in Dahomey, the old warriors who trained the young men always put those who didn't like each other together. The old warriors knew that if they permitted those who didn't like each other to stay apart, their dislike would split the group. If they were put together, and forced to look out for each other, they would rub off on each other and each would become a little like the other. This way, Rufus and Caleb have a chance to overcome their dislike and not interfere with the cohesion of the squad."

After a short time in training, most of us could load and fire almost three times a minute. We could keep it up for over three minutes before we got tired and the rate of fire slackened. We didn't know if we could actually hit what we aimed at, however, because we didn't get target practice. We loaded and fired only blank cartridges, and even using blanks was rare. Usually, we just went through the motions of loading and firing.

The other thing about us was we kept our camp much cleaner and neater than the Confederate camps I had been in. Almost all of the men were very proud to be soldiers, and it reflected in our bearing and the way we wore our uniforms.

We also helped each other whenever one of us had trouble learning some skill. Joe could load and fire faster than any of us and keep it up longer, but he always lagged behind when facing or turning movements were called, especially while marching. On the other hand, Robert always looked clumsy when doing the manual of arms, although he was better at almost everything else. But we helped each other, and soon we looked and felt like veterans.

One morning at the beginning of August, Samson had us fall in for a special announcement.

"The Congress passed a law last month! We can officially be soldiers!" Everyone in the squad greeted the news with great enthusiasm, since we had all been officially enlisted merely as laborers. We drilled with even greater determination and sense of purpose.

Our determination increased when we received news bushwhackers had attacked and captured the town of Independence. Independence was just across the river in Missouri, less than twenty miles away.

However, we were depressed by some other news a few weeks later. Samson again announced the tidings.

"Even though the Congress passed the law permitting it, the War Department still won't allow the enlistment of coloreds. General Lane has been told that the regiment won't be accepted into federal service and the officers won't be given federal commissions."

"I don't care if the off'cers are commissioned or not!" Rufus bristled. "I joined up t' fight, and, by God, that's what I'm goin' t' do!"

"Rufus, don't blaspheme," Caleb said morosely. "The Lord is just testing us. Surely, He would not have allowed us to come this far, only to abandon us. We must pray, and the Lord of Hosts will allow us to be soldiers once more."

It seemed Caleb's prayers were quickly answered, for it was soon apparent General Lane had no intention at all of disbanding us, no matter what orders came from the War Department. The white officers were also apparently unmoved about the withholding of commissions. Most of them were Jayhawkers, like Lane. The Jayhawkers were men from Kansas who had been fighting the pro-slavery Missouri bushwhackers for almost six years. They would continue to fight, with or without federal commissions.

As if to underscore the fact, General Lane gave our battalion an official name. From then on, we would be known as the "1st Regiment, Kansas Colored Volunteer Infantry."

XVIII

One of Colonel Williams' first orders on being placed in command of the First Kansas was that we were to be intensively trained in marksmanship. So, unlike almost every other regiment in the Union army, we shot at targets as often as four times a week. It would take about twenty years for the regular army to catch up to the Kansas Colored when it came to learning to shoot. Not until 1877 would Congress appropriate money to issue 90 cartridges a year per man for marksmanship training.

I already told you about how laborious it was to load the rifles we had back in the Rebellion. What I didn't tell you was how much they hurt to shoot. The Mississippi Rifle was fifty-eight caliber, only a tiny bit smaller than the shotgun barrel on the LeMat carbine, and its cartridge used more powder. By contrast, the Krag carbines we used in Cuba fired a thirty caliber round.

When I fired, I made sure to pull the butt of my rifle back into my shoulder. I had found out the hard way that if I held it loosely when I squeezed the trigger, the rifle would crash back into my shoulder, hard as a mule kick.

We fired at a bull's-eye two hundred yards away. A spotter, in a protective ditch, would raise a long stick with a white circle at the end and hold it to show where the shooter's bullet had gone.

I remember one such day on the target range. I was pleased with myself, for I discovered I was the best shot in the squad. Surprisingly, Charles was the only other man in the squad to do almost as well.

After firing on the range, we usually scrambled for water. Biting open cartridges was thirsty work. The saltpeter in the gunpowder dried out your mouth and the sulphur left a rotten-egg taste.

"You all did good today," congratulated Samson as we guzzled water from our canteens. "Everybody hit the bull's-eye with at least ten out of twenty rounds, and some did considerably better. Now we've been detailed as spotters. Number two men, go report to the Range Sergeant. Leave your rifles and equipment here."

"Tough luck, Charles," said Noah with a wide grin. "I"l just sit here and make sure your rifle don't walk off. I don't think it will too hard a job." Noah, chuckling, made a great show of sitting down and leaning back, as if he were taking a well-deserved rest.

"While you men are just sitting there, you can clean rifles," Samson told us. "Start by cleaning your partner's rifle. Don't start on your own until I inspect and pass your partner's." Charles and the rest of the number two men grinned as Noah groaned. They double-quick marched to report to the sergeant in charge of the spotters.

While Noah started a small fire to boil water to sluice out the rifle barrels, I sat down with Robert's rifle and began to take it apart to clean it. Samson sat down next to me.

"Write to Effie lately?" he asked. I nodded.

"I wrote her twice since we got here and I ain't heard nothin' back."

"I wouldn't set too much store by that," Samson responded. "It's only been a couple months. Mail's slow out here, but when it does come," Samson fished around in his haversack, "it's usually worth waiting for." With a twinkle in his eye, Samson handed me two letters. "The other one is Robert's. Give it to him when he gets off detail." I smiled gratefully as I took the letters, because I recognized the elegant curlicues of the writing on one of the envelopes as Effie's.

I didn't know whether to read it now or wait until later when I was alone. Noah helped me decide.

"Jed, that from a female?" Noah nudged Joe and asked, "D'you suppose that Jed'll read it out loud to us? C'mon, Jed, we're your friends. Read it to us." Embarrassed, I quickly put the two letters in the inside pocket of my coat and resumed cleaning the rifle.

I sat wondering what Effie was doing and what she was learning in Reverend Howell's school. I recalled the night when I had just hugged her close under the stars, until my reverie was interrupted by the shouted order for cease fire.

I had cleaned Robert's rifle and had almost finished my own when the men on the spotter detail rejoined us. I handed Robert his clean rifle and his letter.

"From my wife," Robert said contentedly, taking the letter. Before he could open it, Sergeant Lowrie, the company's fifth sergeant, ordered us to get into formation.

"Fall in, column of twos. When we get back to the tents, you have about an hour to get ready for dress parade." One of Colonel Williams' other innovations was that each day's duty ended with the entire regiment brought together for the formal ceremony to lower the camp's flag, just like in the regular army.

When we reached camp, we heard the news that the Confederates had won another battle, fought on the field near Manassas where the first big battle of the war had been fought. To follow up their victory, the Confederates had crossed the Potomac River to invade the North.

"D'you think if the rebs win a few battles in the North, the gover'ment will end the war?" I asked Samson. The whole squad gathered around to hear his answer.

"It's possible. The rebs don't have to beat the North to win, they just have to keep the North from beatin' them. If the Union army is defeated on its own home ground, I'm afraid that it will give the Copperheads a big boost." Copperhead was the term for people in the North who wanted to end the war and let the South have its independence. "I just hope that Mister Lincoln is strong enough to stand up to them."

That was the first inkling we had that, although the North was immeasurably stronger than the Confederacy, war-weariness might render the whole effort, all the sacrifice and all the death, completely for nothing.

That evening, I could hardly wait for the Retreat Ceremony, the lowering of the camp flag, to end. Finally, the last notes of the bugle call, "To the Colors," died away. Training and duties, except for guard, were over for another day.

I wanted to read Effie's letter before it got too dark. I tore off my equipment and stowed it in the tent, then hurried away, almost to the river. I sat down and carefully slit open the envelope with my clasp knife, unfolded the pages and began to read this letter, which I've kept these past thirty-odd years.

Cairo, Ill.
August 5, 1862

My dearest Jedediah,

> *I hope this letter finds you well, as I am very concerned about you, you being a soldier and all.*
> *I am well, as are mother and Josh and Lucinda and Ella. You would be hard-pressed to recognize Ella, as she has grown so big since you last saw her.*

> *I was glad to get your letter. Nate, your soldier friend, brought it to me. He said to write that Tom will recover and return to duty. He told me about the fight on the bank of the river. I guess you and Samson forgot what Mother and I told you about trying to become heroes.*
>
> *Mother always thinks about you and Samson. Josh is thrilled that you both are real soldiers and would like to see you in your uniforms. When he calls you and Samson the heroes of the riverbank fight, Mother always tells him to hush. She, and I, would rather you both return home safely.*
>
> *I do not know if you heard about the raid mounted by your "old commander," Col. J. H. Morgan. He raided your home state of Kentucky, burning many millions of dollars of property and supplies, and capturing many Union men. I am telling you about it as I would think that your Corporal Wentworth and his brother might still be among Col. Morgan's men.*
>
> *Marcus and Abner presently are "gone south" to conduct another group of passengers to freedom. If only the rumors that President Lincoln intends to free all the slaves are true, then Marcus and Abner will not have to risk their lives and freedom on the Underground Railroad anymore.*
>
> *Please take care of yourself and Samson, and say hello to Samson for Mother and me. We all pray for your safe return. I hope it will be quick, but I will wait for as long as it takes to be with you once again.*
>
> *I have not forgotten the night you kissed me and I never will. Come back soon.*
>
> *Effie*

I recall reading the letter twice more before the light faded. I folded it and put it back in my jacket pocket. For a while, until night fell, I just sat and thought of Effie and Belle and Josh. I remembered Wade and wondered what had happened to Obie. I thought of Maddie and how she taught me to cook. I tried very hard to picture my mother's face.

***

A few weeks later, we were filled with excitement. We were told to take our haversacks with us to breakfast.

"That means only one thing," Rufus exulted. "We're goin' t' be issued rations for marchin'. We're goin' t' war!"

"About time," groused Noah. "I don't think I could put up another day with stories 'bout the raid on Butler."

Earlier in the month, a few companies had been sent to Butler, Missouri to destroy supplies accumulated by bushwhackers. The only fighting had been some shots traded with pursuing horsemen as our men withdrew across the river. The distance at which they shot at each other was so great, no one on either side had been hit. Company B had not been included, but to hear the men who did go tell of it, the battle was more fearsome than Shiloh.

Rufus's prediction was confirmed when, at breakfast, each of us received three days' marching rations: two and a half pounds of salt pork, called "sowbelly" by the men; thirty-six crackers of what was officially called hard bread, more commonly known as hardtack, teeth-dullers or worm-castles; a half-pound of dried beans; a half-dozen apples and coffee, sugar and salt.

Then we were marched to the Ordnance Sergeant to draw sixty ball cartridges for our rifles. Forty went into our cartridge boxes, while the other twenty were reserve ammunition.

Most of us rolled our reserve ammunition and other belongings in our blankets and tied the ends together. The rolled blankets, with rifles, haversacks, canteens and cartridge boxes constituted "light marching order."

I considered taking the LeMat, but didn't want to get into trouble, so I asked Samson whether to take it.

"Take it or you might never see it again," said Samson. I thought he meant that I might be killed, and it must have shown on my face, for he hastily added, "I didn't mean that somethin' would happen to you. I meant, if you leave it, it might get lost or stolen. Got any ammunition for it?"

"I still got twenty-four rounds, plus four buckshot charges."

"Take 'em. The carbine might come in handy. I'll ask Sergeant Lowrie to talk to Captain Crew about it first chance I get." Captain Crew was the officer in command of Company B.

We got into formation. Three other companies were also in light marching order, about 225 men all told. Around mid-morning, we all marched out of camp and boarded a steamboat that took us down the Missouri River and across the Kansas River.

After we disembarked from the steamboat, we again drew up in march formation. Company B was the second company in column. When all the companies were in formation, we started marching south. Abe and Joe started singing work songs and soon the whole company joined in, but after an hour, the singing grew a bit thin and then stopped altogether. We marched on in silence for another hour.

By this time, it was almost impossible to keep my rifle sling from settling in the spot on my shoulder that it had already rubbed raw. I took special care to adjust my blanket roll so the two pieces of the carbine would ride comfortably, but that proved to be impossible. I wished that I had a carbine sling, but I guess that would have just worn a groove in my other shoulder.

Finally, the order to halt was given. Each company was ordered to put two squads on guard, but our squad wasn't detailed.

After a hurried meal, the order to fall in was passed back from the head of the column. We put our equipment back on and slung our rifles. When we fell in and resumed the march, Samson walked beside me.

"Do you have any idea where we're goin'?" I asked him.

"Nope. We weren't told, but I heard a rumor that we're goin' to Missouri. We're supposed to destroy supplies that're bein' gathered by the bushwhackers."

"Just like the Butler raid. Think we'll fight?" I was annoyed at myself for feeling apprehensive, since I had already been in two fights, at Belmont and the riverbank. I didn't count Shiloh anymore, since all I had done there was gather up the wounded after the battle had already moved on. Samson thought for a moment.

"I don't know. I don't expect too many bushwhackers would be around just to guard supplies. On the other hand, I don't think the guards will just let us destroy their supplies. I guess if there is a fight, it won't amount to much. We'll have to wait and see." We walked on for a while before Samson spoke again.

"Did Effie say in her letter how everyone was doin'?"

"Everyone's all right. Nate gave her the first letter I wrote, but it didn't sound like she had got my second letter yet when she wrote this one. She and Josh're still goin' to Rev'rend Howell's school. I guess Belle and Lucinda are still at the mill. Effie didn't say. Ella's got real big. Marcus and Abner went south to conduct a group of runaways north. Belle was askin' about you and Effie said I was supposed to say hello to you."

"Well, are you goin' to?" asked Samson.

"Goin' to what?"

"Say hello to me," grinned Samson.

"Oh. Hello. That's from Effie, not me. You happy now?"

"I just didn't want you to get in trouble, not doin' what Effie asked you to do." Samson's attempt at humor was annoying me all out of proportion to what he was actually saying. I couldn't place why then.

"Effie also mentioned that President Lincoln was plannin' on freein' the slaves."

"I heard that too. I heard he was waitin' for a big victory before he let it be known," Samson replied. "I also heard that there was a real bloody battle last month, up north in Maryland, near some little creek. I can't recall the name. 'Ant' something or other. They say it was even bloodier than the fight you saw at Shiloh. The rebs stayed put the day after the fight, but they wouldn't attack us again and our men wouldn't attack them again, so then the rebs just packed up and went home. I guess Mister Lincoln's still waitin' for his big victory."[22]

The column continued south the rest of that day. Somewhere during the march, we crossed into Missouri. Rufus was elated.

"Let me at the damn bushwhackers. I'll let them know it's a diff'rent game now that we have rifles, too."

"Rufus, I've asked you not to swear," said Caleb resignedly. "Now especially is not the time to imperil your immortal soul."

"Sorry, Caleb," Rufus said sheepishly. "I lost control. If you had known me when I was in bondage here, you'd understand why I got so excited."

"It's a natural reaction and I'm sure the Lord will forgive you," said Caleb kindly. "But, I agree. It will be different now that we are armed and armored with the righteousness of the Lord of Hosts."

We marched until nightfall, then stopped to bivouac.[23] It was my turn to boil the coffee, so while the others lounged around, I gathered some twigs and built a fire.

After I had served out the coffee, I sat back-to-back with Robert, sipping meditatively at my cup. I kind of started to realize why I was so jittery. *Might as well face it*, I told myself, *you're scared*. I would have gone into a blue funk then, but Robert spoke.

"What's it like, Jed?"

"What's what like?" I asked, but I knew full well what Robert was talking about.

"You know. A battle." The eyes of the rest of the men in the squad came to rest on me. I almost fell onto my back as Robert suddenly moved around in front to hear me better.

"It's hard to say. Things seem to happen so quick." I looked around at the eyes of the men, which were riveted on me. It made me uncomfortable and resentful. They were asking me to explain something of which I had almost no experience. Then I realized, as inexperienced as I was, a battle was less of a mystery to me than any of the others.

"Things seemed to be all jumbled up, at least to me. You don't know if a minute just went by, or an hour. You can't see much, because of the smoke. You can't hear much, other than shootin'. Even though there might be a hundred men all around, it's like you're all alone. Things happen, but it kind of seems like they're happenin' to somebody else. Well, maybe not to someone else. You know it's happenin' to you, but in a way, you kind of seem outside yourself." I paused, somewhat self-conscious at all the attention.

"I don't know. That's what it seems like to me," I concluded lamely. They looked at me for a time then looked away, each alone with his own thoughts.

After a while, Caleb softly began to sing. The second time he sang the refrain, Rufus joined in. Their voices harmonized nicely as they sang, "...gonna lay this body down." One by one, the other men in the squad joined in.

I didn't sing, I just sat, thinking. I was angry with myself for wondering, since I had been shot at and shot back, what I was afraid of. As I said before, I wasn't afraid of being killed, because in a way, deep down, I didn't think it would really happen to me. Some of the others maybe, but not me. Samson must have noticed my distress, because he came over and sat next to me.

"You worried about somethin'?" Samson asked with concern.

"Yeah, I am worried," I admitted. "I finally figured it out. At Belmont, even though I was in the thick of the fight, I wasn't doin' the fightin'. At the attack on the riverboat, you and I fought, but we didn't have to fight. It wasn't really our fight. If things went wrong, there was no blame on us and if the fight got too hot, we could just leave.

"This one will be our fight. We'll be the fightin' men and there's a lot ridin' for all our people on how good we do. I'm not scared of dyin' as much as I'm afraid we might fail, that people who think coloreds can't be soldiers might be proved right." Samson looked at me levelly.

"I haven't been this afraid since my father died and I was put aboard the slave ship. But we aren't goin' to fail. As long as we put up a good fight, even if we lose, then we haven't failed. And we'll put up a good fight. You and I will see to that, won't we, Jed." It wasn't a question. I looked into Samson's face and knew that together, we couldn't fail, at least not according to Samson's definition. I nodded.

"Yes, Sam. I know we'll put up a good fight. You and me together."

XIX

A few hours after we had gone to sleep, Samson woke us.

"We'll be moving out soon. Jed, you might as well get the LeMat put together."

When I looked up at the starlit sky, I could tell that it was about four o'clock in the morning. Marcus had taught me to tell time and find my way by looking at the position of the stars.

"Make sure nobody makes a sound, and no fires, not even to light a pipe," Samson continued.

After a cold breakfast out of our haversacks, we got into formation and marched in the darkness. I just walked along without a thought in my head until I suddenly bumped into the man in front of me. He was from the another squad, and it's funny, I can see his face but can't remember his name.

"We're comin' to a ford," he whispered. "Keep your rifle and cartridges dry. Pass it back." He hurried forward as I passed the message to Robert and told him to pass it to the man behind him in turn. I hurried to catch up and almost bumped into the soldier again. A second or two later, Robert bumped into me.

Ahead, I could hear the noise of feet splashing. I lifted up my carbine, rifle and cartridge box then almost slipped on a patch of mud before I was splashing through the water, too. I felt the cold water seep through my shoes and soak the bottom of my pants.

The water got deep enough to reach my waist, and I finally remembered the spare ammunition in my blanket roll. Since my hands were full, I could only hope that it hadn't got soaked. As the water almost reached my chest, it required some exertion to walk and my steps slowed. Gradually, the water got more shallow until I finally stepped onto the muddy bank. I could hear the shoes of the men around me squishing in the dark.

After a few minutes, the column halted. I was all right until we halted, but just standing there, I again felt the jitters. To pass the time, I checked my rifle to make sure it was loaded, then checked the carbine.

The morning clouds purpled, then steadily turned first red, then orange.

Almost suddenly, the edge of the sun poked up over the horizon. A low, rounded hill took shape in front of us. Men disappeared over the crest of the hill, gone so quickly in the early morning light I wasn't sure they hadn't been an illusion.

"Check your rifles to make sure you're loaded and fix your bayonets," ordered Samson. I checked my rifle, even though I knew it was loaded. I rested the LeMat against my thigh as I pulled my bayonet from its scabbard and twisted it onto the muzzle of my rifle. I kept wishing I had a sling for the carbine, to keep it from getting in my way.

Captain Crew came up from the rear, where he had been at a hasty officers' call, then took his position in front of the company, sword in hand.

"The company will advance in skirmish order ahead of the other companies." The Captain spoke in a normal voice, but it seemed oddly loud in the early morning air. "Third squad will form an advance guard two hundred yards to the front of the company."

"Trail arms," ordered Samson quietly. "Follow me. Double-quick, march." We started forward at the double-quick. Behind us, I could hear the First Sergeant, trying not to shout, order "Close it up! Close to the right."

What sounded like a volley, muted yet higher-pitched, washed over the top of the mound.

"Pistols," I said over my shoulder to Robert, but he didn't reply. All I heard was his labored breathing behind me, and my own, as we hurried up the slope after Samson. Running was difficult, with the LeMat in one hand and my rifle in the other. I could hear myself start to wheeze like an old man when we finally reached the top of the mound.

From the top, looking ahead down the slope, I saw a mass of mounted men about a furlong away. They were Confederate cavalry.

A regimental flag showed a substantial number of the enemy were not bushwhackers, but Confederate regulars. The Confederates were trying to get into line formation. They must have been warned by their own vedettes of the our approach.[24]

The enemy force numbered at least five hundred men, probably closer to six hundred. A thrill of fear passed through me as I realized the Kansas Colored Volunteers were outnumbered by more than two-to-one. The sound of Samson's voice snapped me back to reality.

"Work in pairs. We need to keep them from gettin' into formation as long as we can. Fire at will."

I immediately dropped to one knee, laid the carbine down, and took aim with the rifle. I sighted on the man carrying the flag. When I squeezed the trigger, the massive punch against my shoulder reminded me I should have pulled the butt back more tightly.

I peered through the smoke of my own firing as I began to reload. The flag-bearer hadn't fallen. As soon as I fired, Robert ran a few steps ahead, dropped to one knee and fired. In the distance in front of him, I saw a horse keel over sideways, tumbling its rider.

I tore a cartridge open with my teeth. The dreadful taste of black powder filled my mouth and soaked up all the moisture on my lips. I rammed the bullet and stuck a cap on the nipple, suddenly realizing that I hadn't felt afraid since the shooting had begun. It made me feel pleased with myself.

I finished reloading and again searched for the man with the flag, but couldn't see him. I settled for a man waving a saber trying to form the cavalrymen into line, figuring him for an officer. I fired and a second or two later, he arched his back suddenly, almost dropping from the saddle. He kept his seat, but he slumped over his horse's neck.

Again, you might think it funny how the mind works during something as serious as a battle, but I reproached myself for the shot. As I told you, ever since I had helped clear the wounded from the battlefield at Shiloh and had shot the deserter Lem, I had promised to shoot to kill as a mercy to the men I fought. Wounds caused too much suffering.

"You got 'im, Jed!" exclaimed Robert. A few seconds later Robert fired again, but I didn't see the result.

Looking at the Confederate ranks, all seemed confusion. A few riders had been shot out of their saddles or dragged down by their fallen mounts. But then, a few hundred men, most in yellow-trimmed jackets, shook off the confusion and pulled themselves into formation. These were the regulars.

A trumpet blared a call that I recognized from the days with the Kentucky Cavalry Squadron. The front line of the regulars started forward at a walk, and when the interval was right, about a hundred yards, a second line started forward behind them. The bushwhackers rode forward also, in an ungainly mass behind the regulars and on each flank.

I knew in a few moments, the trumpet would order the horsemen to pick up speed to a trot, followed by a canter. When they were about forty yards away from us, the cavalry would charge.

As I bit into a cartridge, I looked around and saw that the company was moving at double-quick step, but was still about a hundred yards away. Moving uphill, it would take them more than half a minute to reach us skirmishing at the top of the mound.

I heard the trumpet order "Forward at the trot" and knew the Confederates would reach us first. It was time for our squad to retreat, but there was no place to retreat to, because the company was also in a skirmish line.

I recalled Captain Morgan's statement about well-formed infantry being invulnerable to cavalry. Infantry standing shoulder-to-shoulder in a square or in a line with guarded flanks could face cavalry. Because there was so much space between each man, a skirmish line could never withstand a cavalry charge. If the horsemen got in among the infantrymen, they could surround individuals and small groups and slaughter them almost at will.

As I rammed a charge home, my knuckles scraped against my sharpened bayonet and were sliced open. I could feel blood immediately start to get sticky on my hand, and wished for ice or snow to slow down the bleeding. Then the memory of the snowball fight against Wade sprang into my mind.

During the snowball fight, Daniel and I had lured Wade, John and Isham into a trap by pretending to retreat. We could do the same here. I looked back once again and saw that in a few seconds, the company would reach the crest of the hill. If they were seen by the rebel cavalry, the plan taking shape in my mind would be ruined. I shouted to Samson.

"Sam! Tell the company to halt where they are and form a firin' line. We'll get the rebs to charge too early."

"What good will that do?" Samson wanted to know.

"When the rebs come over the top of the hill, they'll think they're just chasin' skirmishers. They won't be expectin' a company in line to be so close. When the company volleys, the rebs'll be so surprised they'll just sidle off." *I hope*, I told myself silently. Samson looked at me for a long and maddening moment, then shouted to the squad.

"Take your orders from Jed." He ran down the slope to speak to Captain Crew personally.

"Everybody load, but don't fire," I ordered the rest of the squad. "We need to wait until they get close, then we'll volley. After that, we run."

"Why don't we just run now?" Noah asked tremulously as he reloaded.

"We need to give the company time to form a firing line." I glanced back down the hill and saw the company start to form two ranks, the men shoulder-to-shoulder. I almost shed tears, my relief was so great. My plan might work!

"Ready! Aim!" I shouted as the trumpet ordered the horsemen into a canter. As the Confederate line picked up speed, I searched for the trumpeter to shoot him, but I couldn't locate him. Instead, I aimed at a man with non-comm's chevrons on his arm, but whether sergeant's or corporal's, I couldn't tell at that distance.

The line of advancing horsemen seemed to fill my vision, but I still waited. From the corner of my eye, I could see Abe sneak a wide-eyed look back toward me.

"Wait! Just a little more."

When the line was about fifty yards away from us, I knew the trumpet momentarily would shrill again, this time to order "Charge."

"Fire!" Eight rifles roared. "Now run!" Before the smoke cleared, we were on our way.

Their trumpet immediately ordered "Charge" and the rebs, with a shout, put spurs to their horses to get them to move faster. The sharp crack of pistol shots split the air overhead, as we ducked out of their sight on the other side of the hill.

We came over the crest and onto the reverse slope to see the men of Company B aiming their rifles toward where they expected the rebs to appear. The problem was, we were in the way.

"Down! Get out of their way," I screamed to the squad as they skidded to a confused halt.

I threw myself flat, trying to get clear of the killing ground in front of our firing line. I cursed, having a weapon in each hand and almost flung the LeMat aside. I glanced to the rear one last time just as the charging line of horsemen cleared the crest of the mound and were silhouetted against the morning sky.

Smoke and flame belched from the company's rifles and I was momentarily deafened by the sound.

The Confederate charge came to a complete halt as men and horses crashed to the ground. Here and there, other men slumped in the saddle. Even the unwounded men looked stunned.

I was elated that my plan had worked and almost started to cheer, but then, with a chill of horror, I suddenly remembered the second line of cavalry.

"Get to the top of the hill!" I shouted. "More cavalry's comin'! Get to the top."

The company's line just stood. Most of the men were so overwrought they had not heard me, and even those that did just stood waiting for orders. It was like one of those nightmares where you know you're in dreadful danger, but can't do anything about it. Then Samson's voice blared, sounding louder than a bugle.

"At the cavalry to your front—Charge!"

I heard them give a cheer, actually more a deep growl like that of a bear, as they brought their rifles into the "Charge bayonets" position and ran past me toward the top of the hill. The rebels saw them, wheeled their horses around and galloped away.

I ran forward with the rest of the squad, trailing the company as they came over the top of the hill and onto the far slope. The company quickly formed another firing line.

Down the slope, all was confusion as the second line of Confederate cavalry was swept up by the retreating first line. All were forced back down the slope as red-faced officers and non-comms shouted themselves hoarse, trying to impose order.

"Reload, quickly now!" shouted the First Sergeant. My fingers felt like india rubber as I grabbed a cartridge and my teeth like wood as I bit it open. All around, I could sense the fumbling haste as the other men also reloaded.

The Confederates finally formed another line. Immediately, their trumpets sounded the order to charge.

Company B was now in a desperate race with the Confederate cavalry. We had to finish reloading before the rebels closed with us or we would be massacred.

Reloading usually required about fifteen seconds, but we had started a few seconds before the rebel cavalry began their charge. A horse could gallop a hundred yards over flat ground in less time than that, about six seconds from a standing start. Galloping uphill might add a second or two.

As I drew my ramrod, Captain Crew shouted, "Front rank only, guard against cavalry…guard!" The front rank men stopped reloading. They stood with their feet wide apart, bracing their rifle butts against their hips with the tips of their bayonets held chest-high to a horse. "The rest of you men, keep loading!"

As I looked at the charging cavalry, my heart froze as the realization struck home that Company B would lose the race. I let the rifle fall from my hand, broke ranks and ran.

As I ran, I fumbled with the LeMat. I knew that all the company needed was a little more time to finish reloading and I was determined to buy them that time.

I got a few yards in front of the company, then knelt and thumbed back the hammer. Hardly waiting to aim, I fired, and fired again three more times.

I must have hit something, for part of the center of the charging line collapsed in a tangle of men and horses. The center of the line faltered in confusion for a moment or two, then came on.

Those few moments were all the company needed. Behind me, I heard the First Sergeant shout, "Aim!" I had just enough presence of mind to throw myself flat on the ground as the First Sergeant yelled, "Fire!" The sound of the volley crashing right overhead was even more deafening than before.

I sprang to my feet and was immediately knocked down by a cavalryman falling from his horse. As I shook my head to try to clear it, another cavalryman pointed a pistol right at me. The horse bucked as the man fired, and I felt the bullet whip past my cheek.

Without thinking, I raised the carbine with one hand and fired. A small spot of blood suddenly appeared in the center of the man's chest, just before he fell backward, out of the saddle.

Another cavalryman tried to ride me down. Samson was suddenly at my side, his bayonet-tipped rifle thrust out. The bayonet slid into the man's side and he fell from his horse, almost tearing the rifle from Samson's grasp.

Another horseman charged us. I aimed the LeMat and squeezed the trigger. In an instant, I became frantic as nothing happened. A voice in my head seemed to shout, "Fool!" I hadn't thumbed the hammer back. I cocked the LeMat, but before I could fire, the horse crashed into Samson and me, sending us both sprawling.

I rolled over onto my knees and got up quickly. A man in a gray coat was directly in front of me and I instinctively fired at him. He contorted so wildly I thought he would break in half. Only then did I notice I had shot the man in the back. As if I had the leisure to ponder, I wondered why that realization did not bother me.

Frantically, I looked around for Samson and Robert and the rest of the squad. Samson was trying to fight off a cavalryman cutting at him with a saber, while a horseman with a pistol tried to angle in to shoot him. I steadied the carbine against my shoulder and shot the man with the pistol first.

I didn't wait to watch him fall, but shifted aim to the man with the saber. I irrelevantly noted the "chicken guts" on his sleeve as I fired. The man's hat flew off as the bullet hit him in the back of the head. I winced, then ran to Samson.

"Are you all right?" I asked. Samson nodded.

I looked around and saw that the battle had become a whirling mêlée of infantry and cavalrymen shooting and stabbing and hacking at each other. The Confederates were sure to win such a fight. They outnumbered us and could win simply by trading loss for loss if they had a mind. But they didn't have to do that. With their greater mobility, cavalry didn't have to maintain their formation to be effective in combat, the way infantry did. Looking around, I could see how badly it was going for us.

Sergeant Lowrie was surrounded by three men, one of them an officer. Lowrie stabbed one man with the bayonet, then swung the rifle like a club to hit the officer in the face and knock him from his horse. He swung the clubbed rifle back and knocked over the third man.

Captain Crew stabbed a rider in the belly with his sword. Another rider slashed down at him with a saber. The Captain parried it with his sword, but it broke from the shock. The horseman called on him to surrender, but he refused. Another cavalryman, a bushwhacker, shot him down. Abe bayoneted the man in the side, a moment too late to save Captain Crew.

I ducked under a saber slash, then raised the carbine to shoot, but Samson had already put out his bayonet. The horse carried the man, screaming, onto the point. I heard Samson grunt as the full weight of the man came out of the saddle. Samson quickly lowered his rifle, and the man slid off the blade.

Another rider loomed over us, but the man shifted his attention to something to the rear. I simultaneously saw the cavalryman plucked from the saddle and heard the thunder of what could only be an infantry volley. Turning toward the sound, I saw that the rest of the battalion had finally reached us.

I quickly jumped behind a fallen horse with Samson. A moment later, the second line of the battalion fired a volley. Without a trumpet call or order that I could hear, the rebel cavalry turned away.

From behind the horse, I looked around to see where the rest of the squad was. Just as I caught sight of Charles, he was shot by a fleeing horseman. I fired at the man and knocked him out of the saddle and under his own horse's hooves. Samson and I ran over to see if Charles was still alive. Samson got there first and ripped open Charles' jacket. He felt his chest and shouted triumphantly.

"He's alive!"

Samson pulled Charles up until the wounded man was draped over his shoulder. With me behind him, he ran toward the rear of the battalion, where the surgeon would be. As we ran, a lone horseman blocked our way.

I knew Samson, holding Charles, was helpless to defend himself. I pivoted the carbine's hammer pin as the memory of Lem's shooting rose unbidden. I ignored it and raised the carbine. As the man wrenched on his bridle to ride around us, I fired. The buckshot tore open his chest. Only then did I realize he had only been trying to get away.

The rebel cavalry was in full retreat. The fight was over, and we had won.

So why didn't I feel like cheering?

"Come help me, Jed," said Samson urgently. "We have to get him to the rear." Samson continued to carry Charles to the rear, but I walked over to the dead Confederate.

The dead rebel's face, the eyes still open, seemed greatly surprised. I stood over him, looking but not really seeing, for what seemed like a long time. Finally, I stooped down and gently closed his staring eyes.

I spotted another fallen horseman and walked slowly over to him. I unbuckled his carbine sling and pulled it from his body. It was only when I tried to buckle the sling around myself that I noticed my hands shaking so badly I couldn't even work the buckle.

Dropping the sling, I sat down and sobbed. Maybe it was for Charles, but it wasn't for him alone. Maybe it wasn't for Charles at all.

EPILOGUE

I don't remember the immediate aftermath of the battle very clearly. That was a blessing, as we were left in possession of the field. To the victors, then, fell the task of burying the dead of the vanquished and caring for the wounded of both sides. The dead horses we burned. Our own dead were wrapped in gum blankets. We carried them with us to Fort Scott.

When we arrived at Fort Scott, I wrote to Effie. I have the letter. I probably said as much in the letter as it was possible for me to say about the battle of Island Mound.

You can read it. I have to go inspect the interior guard. I'll be awhile, so just leave the letter on the desk if you go turn in.

I don't know if I wearied you with my narrative, so you don't have to feel compelled to return for more. After thirty years as a soldier, I'm sort of thick-skinned, so it won't hurt my feelings if you don't.

October 30, 1862
Fort Scott, Kansas

Dear Effie,

> *We buried Charles today. You didn't know him, but he was a soldier in my squad. He was killed in a battle with rebel cavalry in Missouri. Our captain was also killed and seven other men.*[25] *They are buried here at Fort Scott. We carried their remains from the island where we fought. Even though it is supposed to be an honor for soldiers to be buried on the field where they have fallen, somehow it did not seem right to leave them there, far from where people would see their graves and remember who they were.*
>
> *As we buried Charles, I thought of the previous autumn, when we buried Heywood Stewart, of the Mercer*

Cavaliers, killed at Belmont. It made me think of all that has happened since this war started. I wonder whether Obie ever made it to the navy, and where Wade is now. I hope that each of them is still alive and well.

In this battle on the island mound, I shot men, two I think, in the back. One was by accident, but the other was not. I also killed a man with buckshot. After I shot the deserter at Shiloh, I never wished to inflict that kind of suffering on a man ever again. But I had to do it to save Samson. The shot was a good one and it killed him instantly, with no suffering. Even so, I am ashamed to have done it. But at the same time, I know that to save Samson, or any of the other soldiers in my regiment, I would do it again.

I am surprised at Samson and me. We have not forgotten that you and Belle said we are not supposed to be heroes, and we are not. But I think we still took to being soldiers pretty well.

There are some things about being a soldier that are most disturbing to me. Even worse than seeing a battlefield littered with its dead is the sound of the cries of the wounded. I remember a Confederate general saying that war is fighting, and fighting means killing. I wish that he were perfectly right! A quick, clean death is much to be preferred to the agony of wounds, of the surgeon's saw, of men without arms or legs for the rest of their lives. I am sorry for Charles, but I am glad that none of the rest of us in the squad were wounded. The thought makes me feel guilty somehow.

We are told that we are the first colored soldiers to have gone into battle. Even if we were not exactly the first, we are numbered among the first. Charles and the seven others were, without a doubt, the first colored soldiers to be killed in battle in this war. That might be a dubious honor, but my hope is that the government will take notice and allow other colored men throughout the North the opportunity to fight for the Union and their own freedom. I know that President Lincoln has proclaimed freedom for the slaves living in the Confederate States. Samson says that it is "ironic" that I am not included in Mr. Lincoln's proclamation, because to keep from offending the border states, it does not apply to slaves from Kentucky, among others.

I have told Samson that it does not bother me, for I do not want us to just be given freedom. Something given can also be taken away. I still think we have to fight for our freedom. In such a fight, our people can be good soldiers. After that becomes known, no one will try to take freedom from us again.

All the same, I wish this war would end. I cannot wait to see you and be with you again. I pray that it will be soon.

Pvt. Jedediah Worth
1st Kansas Colored Volunteers

HISTORICAL NOTE:

The 1st Kansas Colored Volunteers

Based on the date of muster, the 1st Kansas Colored Volunteer Regiment was the fourth colored regiment raised in the Civil War. The first men were enlisted in the regiment in September of 1861, without federal authority by the irascible Jayhawker, Senator James Lane. By August 1862, enough men had been recruited and trained to form seven companies. The regiment was offered for federal service, but the government refused to accept it, stating it had no provisions for enlisting coloreds or Indians. When they fought the battle of Island Mound, Missouri on October 28, 1862, they were still considered state militia.

On January 13, 1863, six companies were accepted into federal service as volunteers under the title 1st Regiment, Kansas Colored Volunteer Infantry. On April 18, 1863, the regiment suffered 172 casualties in a hour's fight at Poison Springs, Arkansas. It was alleged that men of the regiment captured by the Confederates had been murdered. The Confederacy officially denied the allegations. Even so, the 1st and 2nd Kansas adopted the rallying cry "Remember Poison Springs!" Many men in colored regiments took solemn oath to avenge Poison Springs and the more well-known massacre of colored troops at Fort Pillow, which had occurred the week prior.

After Poison Springs, the regiment served under Major General James Blunt, a friend of Lane and another Jayhawker. On July 2, 1863, at Cabin Creek in Indian Territory (now Oklahoma), the 1st Kansas attacked an entrenched force of Confederates and drove them from their earthworks. The battle was the first in which colored and white troops fought side-by-side.

Blunt followed up the victory at Cabin Creek with an attack on a Confederate force larger than his own at Honey Springs, Indian Territory. On July 17, 1863 (the day before the 54th Massachusetts made its celebrated assault on Battery Wagner), the 1st Kansas held the center of the Union line and advanced, under fire, to within fifty yards of a Texas regiment. The two opposing sides traded volley fire for about twenty minutes, until the Texans broke and ran. The 1st Kansas pursued and captured the Texans' colors.

The 1st Kansas was finally accepted for federal service on December 13, 1864, as the 79th Regiment (New), United States Colored Troops.

ENDNOTES

[1]. Tom Mollineaux was an American Negro prize-fighter who won renown in Great Britain, the home and pinnacle of the prize ring, for his skill and for being robbed of the English championship through trickery during a bout in 1814. The bout to which Worth refers occured circa 1808 in New Orleans. Mollineaux, beaten almost literally to death by his opponent in a no-holds-barred match, rallied to win when his master, who had bet heavily on the outcome, promised him his freedom as a reward for victory.

[2]. Worth is referring, of course, to Lieutenant Colonel George Armstrong Custer. Custer's treatment of deserters (they were shot out of hand) is well documented.

Many frontier cavalrymen, white and Negro, resented the preferential treatment meted out to the 7th Cavalry because of Custer's standing with the press and with General Sheridan, who commanded the Department. The 9th and 10th were often supplied with cast-off horses and worn-out equipment discarded by the 7th, but that also sometimes happened with white regiments.

An incident that occurred during the Christmas of 1869 would also have been galling to Negro soldiers. The 10th was posted to Fort Riley, Kansas with the 7th at the time the post was being constructed. Of course, the 10th ended up doing almost all the hard labor.

Custer refused to have the men of the 10th celebrate Christmas with his troops, and the 10th was forced to use a vacant warehouse for its celebration. Worth's attitude is understandable, but this incident occurred while he was still a non-commissioned officer with the 9th Cavalry.

Ironically, the 7th and 10th were the two regiments brigaded together to form the 2nd Provisional Cavalry Brigade during General Pershing's "punitive expedition" into Mexico to suppress Pancho Villa and his bandits.

[3]. Some literary opinion sets the action of *The Red Badge of Courage* during the battle of Chancellorsville, May 1 through 4, 1863.

⁴. Worth is referring to a poem, "Sambo's Right to be Kilt," that at first glance appears to be a slur on the ability of Negroes to be soldiers. However, the man who authored it, Major Charles G. Halpine, was committed to the enlistment of colored troops. He had been an officer on the staff of Major General David Hunter at the time he raised the first colored regiments admitted into federal service.

Major Halpine's ditty, published under the nom de plume of "Private Miles O'Reilly," is actually a sly argument for the enlistment of coloreds, made as an appeal to the more venal motives of whites. It was set to music, using the tune of a popular Irish song, "The Low-Backed Chair."

It was first performed on January 13, 1864 at Irving Hall in New York at a reception for the officers of Major General Thomas Meagher's Irish Brigade. The text was published as an editorial in the New York *Herald* shortly after. The text is reproduced below.

> Some tell us 'tis a burnin' shame
> To make the naygers fight;
> An' that the thrade of bein' kilt
> Belongs but to the white
> But as for me, upon my soul!
> So liberal are we here,
> I'll let Sambo be murthered instead of meself
> On every day in the year.
> On every day in the year, boys,
> And in every hour of the day;
> The right to be kilt ''ll divide wid him,
> An' divil a word I'll say.
>
> In battle's wild commotion
> I shouldn't at all object
> If Sambo's body should stop a ball
> That was comin' for me direct;
> An' the prod of a Southern bagnet,
> So ginerous are we here,
> I'll resign, and let Sambo take it
> On every day in the year.
> On every day in the year, boys,
> An' wid none o' your nasty pride,

> All my right in a Southern bagnet prod
> Wid Sambo I'll divide!
>
> The men who object to Sambo
> Should take his place an' fight;
> An' it's betther to have a nayger's hue
> Than a liver that wake an' white.
> Though Sambo's black as the ace of spades,
> His finger a thrigger can pull,
> An' his eye runs sthraight on the barrel-sights
> From undher its thatch of wool.
> So hear me all, boys darlin',
> Don't think I'm tippin' you chaff,
> The right to be kilt we'll divide wid him,
> An' give him the largest half!

[5]. In talking of John Brown's murder of "Missouri men," Wade Wentworth is apparently referring to the "Pottawatomie Massacre." Although five Southern settlers were killed, the incident actually took place in Kansas on May 24, 1856.

The reference to the attempted slave rebellion is obviously to Brown's raid on the federal arsenal at Harper's Ferry, Virginia (now West Virginia) which took place October 16 through 18, 1859.

[6]. The first model LeMat had the elaborate trigger-guard described by Worth, but was never produced in the numbers that the simplified, and more common, second model was.

The carbine acquired by Wade Wentworth must have been a prototype. Most LeMat carbines, of which very few were made, seem to not have been produced until after Colonel/Doctor (both titles seem honorific) LeMat had displaced to France.

[7]. Governor Beriah Maggoffin of Kentucky issued a proclamation of neutrality in May, 1861. In September, 1861, a pro-Union legislature set aside the stance of neutrality, and Magoffin resigned in protest on August 18, 1862.

[8]. Not only did many of the Confederate soldiers at Union City have

obsolescent flintlocks as described by Worth, many were not even armed at all. Almost a year would pass before the western Confederates were fully armed, by weapons captured from federal soldiers or run through the blockade. Southern industry did manufacture copies of the U. S. Springfield and British Enfield, but never in sufficient quantity to supply their troops adequately.

[9]. Officially Battery A of the 1st Tennessee Light Artillery, but known as Rutledge's Battery after its commander, Captain A. M. Rutledge. Its armament was four 6-pounder smoothbore cannons and two 12-pounder howitzers. The unit's losses were so severe at Shiloh that it had to be amalgamated with McClure's Battery.

[10]. Inventors of "quick-firing" guns and "machine-guns." Richard Gatling invented his first model gun, which operated by turning a crank, in 1862. An improved version, using Colt metallic cartridges, was adopted by the U. S. Army in 1866 and remained in use through the War with Spain in 1898.

The assaults during the Battle of San Juan Hill and Kettle Hill, in which Worth was a participant, were supported by Gatling guns.

Hiram Maxim and John Browning invented "true" machine-guns. Maxim invented a gun in 1885 that used the force of its own recoil to operate. In 1895, Browning designed a gun that used pressure from the gases generated by the exploding powder.

[11]. The officer seen by Worth appears to have been Captain John Seaton of the 22nd Illinois. Seaton took some pride in his company's proficiency in skirmishing tactics.

[12]. Brigadier General Gideon J. Pillow seemed to make a habit of hiding behind trees, repeating his performance at Murfreesboro in January, 1863. In between Belmont and Murfreesboro, he briefly commanded Fort Donelson.

He received command of the post from John B. Floyd, who vies with Pillow for the title of the biggest scoundrel to hold the rank of Confederate general. Pillow immediately turned over his command of Fort Donelson to Simon B. Buckner, leaving him to surrender to General Grant, while he and Floyd fled.

[13]. A step that was sometimes included in the reloading sequence was running a "worm" down the barrel to remove any bits of smoldering cartridge bag

still remaining. Either the Confederate cannoneers were confident that sponging alone was enough or were too hurried to take the extra step of worming.

[14]. Also known as Mill Springs or Fishing Creek, the battle took place on January 18, 1862. The Confederate general, Felix K. Zollicoffer, was killed in a bizarre incident. Zollicoffer, studying the terrain, rode up to a body of federal cavalry that he apparently mistook for Confederates. Because he was wearing a voluminous white raincoat, the federals had no idea that Zollicoffer was an enemy. When they fired on Confederate troops, Zollicoffer reprimanded the federal commander for shooting at " his own men." At that point, Colonel Fry of the (Union) 4th Kentucky realized that Zollicoffer was a Confederate, drew his pistol and shot him dead.

[15]. Nathan Bedford Forrest commanded the Confederate troops who massacred the mostly Negro garrison at Fort Pillow after its surrender. He reportedly was the founder of the Knights of the White Camelia and one of the guiding lights of the Ku Klux Klan.

[16]. Although the 83rd Ohio was indeed part of William T. Sherman's division at this time, unlike Confederates, the federal army did not usually name formations after the commander. Either these soldiers were proud to be under Sherman's command and so mentioned his name or perhaps Worth's memory is playing tricks on him. Then too, Worth was never an admirer of Sherman because of his attitudes toward Negro soldiers and his treatment of them while he was Commanding General after the war. Perhaps it gave Worth satisfaction to know that it was Sherman who was surprised at Pittsburgh Landing.

[17]. Franklin Gardner, later a Major General. He commanded the Confederate garrison at Port Hudson, where two colored regiments, the 1st and 3rd Louisiana Native Guards, were destroyed in gallant but futile assaults.

[18]. "Moses" was Harriet Tubman (1820?-1913), who is credited with guiding to freedom more than 300 Negroes in the decade from 1850 to 1860. During the Rebellion, she also served the Union cause as a nurse and a spy.

[19]. The slave trade at this time was centered on the Bight of Benin in the

Gulf of Guinea on the western coast of Africa.

One of the reasons that Miner must have been so traumatized by his enslavement, apart from being a member of the ruling-class, is that only a handful of the Fon people of Dahomey had been enslaved, at least by Europeans.

In the early seventeenth century, the Fon began to establish a militaristic state to avoid the depredations of the neighboring Yoruba, who captured them for slaves. King Gezo of Dahomey quickly recognized that his people could remain independent of both the Europeans and their neighbors through force of arms. This meant he had to obtain firearms from the Europeans, but they would only trade them for slaves. The Dahomeans began to enslave the peoples of the interior. Though it was an odious business, it was perhaps the only possible course, given the military and political reality, available for Dahomey to preserve itself as a nation and protect its people.

As Miner says, the Dahomean army was well-trained and feared throughout Africa. The royal guard, the *Fanti*, was composed of exclusively of women, but the "regular" army echoed the guard in having all-female units: the *Nyekplehhoteh*, the "razor women" were armed with swords that folded into their scabbards like razors; the *Gulonetoh* used British-made muskets; the *Gohento* or archers were exclusive to the Fanti; the *Agbaraya*, armed with blunderbusses, were almost like Napoleon's Old Guard: older, veteran troops who were committed to battle as the last do-or-die reserve; and the *Gbeto*, all of whom had killed an elephant with a spear and many of whom had scars inflicted by tusks.

It is perhaps ironic that King Gezo, who ruled Dahomey for some forty years, died a year or two after Miner's enslavement and exile.

[20]. Miner's explanation of the cause of the Rebellion may seem simplistic, but in the half century since the Rebellion ended, Southern apologists (and now with the tacit approval, if not encouragement, of the Wilson Administration) have spent a great deal of effort manufacturing explanations other than slavery. "States' rights" is the most noble-sounding, while others, such as differences over tariffs, are more venal.

That slavery alone was the cause of the Rebellion is evident in most of the seceding states' ordinances of secession. South Carolina, home of the most ardent secessionists and the first state to secede, has exposed the prevarication inherent in any other reasons. The third paragraph of its ordinance, in which the reasons for secession are enumerated, refers to nothing else but the United States government's interference with the rights of property in slaves, and then complained of "…an increasing hostility on the part of the non-slaveholding States to the institution of slavery." Mississippi declared, "Our position is thoroughly identified with the institution of slavery…a blow at slavery is a blow at commerce and civilization." Alabama's secession ordinance gave only one reason, that the Republicans were a "sectional party avowedly hostile" to the state's "domestic institutions." Georgia's Declaration of Causes cited "…complaint against our non-slave-holding confederate States (meaning the Union) with reference to the institution of African slavery" and further cited the prohibition of the extension of slavery into the territories as their grievance. Texas complained of abolitionists, Northern states and Republicans threatening "…the ruin of the slave-holding States." The Texas declaration went on to state, "We hold as undeniable truths that the governments of the various States, and of the confederacy (Union) itself, were established exclusively by the white race, for themselves and their posterity: that the African race had no agency in their establishment; that they were rightly held and regarded as an inferior and dependent race, and in that condition only could their existence in this country (U.S.) Be rendered beneficial and tolerable."

Reading the Confederate Constitution might also be instructive, especially for the states'-righters. It is almost a direct copy of the United States Constitution, with the notable exception of the protection of slavery. On the other hand, it seemed compelled to clutch a "moral fig-leaf" by specifying that the overseas trade would be suppressed.

The unimportance of states' rights compared to the right of slavery is amply demonstrated by the Constitutional clause that the right to "transit and sojourn" slaves would be "unimpaired by any state or local ordinance."

That states' rights was a sham is even more forcefully revealed by the systematic suppression of civil liberties, over state protests, conducted by the Davis Administration. In short order, citing the "necessary and proper clause" of the Confederate Constitution as authority, Jefferson Davis suspended habeas corpus (allowed under the Constitution only in the event of "invasion"), imposed conscription, held citizens without trial on the mere suspicion of "disloyalty" and enacted martial law in several major cities, where courts martial went so far as impose and carry out the death sentence on civilians.

[21]. They were fugitive slaves, many of mixed blood, who had taken refuge with the Sac and Fox Indians. Benjamin F. Van Horn suggested making the effort to recruit them. General Lane commissioned Van Horn a lieutenant and put him in charge of the recruiting operation. Pleased with the number of recruits, Lane formed them into a single company with Van Horn as the company commander.

[22]. Miner is referring to the battle of Antietam, which took place on September 17, 1862. Despite Miner's view, this victory precipitated the issue of the Emancipation Proclamation.

[23] Worth's account seems a bit confusing about timeframes. The regimental history of the 1st Kansas indicates the expedition set out on Sunday, October 26, 1862. The steamboat ferried the detachment across the Little Osage River, then they marched for about twenty miles before bivouacking for the night. The next morning, the march was resumed and continued until Dickie's Ford was reached about two o'clock in the afternoon of October 27. There, the detachment forded the Osage River and continued on about three more miles. They halted for the night and constructed a low breastwork, dubbed "Fort Africa" by a few of the troops.

The following day, October 28, was devoted to scouting the exact location of the Confederate force. Although Worth makes no mention of it, that duty probably fell to Van Horn's company of mixed-bloods.

[24]. The Confederate regulars were the 2nd Missouri Cavalry, under the command of Lieutenant Colonel (later Brigadier General) Francis Marion Cockrell. They had just attacked the men the Worth had seen cresting the mound at first light, a small detachment under Lieutenant Joseph Gardner. Gardner's men had advanced unsupported for almost half a mile then, attacked by the Confederate cavalry, they took cover in a farmhouse. Worth's company was ordered forward to cover their retreat. As the Confederates shifted their attention to Worth's skirmish line and its supports, Gardner's men took refuge in a small ravine on the near side of the mound, from which they made a stand.

[25]The others were Corporal Joseph Talbot and Privates Marion Barber, Samuel Davis, Henry Gash, Thomas Lane, Allen Rhodes and John Six-Killer.

Printed in the United States
22050LVS00004B/139-144